Wisdom of the Horse

A novel

Suktanka Woksopa!
Cali Canberra

Cali Canberra

Published by:

Newchi Publishing
11110 Surrey Park Trail
Duluth, GA 30097
770-664-1611
calicanberra.com

This novel is a work of fiction. Any references to real people, living or dead; and real events, businesses, organizations, and locales are intended only to give the fiction a sense of reality and authenticity. All names, characters, places, and incidents either are the product of the author's imagination or are used fictitiously, and their resemblance, if any, to real-life counterparts is entirely coincidental.

Copyright © 2006, by Cali Canberra

ISBN: 0-9705004-4-0

All rights reserved.
No part of this book may be reproduced or transmitted in any form or by any means, electronic or mechanical, including photocopying, recording, or by any information storage and retrieval system, without the written permission of the copyright owner and the above Publisher, except where permitted by law.

First Edition

Printed in the United States of America

Trading Paper, Never Enough! & Buying Time

expose the insider secrets of the high-stakes world of the horse business.

Cali Canberra's first three hit novels weave intricate relationships between influential horse breeders and trainers who lure in celebrities, successful business people and Wall Street tycoons, eager to spend millions on horses.

A CREATIVE BLENDING OF
JOHN GRISHAM & DICK FRANCIS...

ACKNOWLEDGMENTS

Thanks to my husband and daughter for their sense of humor, tolerence, support, and encouragement. Thanks to my horses, especially Cabaret, my inspiration to write this story.

And most importantly, thanks to my loyal following of readers who make my writing career possible.

Wisdom of the Horse

We are not humans having a spiritual experience.
We are spirits having a human experience.

PROLOGUE

Many cultures have a common thread in their thoughts on suicide – the fear that the spirit/soul might leave the body before some sense of peace or completion has been experienced. For this reason, many cultures forbid suicide. He wondered, who is to say that a person's attachment to life should be stronger than anything else in the world? What about terminally ill people who don't want to prolong an agonizing death? He understood the anguish, determination, and dignity that can compel the dying who choose assisted suicide.

Murder. That's what the law called it. Murder. The law would not consider that he helped people live out their last functional weeks and months as peacefully, spiritually, and productively as possible. All they would see is a murderer. His conscience was clear about what he did. In fact, he felt good about it in one way because most of the time the terminally ill were turned down by their closest friends and family when they pleaded for help in the transition to the spirit world.

His problem was with the guilt he sometimes felt over profiting from the death of his clients. He was in the highly lucrative viatical settlement business. For an investment, his company purchases life insurance policies at a discount from individuals in the late stages of a terminal illness.

When he got to know a client he offered them his wisdom on the transition from life to death. He taught them how to accept that death was coming and how to prepare emotionally and spiritually. If the client was physically able, he encouraged them to help nurture animals – ideally, horses. Even if the client wasn't able or interested in being with animals, he guided them by sharing what he had learned from the Native American pathways

Cali Canberra

and Eastern philosophy about departing from Earth.

From time to time, he became close to a client and they would discuss assisted suicide. Many terminally ill people desired to avoid future suffering, but if no one was willing to help them die when the agony was severe, it meant they must take their own life while still mentally and physically capable of doing so. In taking that course of action, they would cut off an unknown amount of tolerable, if not pleasant, life. He discovered that with his guarantee to help if the pain became brutal and relentless, many clients could hang on and experience the natural route to death.

When clients pleaded with him to end their suffering, he would be told in advance at what point in their illness they wanted to die, such as when they couldn't think clearly and couldn't eat and breathe on their own, or when they were taking so much morphine they couldn't feel anything, good or bad. A terminally ill person thinks that when he gets to a certain point, he knows that is when he wants to die. Then, that point comes, and they think they can handle more - as a result, they choose a different point. He called it *'moving the line in the sand'*. He honored their wishes and did the kindest thing a person could do for another living being: help him die with dignity before the pain became absolutely unbearable and his body withered away.

Chapter 1

Grayson Solvan inhaled the aroma of the crisp, fresh air as he mounted Chief, his muscular copper-colored chestnut stallion. Today, as he adjusted himself in the saddle and gathered the hand-braided romal reins, he was interrupted by his ringing cell phone. The caller ID showed it was Misty, his secretary.

"Mr. Solvan," Misty said solemnly, "I'm sorry to bother you, but Lou Pannetta called. He needs to see you as soon as possible."

A hot lump formed in his throat then sank to his chest. "Thanks for calling. Is there anything else?"

Misty hesitated. "No, sir. Enjoy the farm."

"I always do. Create a nice day."

He didn't want to deal with the outside world. Not anymore today at least. Sitting straight in his saddle, he tried to clear his mind of the obstacles he would need to overcome to ensure his lifestyle would continue - and so that he wouldn't end up on death row. Texas was known as a state that didn't mind executions.

He powered off his phone and opened his spirit to the wide-open sky. At the farm, he and Chief could simply *be*.

The even-tempered stallion collected himself without a cue from his rider. Chief knew that arena riding meant to flex his poll and round out his back as he reached his hindquarters deeper under himself. The stallion walked down the fence line unconcerned about the hawk on the corner post.

After two laps at a walk and jog to make sure his horse was sound, Grayson completed the reining horse pattern that won him the 2003 NRHA Futurity Championship. When he finished the pattern, he opted for a scenic ride to the cattle pasture. Chief's ears perked up as they headed out the arena gate. The stallion

Cali Canberra

eagerly entered the depths of the forest, trotting down the wide pine-needle-covered dirt trail. The buzz of grasshoppers seemed amplified and the strong scent of honeysuckle hung in the air.

A half-mile into the ride, the sun glided behind a group of billowing clouds. A brisk breeze swept in announcing the change of seasons. The chill sent goose bumps down Grayson's arms as the wind pulled at his long-sleeved denim shirt. The unpredictable weather in Kiamichi Country of southeastern Oklahoma was no surprise to the Texan. Today, the cool air and the rustle of wind through the leaves were the right ingredients to rile up the precocious Quarter Horse. Chief searched the shadows looking for monsters behind trees and boulders. When the horse was younger, he spooked at imaginary horrors but now, with more maturity and mileage, he settled for simply staying on lookout with flaring nostrils, pointed ears, and arching neck. When Chief was buoyed up by the exhilaration of anything, Grayson let him work it out by climbing a steep grade or galloping on a loose rein until he got it out of his system. If a rider tried to hold him back, Chief braced against the bit and took off bucking.

As the wind blew harder and the clouds drifted away, Grayson abandoned his plan to ride out to the cattle pasture. He turned onto the sand and loam trail running parallel to the river and then imperceptibly squeezed his calves and gave the horse his head. The horse flicked his ears back. Twelve-hundred pounds of horseflesh exploded into action with a pipe-opening gallop, letting out some pent-up steam for himself and his rider.

A mile or so later, recalling that Chief had a new set of shoes, Grayson took the Bobcat Trail to the right and galloped the powerhouse up the stone-riddled slope. The horse navigated his own way, never taking a single misstep. He had been shod since he was a two-year-old, leaving his hooves with very little feeling in them. The subject of horse shoes was a point of contention between Grayson's old ways of horsemanship and the ways of natural horsemanship he had adopted. His horses wore shoes all of their lives and became tender-footed when he tried to let them go barefoot. Although convinced that barefoot horses are healthier,

Wisdom of the Horse

he still felt guilty knowing his horses were sore because their feet needed to be toughened up. Chief was the only one of his riding horses with his shoes replaced - Grayson didn't want down time with his favorite horse until at least two other horses he could ride hard were toughened up to do the job. For the most part, the ground in southeastern Oklahoma was hard and unforgiving, and the majority of the mountain trails were rocky. He had spent thousands of dollars and hundreds of man-hours creating a mountain trail system cleared of rock and replaced with good footing, but he couldn't justify doing the same to every mountain trail on the four-thousand acre property. Fortunately, there was plenty of pastureland to ride on with good footing, but the wilderness experience could really only be appreciated in the mountainous terrain.

At the crest of the long rocky trail they frightened a herd of grazing antelope. Chief's eyes bulged. The antelope scampered off into the hardwoods as Chief snorted nervously. Grayson stroked Chief's sweaty neck to calm him down and they eventually walked off as if nothing had happened.

Finally, the wind dwindled to a gentle breeze. A few minutes later they arrived in a lush valley - a hundred acres of gently swaying grass dotted with a cross-country course of rustic jumps. Two mowed acres of carved out flatland contrasted the expanse of rolling hills and deep woods. In the center of the valley a perfectly graded sand arena with a jump course and covered viewing deck stood out like a glistening diamond on a piece of draped green velvet. The pristine land glowed with foliage almost blinding in its brightness - vivid amber red cedars, harvest gold elms, and dark purplish black gum trees set in the field of tall nut clover and panicum grasses.

From the distance Grayson squinted into the sun and admired his wife, Laura, astride Touché, her most promising Warmblood. Over the last several years she had become a formidable competitor in Three-Day Eventing - an equestrian competition consisting of dressage, cross-country jumping, and stadium jumping - equated to a triathlon. Laura, a record-holder

Cali Canberra

NCAA competitive swimmer, tore her rotator cuff during her senior year on a swimming scholarship at Stanford. The injury devastated her; she'd have no chance to compete in the Olympics - a lifelong aspiration. She grew up with a fiercely competitive spirit, both as an elite athlete and a student. As an adult, horseback riding would be her only chance to compete in the Olympics. She'd do whatever it took to attain that goal and make her dream a reality. She wasn't afraid to spend the money or do the work required to have a fleeting chance at glory.

The sun created creeping shadows on the jump course. Grayson was interested to see what effect they would have on Touché's performance. Before Laura bought Touché he was proving himself hard to beat in speed classes. The first time she test rode him the poles were set at 3'6" - he felt unstoppable and made the jump course feel easy. The animal's natural inclination was far from subdued, but that's what Laura was ready for. She wrote a check for $350,000 that day without so much as a veterinary pre-purchase exam.

This afternoon, after one playful buck, Touché concentrated on his job. Surged with power, he jumped a fluent, immaculate round with perfect rhythm. In schooling sessions the horse jumped with neatly folded legs high and wide, never rushing - but under the pressure of competition, Laura became nervous and caused the horse to feel insecure.

Grayson rode toward the arena to get a closer look. Laura went for a long spot, but she placed the horse a little bit far off the base of the jump. It was obvious Touché thought it wasn't quite right, but he still jumped it clean.

David O'Conner, an equestrian Olympian and the president of the U.S. Equestrian Federation stood with his arms crossed in the middle of the ring, his analytical eyes scrutinizing every movement of horse and rider. As a result of what Laura considered her most dismal performance at Devon, she hired O'Conner to assess her and her horse's abilities. After evaluating the string of horses and sorting out the awkward ones, O'Conner agreed to work with Laura and her daughter Heather so they would be better prepared for Wellington, Devon, and Rolex. If she didn't start placing higher, Laura planned to quit competing. She was sure that with the right instructor she and her horses could manifest the spark of brilliance needed to win against stiff competition.

Laura and her kids (from her first marriage) immersed themselves in the elite horse world as Grayson did everything in his power to fit into their lifestyle while remaining true to his own interests. For the moment, astride Chief and overlooking the expanse of the jump course, Grayson simply wanted to relish the one-time dream life that had become his reality.

Chapter 2

Leaving their Oklahoma ranch on the private jet, Laura, exhausted from riding, kicked off her shoes, sprawled out on the sofa and sighed. "I've got to talk my father into keeping the plane. I can't imagine living without it," she said as if she were referring to living without an automobile.

Grayson moved to the sofa, positioned himself at her feet and began massaging her soles and ankles. "He wasn't serious when he said he's going to sell it. Don't worry."

"Yes, he was. You know he hardly uses it anymore."

"He'll never sell it. You'll inherit it before that happens. He's eighty-two years old. The old man's not going to live forever."

"He might. He's never been sick a day in his life. Anyway, if I inherit it, I'll have to sell it. I don't have the kind of money it takes to maintain a Gulfstream. You better hope he lives forever!"

"We'll have the money," Grayson said without further explanation. He never worried about a lack of money. He only feared experiencing a poverty of purpose.

Laura hoped her husband wasn't assuming he would control her money. That's why they had a prenuptial agreement - to protect her from losing her assets and all she would inherit.

Laura squeezed her toes into a fist when he dug his thumb into her insole. "Ouch!" she screamed playfully. "Daddy said we use it more than everyone else in the family combined. He thinks we're starting to act like we're entitled, and he doesn't like our attitude about it."

"Your father can't seem to grasp our hectic schedules."

In addition to using the plane for business, Laura, Grayson, and the kids flew back-and-forth from their home in Dallas to the

Wisdom of the Horse

Oklahoma farm, and all of them flew to different horse shows. They needed the plane.

Laura sat up abruptly. "I'm seriously thinking of selling the spas. There are so many opening up everywhere."

Ten years earlier, Laura opened day spas catering to women without the time or the money to stay at exclusive spa resorts. Her father approved her business plan and funded the start-up. The business was successful in the sense that she had opened thirty locations nationwide, and although very few of them generated a significant profit, at least none of them lost money.

Grayson beamed. "You've met the challenge of developing your business. You know you're bright and capable of doing anything you set your mind to. Sell out and concentrate on the horses. That's what you and the kids enjoy the most anyway."

Laura nodded. "I think I'll redirect my time into being in the horse business."

"The horse business?" Grayson said, surprised at her reply. Although he would never tell her, he hoped she wouldn't. In his opinion, for the most part, the horse business revolved too much around perceptions of reality. So much of the business was so consumed with image that substance rarely mattered.

"Yes."

"I meant that you should simply enjoy working with your trainers and riding your horses - competing - and going to the kids' competitions."

"And yours?" she said playfully.

"That would be nice," he said, trying not to sound as if he felt neglected.

"I don't like all that cowboy stuff. You know that."

"Quarter Horses aren't all about 'cowboy stuff'! I've told you a million times - there are plenty of English classes."

"I know," Laura agreed. "But it's not the same as what I do."

"Are you saying you and your horses are superior?" he said playfully. He never argued the value of their riding disciplines, sensing such arguments would put distance between them.

"It goes without saying," she shot back, and then gave him a flirtatious wink. In her opinion, preparing the horse and rider for eventing is the ultimate challenge for a serious equestrian.

"A lot of the riders aren't cowboys as you call them."

"Don't get so defensive."

"I'm not. It's just that there's more to the horse world than eventing."

"I know that," Laura shot back. She had never discouraged her son, Brett, from showing his Polish-bred Arabians in English Pleasure, Park, and Reining. Her father rode western, so she never discouraged Grayson's involvement with Quarter Horses. In fact, she had admired his show record in Western events. Over the years, Grayson had won reining and cutting horse championships at Quarter Horse Congress and the AQHA World Championships.

As long as the family all loved horses, she was fine. They needed to have something in common. The horses were ideal – as was the time they all spent together at the farm.

He lightened up. "So, what are we arguing about?"

Laura didn't realize she had sounded ticked off. "We're not arguing. I was saying that I think I want to be in the horse business - not just own and ride horses. I'm not depressed or anything, but I feel like there's something missing in my life - I'm just not fulfilled like I want to be."

Grayson understood. He had sensed her recent discontent and had been in the same place emotionally many times in his life. "Why don't you make a professional appointment with Shin?"

She bit her bottom lip as she gave his suggestion some thought. "I don't need a therapist. I'm just saying that I think I want to be in the horse business."

"In what way? Buying and selling? Breeding? A public training operation?"

She tilted her head. "I don't know. I'm trying to decide."

"So, just enjoying them isn't enough for you anymore?"

"Not with the kids growing up and becoming more independent. I need something more, like what I have with the spas. But with horses, the business would actually be meaningful."

"You don't need to make money. I make plenty."

Wisdom of the Horse

You mean I have plenty from my trust and you hope I inherit more, she thought. "I know you do, but it's not about the money. I can't explain it."

"I understand. The safety of the known stifles the experience of life. You want to do something different to help you make sense of your life outside of your family." He knew first-hand that when you stretch yourself you discover an energy source within you that allows renewal.

She rested her head on his shoulder and wove her fingers through his. "I wish I could think the way you do and communicate my feelings like you do. You're so eloquent - it makes me feel so simple. I guess simple is the only word I can think of to describe it. Simple, or shallow."

"Don't think that way," he said almost in a whisper. He kissed her forehead and looked deep into her eyes. "The more you allow yourself exposure to the things I'm involved in, the more it will be internalized and the more you'll benefit. Just remember, what you know matters less than what you feel. The mind, body, and spirit are chemically connected. It only stands to reason that you need to stay aware of how your heart feels."

"Is that what you do? You seem so together now," she said, hoping he wouldn't be insulted. As a result of facing emotional challenges, Grayson went through a metamorphosis. She loved him when they met and married, but now she admired him too.

Grayson didn't point out that her world view was limited, but he felt compelled to urge her to expand her awareness. "Why don't you spend more time with Shin - not related to therapy, but just being with her when she works with the horses - and spend more time with Tate and Thundering Cloud? You've already learned a lot from them." The Crow family shared their wisdom about life, animals, and nature. Since befriending them, Grayson's inner chaos had ended as he developed a whole new relationship with nature and his horses. He now lived a purposeful and meaningful life and he continued on a journey of discovery.

"I am interested in the Native American ways," Laura admitted to him for the first time.

"It's not just Native American ways," Grayson said while he had her attention on the subject. She usually had no interest in anything spiritual, ritualistic, or philosophical. "They'll guide you in ways that at the core are universal to all ancient spiritual practices—including Taoism, Buddhism, and Hinduism. They all have many common beliefs. The very essence of the beliefs are what are important. Not the details."

Laura nodded. "I suppose you're right."

"You need to stop tuning out the longings you feel. You need to confront them and act on them."

"That's why I think I want to be in the horse business instead of the spa business."

Grayson was in the process of developing a hospice and a horse rescue program on the five hundred acres adjacent to their farm. He was grateful to be financially and physically in a place where few others would have the opportunity. He stroked her back. "How about helping out with the rescue horses?"

"Maybe. I've actually been considering that. I was thinking about how now that some of the rescue horses are gaining weight, you ought to start buying tack. If I were you, I'd start looking for used saddles. With so many horses coming and going, you'll need every size and style."

Grayson had already ordered a dozen new Tucker endurance saddles - rider comfort was critical, especially for new equestrians and those not in good physical conditions. The gel seat and the tree design made them versatile for horses and their passengers.

"I gave Joel cash to take to some of the shows. There are always people with used saddles for sale."

Joel had worked on the farm for almost a year. When he was released from his last stint in jail he didn't have a place to live or anyone to turn to for help. His last foster family, whom he had kept in touch with as a young adult, wouldn't have anything to do with him, having given up hope that he could change his ways. Joel's extensive juvenile record was followed by two DUI's, a breaking and entering arrest where the charges were dropped,

Wisdom of the Horse

and then two breaking and entering convictions - the last of which sent him to prison. Upon Joel's release, his parole officer suggested he try to find a job that provided housing, such as at an agricultural business. There were a lot of cattle and horse operations in Oklahoma. The day after Joel regained his freedom, Grayson ran help wanted ads in a dozen newspapers throughout the state. Joel called him, told him of his record, and swore that if he could get one more chance to succeed he would be a changed man. Grayson was convinced anyone could change with proper guidance and support. He hired Joel based on the telephone call and hadn't regretted his decision.

Laura shook her head at the idea of Grayson giving Joel a substantial amount of cash. "I hope you're making him get itemized receipts with the contact information of the sellers."

"No. I'm not going to do that. He needs to know that he's proven himself trustworthy. He's started a new life and I'm proud of him. I've enjoyed mentoring him, and so has Bruce," Grayson said, referring to their farm manager.

"If you're comfortable," she said, "then I am too." Her husband had evolved into a man born to heal the spirit. Sometimes she thought it was one of the few things that gave his life any meaning.

"He's a good kid. He just needs people to believe in him."

Laura nodded. "By the way, did you read the article in *Natural Horse* magazine about the PMU horses? They use the urine from pregnant mares to make Premarin®." As many as eight million post-menopausal women have been taking the drug for hormone replacement therapy to alleviate the symptoms of menopause.

"I didn't read anything about it. What's the big deal about using urine from pregnant mares?"

She shook her head. "The harvesting of the urine requires about 70,000 pregnant mares to live in five-foot standing stalls, each with a bag attached to the base of her tail to catch her urine. What's even worse – the byproduct of doing this is thousands of foals being sent to slaughter."

Grayson turned pale at the thought. "Why don't they sell the foals to people who will raise them and ride them?"

"They just don't. It's sickening. They just want to get rid of the byproduct as quickly and easily as they can."

"That's horrific," Grayson said, appalled. "Hasn't this been made public outside of the horse community?"

"Not that I'm aware of. I don't really know. I think we should adopt some of those mares."

He didn't need to consider her idea any further. "Definitely."

"I wish you could join us on the camping trip. A couple of my clients will be there for the sweat lodge," Grayson said.

"Maybe another time. I wish it didn't conflict with Brett showing," she said, referring to the U.S. Arabian Nationals in Louisville, Kentucky.

Grayson had planned on watching Brett and his horse, Accomplice, compete for the reining horse championship, but when Brett decided not to risk the gelding's health after his colic episode, Grayson cancelled his plans and rescheduled the camping trip for the same dates. They originally planned on camping the last weekend in October, but that timing would be more likely to have inclement weather.

"Brett wants me to meet this man who has Dutch Harness Horses. Apparently he's looking for a silent partner."

"I've never heard of Dutch Harness Horses," he said dismissively.

"The pictures look interesting. I promised Brett I would meet the man," she said.

"Why are there going to be Dutch Harness Horses at the Arabian Nationals?"

"I don't think the horses will be there. The guy - his name is Greg Bordeaux - crosses them with Arabians. He was a big-timer back before the tax reform. Brett said he more or less disappeared from the public eye for the past decade as he reorganized his life, got remarried, and some other long saga I really didn't pay much attention to. Anyway, Greg's going to be at the Nationals and I promised Brett I'd at least hear a proposal and maybe go to his

Wisdom of the Horse

farm - it's about an hour away from the show grounds."

Laura wasn't just going by what Brett had said about Greg. She had heard Bordeaux's name over the years through her ex-husband, Drew, who had dabbled in various breeds of horses, including Arabians and Half-Arabians in the early eighties. Drew gathered small groups of investors together (usually from their country club in Dallas) to form partnerships to speculate on a few horses at a time. They'd pay Drew to find undervalued horses, get them in prime condition, maybe bred to a popular stallion, and then try to get the horse consigned to a February Vintage Arabians auction in Scottsdale. They made incredible profits from time to time. They never lost money on the Polish Arabians with bloodlines tracing to the Vintage Arabians program. The best part was, they never took possession of the Arabians, leaving Laura's farm an exclusive and private showplace for her eventing horses.

Eventually, some of Drew's banking and oilmen cohorts pushed him into trying to do the same thing in Texas so they could easily visit the horses that they were risking so much money on. By private invitation, the group attended an elaborate presentation about investing in Egyptian Arabians through a bloodstock agency where the principal owners were a Class 'A' Judge and a successful trainer who owned a prestigious farm in Waco. To top it off, the bloodstock agent was very influential in the Pyramid Society, the Egyptian Arabian breeder organization. Against Drew's better judgment, the group bought five Egyptian horses. They lost most of their money. Next, they tried investing in Russian Arabians with a prominent farm in Baton Rouge, Louisiana. It turned out that their investment was a scam. Eventually, Laura got so fed up with Drew's get-rich-quick-and-easy mentality she didn't even want to hear about what he was doing.

"If Bordeaux's so experienced, why does he want a silent partner?" Grayson asked, confused.

Laura rolled her eyes. "I don't know exactly. Brett said he really only had one major client - some heavy-hitter from Southern California – and the client was bailing on him for some reason. I'm not sure really. Something about Greg relying on just one client to spend enough money to support his horse venture."

"Sounds like a bad move on his part," Grayson said.

"Brett pleaded with me to meet him. He's convinced this guy is on to something with the Dutch Harness Horses, and he acts like Greg is the next best thing to God. Who knows? All I could do is to tell him I'd listen."

"Write down this guy's name. I'll call one of my private investigators to check him out and dig up details on his background. You should know more about him before you seriously consider a proposal."

Laura wrote the name Greg Bordeaux on a slip of paper, folded it in half, gave it to her husband and then cuddled up to him, molding her body to his.

Chapter 3

The smells in the ICU triggered Grayson's gut-wrenching memories as he walked down the corridor. The door to Lou's room swung open just as he approached. The nurse exited, eyed Grayson up and down, and wondered if he were immediate family. He wasn't.

Grayson walked into the room, a hesitation in his steps. It had been a long time since he saw anyone with tubes in their arms, surrounded by beeping medical monitors and equipment sending reports on vital signs. He felt the heat rise in his face as the memory of Lana hit him like a punch in the stomach – the last time they were together was the most transforming event of his life.

Today, in the stark institutional room, Lou lay before him with dark sunken eyes, his pale white face nearly translucent. Since Grayson last saw him, his muscles wasted away, accentuating his emaciated frame – his skull protruded beneath his face, making him appear skeletal. It was somber and strange.

Grayson noticed how the blood pressure cuff looked enormous on Lou's withered frail body. Saline and sedatives dripped from the IV in his paper-thin veined arm. The bag attached to the catheter was empty. The nurse must have just changed it. The ebb and flow of Lou's life was artificially controlled by the breathing tube in his nose and his throat. It's not what he wanted. That, he knew for certain.

Grayson lowered the bedrail and gently sat on the edge of the mattress. Lou reached out a hand hoping his brittle yellowed fingernails weren't repugnant. For a moment, tension grew in Grayson's body then quickly evaporated. He cupped Lou's hand between his own and looked straight into his friend's eyes. He just knew the blood drained from his own face as he did so, but he hoped it went unnoticed. His instinct was to hug Lou, but Lou's prominent collar bone and shoulders looked as if they might snap if he wasn't as gentle as he knew he'd need to be.

"I got here as soon as I could," Grayson said finally.

Lou nodded. "I told Carol not to bring me," he said with great effort as the cords of his neck tightened.

"You've always known she didn't agree with you."

Carol told her husband that she could never live with herself if he signed a DNR order. There was no way she'd agree to withhold life-saving measures. She firmly believed that with enough prayer and pure will there was always a chance that things could get better.

When Lou began experiencing the rapid deterioration of the quality of his existence, he confided to Grayson that he lost his tenacity to continue clinging to life. His inner fire was extinguished. There was no hope. He didn't want to linger. He didn't want his family to live that way.

Lou's throat constricted, making it nearly impossible to communicate. Pronouncing each word seemed laborious. "It's my time. I'm ready."

Grayson stood. His face was carved with grave sorrow as he delicately pulled the vial and syringe out of his jacket pocket. He stuck the needle in the vial, angled it just so, and pulled back the plunger. With the syringe full he answered his friend's plea. Lou, an oncologist, was ironically dying of colon cancer. He gave his instructions – when the time came, Grayson was to inject the prepared combination dose of pancurium bromide, potasium chloride, and sodium pentothal into the IV. Without a doubt, it was time.

Grayson's hands trembled as he simultaneously said goodbye to Lou and injected the IV.

His eyes vacant, he left the room and the hospital as quickly as he could, thinking about how two years earlier, it was Lou who first posed the question to him - why is it that when inevitable death is imminent it is legal and morally acceptable to make the decision to refuse forms of treatment that would only prolong life - yet, when it comes to actively helping someone with a terminal illness to die, it is murder?

Chapter 4

Feeling a wild helplessness in her chest, Cia drove toward town counting the telephone poles on the two-lane highway. She didn't know why she bothered - there were always 87 poles between the end of her long gravel driveway and the farm and ranch store. Actually, she knew why she was counting. It was the same reason as always - the unsettling fact that her life was in shambles, and she was willing herself not to drive off the road - not to end up like a crushed aluminum beer can at the bottom of a steep gully. With an expression of permanent weariness she blinked in double time, her eyes dry, grainy, and completely cried out.

By the time she approached the outskirts of town, she found herself plagued by the recurring acceleration of her own heartbeat. Her stomach clenched at the idea of her underlying truth - she was sinking deeper into emotional quicksand. She wanted a physical reason for the ache inside, but she knew there was none. She tried so hard, but she couldn't suppress the deep ache invading her body, stealing her courage and will to go on. She could turn around and blow off her appointment like last week, but today, for a change, the fatalistic knot in her gut wouldn't let her back down from starting to face her demons. This was the eleventh appointment she had made, but the first one she hadn't cancelled. If she didn't keep this appointment she was afraid she would leap from the ledge of sanity.

Driving past the bleak faces of old buildings, some even boarded up and closed for good, Cia glanced at the plastic digital clock affixed with two-sided tape to the cracked dashboard of her Toyota Corolla. There was just enough time to grab a chocolate shake at Elvin's. As she pulled around to the drive-up lane she

Wisdom of the Horse

almost rear-ended Harry in his stalled out old pickup truck loaded down with trash bags and a mangled aluminum chair. Once the ignition finally turned over, Harry's old heap sputtered out a noxious odor that nearly triggered Cia's gag reflex. He ignored her and drove off, undoubtedly to the bar down the block.

Elvin's hand-written 'broken speaker' sign was still duct taped to the menu board. Cia drove directly to the takeout window.

"Your usual Cia?" Melba said with a southern drawl, wiping her hands dry on the seat of her polyester pants. She couldn't help but notice the dark bags under Cia's eyes.

"No. Just a shake. I'm in a hurry."

"It's on the house, sugar. You look like you could use it."

She yelled for a double chocolate shake and handed Cia a straw and napkin. Cia winced, thinking about how pitiful she must look if even Melba felt sorry for her.

A few winding miles later she loudly slurped the last few drops of her shake from the bottom of the wax coated cup. She parked on what remained of the cracked asphalt at the county mental health center. The decrepit building was lined with wind etchings from years of neglect. She slammed her car door as hard as she could so the door would catch. It didn't work, so she gave it a kick in just the right place to insure it wouldn't swing open and hit the Impala next to her - even though the owner probably wouldn't have noticed through the other dents and nicks covering the car. In the recess of her mind she thanked heaven her parents couldn't see her life deteriorating before their eyes. They tried to keep her in college by offering to buy her a new Mustang convertible. She refused, insisting no one found true love more than once. She found her true love in Jeffrey. Her parents still hung up on her when she called. When they threatened to disown her if she married Jeffrey, she never believed they were serious. Just because he wasn't Jewish, they wouldn't accept their relationship, let alone her marriage. All her life they ingrained in her that she must marry a Jew.

Minutes after parking she sat morosely on a metal folding chair in the waiting room filling out a questionnaire about her moods, her eating and sleeping patterns, and the reason she sought counseling. Her stomach felt hollow as she contemplated a simple explanation. She wrote, 'I'm here because I'm broke.' The statement was true in more ways than one. As far as she was concerned, she was a hopeless case, but Jeffrey said she just needed to talk to a professional. She had to at least try.

Right on schedule, Shin, a young woman with a dark, flawless complexion and deep brown eyes entered the waiting room wearing Birkenstocks, tattered stone-washed jeans, and a loose fitting ruby-red cotton tunic with a scooped neckline beaded with traditional Olivetta Bibiplicata "Purple Olives"- once the most common shell beads created by Coastal Natives.

"Cia?"

"Yes," Cia answered nervously, dreading spilling her guts to a stranger.

"I'm Shin Crow."

Cia nodded, the sorrow on her face evident. She followed the slender, lithe woman down a dank, narrow, pale yellow hallway. Each step made her wonder if she had made a mistake in coming to such a depressing place. Then, entering the open office door, the fatigue lines surrounding her eyes and mouth faded. A look of puzzlement crossed her face. She was transported to another place and time.

Shin's dark eyes sparkled when she said, "Make yourself comfortable." She began to read the form Cia had filled out.

Cia sank into the cowhide chair, entranced by the ambiance of the cozy room. The hypnotic sound of Mozart and the fragrance of cedar incense drifted through the room. Calming water trickling down the stones of a small fountain in the corner instantly put her at ease. Cia explored the room with her eyes. The fawn-toned walls were simply decorated with pottery on free-standing antique barn-wood wall shelves. A Native American blanket hand-woven in earth colors hung on the largest wall. Next to a bleached buffalo skull, a Navajo rawhide quiver hung on the wall behind Shin's desk. Books, stones, and candles covered the aged wrought iron coffee table. A lamp made from

Wisdom of the Horse

antlers and a hand-carved Peace Pipe with intricate beadwork on the handle sat on the petrified wood end table.

"I feel so at ease in here," Cia commented, almost in disbelief. Her mind buzzed with regrets for canceling her previous appointments.

"Me, too."

A long silence passed as the heaviness of her fatigue washed over her like a wave in the ocean. "It's euphoric. I'm afraid I might just fall asleep."

"You don't sleep well," Shin acknowledged, reading the questionnaire.

"I can't remember the last time I've slept well for more than a night or two. It's been years."

"Would you like to go to sleep now?" Shin asked in her mesmerizing voice.

Cia looked stricken. "I'm not going home to take a nap now that I'm finally here. You must know I've cancelled about a dozen appointments."

Shin looked deep into Cia's eyes as if she were looking into her soul. "I meant - would you like to sleep now? Here in this room? The sofa is very comfortable," she said, directing her gaze toward the back wall.

"I'm here for therapy. Not for a nap," Cia responded. She wondered if her answer was a test to see how much she really wanted help.

"A rested person is better in touch with their feelings. Sleep deprivation can cause emotional and physical problems."

Cia nodded, instantly glad she had chosen Shin for her therapy. Her eyes held an empathy she never expected.

"But what about your next appointment? I'm only scheduled for an hour."

"You can sleep here as long as you'd like. I have two other rooms," Shin assured her.

Relief reflected in Cia's tired red eyes. Shin led her to the wide worn suede sofa. Cia laid down, closed her eyes, and adjusted the down pillow under her head and neck as Shin covered her with a cozy heavy blanket.

From the room next door, Shin dialed the phone.

On the second ring a man answered. "Costa's." His first instinct was still to say Mathews, but he never let it slip.

"Jeffrey Costa, please," Shin said.

"Speaking."

"Mr. Costa. My name is Shin Crow -"

He cut her off. "Is my wife hurt? I told her I'd drive her -" he said weakly, unable to keep the quaver from his voice.

She broke in immediately, sensing his panic. "Your wife is fine. I wanted to let you know that she's in my office, asleep. If it's not a problem, I'd like to let her sleep as long as her body tells her to."

Jeffrey furrowed his brows. He paused, his face stiffened. "Asleep?"

"Yes. She's suffering from a state of exhaustion as a result of sleep deprivation," she said in a non-accusatory manner.

"I know. She won't take the sleeping pills her doctor prescribed, and I can't seem to—"

She interrupted. "I'm not blaming you for her lack of sleep, Mr. Costa. I'm simply informing you that she's safe and asleep in my office. Would it be a problem if she stays here?"

"Well, no. I suppose not. I'm just glad she finally got to your office. You come very highly recommended and I've been trying to get her to see you. Wasn't her appointment scheduled for fifteen minutes ago?"

"Yes."

"So you bring a patient to your office and suggest they go to sleep?" His anger was braided together with strands of reason.

"No. Not normally. But this is what your wife needs. She's so exhausted I didn't have the opportunity to actually talk with her. I see on her patient questionnaire that you have a daughter. Is someone available to take care of her?"

Jeffery wondered if Cia had told Shin that she had thoughts about suicide. She had never told him directly, but there were hints and he didn't know how to handle it other than urging her to see a therapist.

"Our daughter is with me. I work out of the garage at our house. It's no problem. I'm just glad Cia's finally getting help."

"Does your daughter have that flu bug? I hear it's spreading all over the schools."

"No, she doesn't have the flu bug," he said, wishing that's all that was wrong.

Shin looked out her window. "I'll let Cia sleep and have her call you when she wakes up."

"Thank you. Thank you very much."

"One more thing. Cia didn't fill out the information about your health insurance."

"We don't have health insurance. Can't afford it. Isn't the county program for people who can't pay for medical expenses?" Not only could they not afford it, but even if they had the money they would need to show valid identification to get the insurance. That wasn't going to happen.

"Lots of people with insurance use our services also. And people without insurance pay on a sliding scale based upon what they can afford."

"We can't afford anything." Adversity had become a way of life.

"The forms Cia filled out indicate she's not employed, but you own your own business. Certainly you can afford to pay something on a sliding scale."

"My wife isn't employed because we home-school our daughter."

"You own a business."

"That doesn't mean I make much money," he said, a strong tension taking hold. "I own a television repair shop and I can barely pay the bills. There's not as much business as you think in a small town like this. If people own an old set needing repairs, they're only repairing it because they can't afford a new one. If they can't afford even a low priced new set, I can't charge these people that much to repair..."

She sighed. "I get it. I'll see what I can do."

"Ms. Crow?"
"Shin."
"Fine. Shin – please help my wife."
She heard unmistakable pleading in his voice. "Like I said, I'll see what I can do."

Chapter 5

Cia woke up on the sofa. Now that she was at eye level with the coffee table she noticed the kachina dolls. She hadn't recalled them being there before. She had no idea how long she had slept - perhaps it had been an hour or two, but she felt rested for the first time in months. If only she could sleep that sound at night. Across the room, Shin was deep in thought writing an article about holistic health care for horses. The deadline for the magazine was in just a couple of days. When she first began writing for equestrian magazines she was enthusiastic, but after the first several articles she realized it wasn't the kind of writing she really wanted to be doing. She dreamed of writing fiction, utilizing her creativity in a way not possible with non-fiction. If her older brother hadn't started his career first and become so successful, she wouldn't have hesitated to pursue her dream.

"Thanks for letting me sleep. I was desperate for a nap."

Shin smiled. "That was a long nap."

"Do we have time to talk?"

"Not this morning, but if you can come back at around five, I'll have all the time you want."

Cia was momentarily confused and then realized Shin was wearing a burnt orange-colored blouse and a necklace with an ancient Chinese coin pendant. When she had seen her last she was wearing a dark red top, a different style. "How long did I sleep?"

"Over eighteen hours. I'm impressed at your bladder control."

"Eighteen hours?"

"Yes. You're sleep deprived."

"You've been in here with me for that long?"

"No. I met with my other clients in the room down the hall. Then I checked on you before our group met last night. We meet from seven until ten. I checked on you again after group. You were still out like a light, so I went home for a change of clothes and another pillow and blanket. I slept on the sofa in the other room - with the door open so I would hear you if you woke up. I've been up since six this morning."

Cia felt a sharp stab of regret. "My husband must be worried sick. He probably thinks I've gone off and slit my wrists or something. He's probably called the hospital."

"Calm down. I called him after you fell asleep yesterday, then I called again last night. He's glad you're getting sleep. Can you come back at five?"

~ ~ ~ ~ ~

"Instead of taking a bath, do you want to try to come outside and play in the swimming pool?" Jeffrey asked his daughter. They had just bought an above-ground pool at a garage sale, hoping to entice her to use the fun floats and the water volleyball game.

Elizabeth glanced out the front window and then the kitchen window. "No. I want a bath," she answered without giving the swimming pool suggestion serious consideration.

"Mommy's going to get happy!" she told her father as she finished eating her hot dog. She always finished the other food on her plate before she ate her macaroni so she could make designs on the plate with her noodles. She loved arts and crafts - it was something she could do without going outdoors.

Jeffrey smiled at her, skillfully hiding the sadness he felt. A child deserved a happy mother. For that matter, a husband deserved a happy wife. And Cia deserved to be happy. Half of this was his fault. Years ago he could have made a good living honestly, but he got adventurous and greedy. Not a good combination. As a result, their lives would never be the same.

Wisdom of the Horse

"How many times will Mommy see the lady who is going to make her happy?"

"How ever many times it takes, honey."

"I'm happy and you're happy. Why isn't Mommy?"

"I don't know, sweetie, but you know she loves you. And, I love you. Speaking of happy, honey – I would be even happier if you'd play in the pool with me."

"No way."

~ ~ ~ ~ ~

Although Cia was anxious to meet with Shin, a rising apprehension grew inside. Terror spread in her belly and chest as she wondered if Shin would be asking specific questions, like: what's the worst thing you've ever done in your life? She sensed a growing tension in her muscles. Deep inside, dread pulsed through her veins.

In her normal haze of depression she arrived fifteen minutes early. This time she was led to a different room. Serene flute music played in the background. A stunning Trigram hung on one wall. In the east corner, a large fountain slowly trickled water over smooth black stones. Crystals in the shape of mythical creatures were displayed on the southwest wall. A modest collection of Yin and Yang symbols lay scattered about the room, as were artful objects made of wood. Scented blue, red, and green candles were lit. An aquarium was a serene home for a variety of brightly colored fish. A prism and a cut crystal hung in front of the window creating a bright spectrum of colors. A rectangular jute mat covered the vinyl tiled floor.

Shin sat on top of a plush, thick amber pillow with her knees tucked under herself. Cia, feeling numb and helpless, followed Shin's lead, lowering herself cross-legged onto an enormous pale blue floor pillow at the low, round glass-top table in the center of the room.

Shin poured two cups of mint flavored green tea that had been steeping in a deep brown pottery tea set imbedded with symbols of the five elements. "I was in the mood for this room," Shin said simply, and then sipped her tea.

"It's beautiful," Cia said, her face a mask of anguish.

Shin gave Cia a minute of silence and then spoke in a mesmerizing tone. "As of this moment you can shed your old ways of thinking, like a snake sheds its skin."

Cia ran her fingers over the Ancient Chinese coins placed in a bowl next to a marble sculpture of Confucius. A worn copy of the *I Ching, The Book of Changes*, one of the most important books in the world's literature, sat open on the table.

Eventually Cia gave a withering look and said, "I don't have a problem with my thinking. I have a problem with my feelings. With my emotions. I can't remember the last time I felt happy."

"The way you think and the things you think about trigger emotions – good or bad."

Her chin began to quiver. "I guess you're right."

Noticing Cia's shallow breathing, Shin provoked a strained silence.

When Cia realized Shin had no intention of responding to her statement, she elaborated. "It seems like I'm having a good day if I'm not thinking about running away from this shit hole of a town and from everyone I know - or if I'm not thinking about dying. I can't stand it. I can't take it any more."

"When you say you can't remember being happy, do you mean months or years?"

"Years," she said slowly, now hugging a small fringed pillow on her lap and rolling a piece of the fringe between her fingers.

"What triggered your feelings?"

"I have no idea. I don't know why I feel this way," Cia said, unable to admit her deepest turmoil.

"Tell me about your family life."

Images of losing Elizabeth and winding up in prison spun through her mind. A dull stabbing pain shot through her chest at the thought. "I don't want to talk about my family. I'm here to talk about me."

"Your family is part of who you are. We don't need to talk

Wisdom of the Horse

about it now, but we will need to, soon."

Cia looked at Shin with a placid expression. All she knew was there was no way she was going to tell her therapist or anyone else about Elizabeth. They would lock her up if they knew. It was her destiny to live with the consequences of her actions.

"I guess one of my problems is about the lack of money," she murmured. A hot sinking feeling grew in her chest. "We used to live extremely well. Now, we barely make ends meet. I feel like we're drowning and it's just a matter of time before we're out on the streets. I'm scared to death of being homeless." If only she and Jeffrey could get credit cards again. That would help a lot, but they weren't willing to steal someone else's identity, even though Jeffrey, an electronics and computer wizard, could probably figure out a way to do it without being caught.

Shin nodded, wordlessly acknowledging that financial problems can cause feelings of desperation. "Do you think money would make you happy, or do you think the lack of money only makes your personal problems worse?"

Her throat felt tight. "I know money doesn't buy happiness, but life feels so hopeless when I can't see an end to being broke."

"I understand, but do you think your core problems would still exist even if you had plenty of money?"

She slouched from the weight of the question. Her voice quavered. "Probably." Her problems with Elizabeth would be the same even if she and Jeffrey were millionaires. For a start, she'd just like to check one thing off the list: being poor.

"We can't change your financial problem right away, so I suggest we address other areas of your life."

"I don't have a life," she said, her chin quivering. "I rarely leave my house except to go to the grocery store or to Pizza & More or Elvin's for burgers." She rarely even spent time in her own yard because Elizabeth wouldn't join her and she didn't want to leave her daughter in the house alone.

Shin reached for a pad of paper and a pen."What are you interested in?"

"I don't know. That's part of the problem. I'm not interested in doing anything. I'm too exhausted and I ache. When I exercise or clean house my body aches worse, so I don't do much of anything," Cia explained as her fear of talking to a stranger dissipated.

"You ache in what way?"

"My joints ache. It takes all of my effort to get through the day," she said, her lips trembling. "Everything's like a big chore, and there's nothing I want to do for enjoyment. I can't think of anything fun or interesting to do that doesn't take money to do it. So, I just think about escaping or dying. I can't stand it."

Shin took notes resembling bird scratching.

"What do you hope to achieve with therapy?" Shin asked directly.

Cia thought about it as she sipped her tea. She liked how Shin didn't make her feel as if she had to rush her answers. "I don't know. That's why I've cancelled so many appointments. I feel like it's hopeless to think things can change or that I can change. I feel so out of control."

"I asked what you hope to achieve, not if you think you can achieve."

No longer sounding subdued, Cia said, "What I want to achieve is some sense of purpose to my life – and genuine happiness. All I know is - I don't intend to come here and just spill my guts to you. I want you to give me guidance. And answers. If I just needed to talk, I can do that with my husband. I need more than that. I really hope you can do something besides ask me questions and listen to my problems."

Shin accepted her skepticism not as a criticism but as an opportunity. She detected Cia hid behind well thought out words. "It's good you came, then. I call myself a spiritual psychologist and I prefer to work on a client's whole life - not simply emotional problems."

Cia nodded, not admitting she didn't quite understand what Shin meant.

Shin rested her hand on Cia's leg for a moment. "The isolated life you've been living isn't working for you, obviously."

Wisdom of the Horse

Cia nodded, wishing she had eaten before she left the house. "It's going to be painful to heal your heart. You can avail yourself of our relationship, or you can remain closed up in isolation," Shin said, hoping to provoke a strong reaction.

"I want to try to work with you," Cia said, almost pleading.

"The pace of guidance, whether from me or anyone else, is like peace of mind. It begins internally. We can visit as often as you want, but for you to benefit from our time you must internalize what I teach you. I won't let you come to me and kill time just to appease your husband. I promise you, if you're open and honest there will be a pivotal point that will shift what you are doing with your life from being insignifcant to being something of great consequence."

With a tired, wary look in her eyes Cia said,"That's what I want to do. How do I start?"

"First, you must put your feelings and thoughts into perspective. It's the only way you can expand who you think you are. A depressed person doesn't like who they think they are, so that's one of the things we need to work on first."

Cia exhaled a deep breath feeling comforted by what she heard and how Shin spoke. "I definitely don't like who I am – I don't even feel like I'm 'somebody'. I feel like I'm just a blob, reluctantly living from day to day."

"Do you ever go to church?" Shin asked.

Despising organized religion, Cia tensed. Thoughts of Shin advising prayer ran rampant through her mind. There was no way she would do it.

"No, I never go to church." Or synagogue, she thought. Even if she wanted to, there probably wasn't a synagogue for hundreds of miles.

"My church is being out in nature," Shin said to Cia's relief. "Do you like being outdoors?"

Cia shrugged, thinking the question had no real importance. "Sure."

Shin disliked being indoors when not absolutely necessary. "It's so beautiful this time of year. What would you think about us having sessions outdoors when weather permits?"

Cia hid the disappointment she felt. "Fine with me." Being in Shin's office reminded her of the luxury hotels she and Jeffrey used to stay in. She loved the ambiance. It was nothing like their rental home furnished with a stained vinyl couch and love seat, second-hand coffee table and end tables that didn't match or look good together, and peeling, shiny brass lamps and light fixtures. Her kitchen table and chairs were patio furniture.

"I think it's easier to get in touch with your spirituality outdoors," Shin said.

"I'm not spiritual. I just want to feel happy and I just want to find a purpose," Cia said quickly as her mind instinctively rebelled.

Shin stood to reach into a wooden box near the door. She brought out a bag of dark Belgian chocolate, setting the mouthwatering homemade candy on the table. Speaking with a silken, buttery voice she said, "Spiritual doesn't mean religious. I think of spiritual as an ethical and practical way of living in harmony and with peace of mind."

"Oh. Well, if that's what you mean, I do want those things."

Shin sat down again, this time with her legs out straight. She bit into a piece of chocolate and savored it, letting it melt in her mouth as she gave Cia a moment to think. "When you begin to heal your life you gain the wisdom of awakening to who and what you are. It's a wonderful feeling."

Cia could only dream of the day. She ate a piece of chocolate, waiting for Shin to continue.

"I'm a practicing Buddhist and I practice Native American traditions. You know, in America it's a melting pot – and there are so many different kinds of spiritual practices, but the essence is the same. It's our diverse cultural reality."

Mystified, Cia listened and stretched out her legs. "What's this got to do with my problem?"

"What is your problem?"

Cia didn't answer.

Shin placed a hand on Cia's leg again. "See, life can't be

Wisdom of the Horse

solved by identifying something so simply. People need to connect to a higher source in order to attain at least some sense of peace, to feel a purpose, and to feel happy."

"It sounds so out there," Cia said, her face assuming a blank expression.

"The point is - the connection to spirit is so real that it will give you the strength to reach for anything you want. In your case, at this time in your life - for the will to live," Shin told her, keeping the concept uncomplicated.

"Fine. I'll trust you. Where do I start? How do we start?"

"By being honest."

"What do you mean?" she said, hoping she didn't sound defensive. Shin sipped more tea and wiped her lips with her slender finger. "You can't be a truth seeker without being a truth teller."

"How do I start wanting to live - actually looking forward to living?" she asked, not wanting to think about the truth.

"There's not an actual starting point that's the same for everyone, but I do know that however you gain peace of mind, that's when things are good. When you have peace of mind, it's the clean slate upon which your new life can be written."

Frustrated by the answer, Cia tapped her bitten fingernails on the glass table top. She missed the days of professional manicures and pedicures. "How do you gain peace of mind?"

"It's a lot of work. For one thing, I suggest meditation. First, you have to hold yourself in a quiet receptive state. Meditation and your therapy with me will go through the same sequence of actions. There is a process of descent, encounter, reconciliation, and then transformation. You need a life transformation."

Cia couldn't achieve a quiet mental state if her life depended on it. She'd tried on and off for years. Each legitimate attempt caused the reverse to happen. Uncontrollable thoughts popped into her mind – anything from wanting to die to wondering who came up with the idea of toilet paper on a roll and if he gets a royalty for each roll sold. Thoughts of her marriage surviving and of her favorite kind of candy bar. Memories of a fun filled day snow skiing in Aspen with her parents when she was a teen, and memories of herself and Jeffrey driving off in their car with a baby in her arms for the first time. Random thoughts - silly, sad or scary. Still, every time she tried to quiet her mind the session ended the same – with her heart ballooned in her chest and triggering a storm of emotions. Internal darkness became her constant companion for days afterward. For her daughter's sake, she snapped out of it, trying to be a good mother and wife, but there was always a longing that couldn't be satisfied. An emptiness. A sense of quiet desperation.

Shin's eyes lingered on Cia. Like most of her clients, Cia didn't have a common frame of reference. Shin grew up meditating and spent peaceful time in solitude, listening to nature and the spirits with a receptivity that put her at ease. When troubled, she was able to take her mind to a quiet, receptive state in order to find answers or, just as important, to let go of the need for answers.

Cia's eyelids began fluttering, her energy level running on empty. "Can you teach me how to get into a quiet receptive state?"

"I believe I can," she answered with easy optimism.

"I hope so."

"The world mirrors your level of awareness. Among other things, in our sessions you'll learn to become aware of your thought patterns and how to redirect negative thoughts. You'll learn to replace bad feelings with good feelings - that will help with your depression. To start, I suggest you pick someone worthwhile to emulate and then begin acting in the ways you would assume that person acts."

There was no denying the intelligence in Shin's eyes, Cia thought. "Who do you suggest I emulate?"

"That's your decision. Simply coming up with ideas will move your mind into positive thinking. It's part of the journey."

"That makes sense. I'll do it," Cia said, her face now resolute. In the dark center of her mind, she felt capable of following Shin's suggestion. Her first instinct was to emulate Shin, but she knew she should give it more thought before making a commitment.

For the next fifteen minutes the women laid down flat on the mat. Shin taught Cia how to release endorphins by placing the tip of her tongue on the roof of her mouth as she breathed. Next, they worked on purposeful breathing – inhaling deeply through the nose, filling the abdomen, and slowly exhaling through the mouth until the ribs collapsed. With the meditative background music and incense burning, Cia was able to temporarily release the sadness that punctuated her life.

Cia liked Shin, but was baffled by the lessons Shin planned to impart. For now, she was reluctant to continue. "I'm tired and I didn't eat dinner. I think we need to continue on another day."

Shin wasn't willing to let Cia go home without accomplishing something. "You're definitely suffering from exhaustion caused by sleep deprivation. That's where we need to start. You need to get in a regular sleep routine."

"I'm not taking sleeping pills. I've tried them and I hate how I feel drugged the next morning. It's worse than simply feeling tired."

"Have you tried herbal remedies to help you sleep?"

"No."

"I agree with you about not taking sleeping pills. I'd like to set up an appointment for you to meet with my mother."

"Your mother?"

"Yes. I hope you'll keep an open mind. My mother practices Traditional Chinese Medicine. She can help you with your physical issues while I help with your emotional issues and spirituality. The mind/body connection is indisputable."

Cia's eyes sparkled for the first time, but her smile still had a sad edge to it.

"Your mother's Chinese? I thought you looked like you might be Native American. I studied Native American history in college. I've always had a fascination with learning about different cultures."

Finally, Shin learned something about Cia's interests.

"You have a good eye. Actually, mother is Chinese. And, my

father and half-brother are American Indian. My parents are healers and are into preventive medicine. When you studied, did you learn about shaman?"

"No."

"That's too bad. Anyway, my mother will evaluate your diet and energy fields. They're a critical component of your physical and emotional health."

"Look, I know I might need to lose a few pounds, but it's not going to make me happy just to get down to a size six. It's not like I'm fat and hate myself for it. I wear a size twelve, and that's fine with me. I need a shrink - not a health program."

"Everything has to be in balance to function correctly. If you're serious about needing me as a shrink, trust me and keep an open mind. Can you do that?"

"I don't know. It's not that I'm closed minded, but it's not what I'm here for."

"Would sleeping well benefit you?"

"Of course."

"Would having energy benefit you?"

"Yes. Of course."

"Would living without aches and pains make your life easier?"

"Yes."

"And getting to the root of your emotional problems - would that benefit you?"

"Hopefully."

"I think you're intelligent enough to know that if you can identify what your core problems are, then you can work on them. Conversely, if you don't know what's wrong, you can't fix it. Am I correct?"

"Yes."

"Does it make sense that you will think more clearly if you're rested and pain free?"

"Of course."

"Therapy won't give you sleep or take away your pain. We could talk all day every day and if nothing else in your life changes, you'll still be depressed and in pain. Maybe the depression won't

Wisdom of the Horse

be as severe, but believe me, you'll still be depressed."

"Okay. I get it. I'll see your mother. Does she give you a referral fee or something?"

"I don't get a referral fee," Shin replied good-naturedly, "but it makes my job easier if my clients work on their whole lives. Speaking of fees, we need to discuss my compensation. From what your husband told me, both of you assumed the clinic provides free services. Unfortunately, we can't afford to do that. I know it's uncomfortable, but it's something we need to address."

"I don't know what there is to address," she said in a clipped voice. Holding back her tears she added, "My husband and I can't pay all the bills we already have. There's no way I can pay you, and I'm not up to getting a job. Besides, where would I work in this little town anyway?"

"Do you like animals?"

"What?"

"Do you like animals?"

Cia shrugged. "Sure. Who doesn't?"

"My parents own a small farm and there's always work to be done. Believe me, I understand about money problems," Shin said, thinking about her own mounting credit card debt.

"I guess I could try to help out if I can physically stand it and can muster up the energy. My feet, wrists, and fingers usually ache. But I'll try, if that's how we can work out your compensation." Jeffrey would understand why she had to be away from the house and Elizabeth. This would be a perfect excuse.

"If you'll listen to my mother and do what she says, you'll be pain free and energetic before you know it. Can you meet with her tomorrow?"

Cia's instinct was to put her faith in Shin.

Chapter 6

Jeffrey took Elizabeth to his repair shop, a converted enclosed two car carport attached to the house.

"We don't have many televisions to fix," Elizabeth said, shaking her head in frustration in the same way she so frequently observed her mother doing. To at least get her out of the main part of the house, Jeffrey let her help him by handing him tools and parts and by spraying the can of Dust-Off.

"Three of them are hopeless," he said. "I'm keeping them because we might be able to use the parts."

Elizabeth wandered to a small back room, almost a closet, and pulled a worn canvas tarp off of what she thought was going to be a television.

"What's this, Daddy? I've seen these on TV."

He smiled at her curiosity as he joined her. "It's a slot machine. People put coins in and pull the handle or push this button. And then, those squares change their pictures. If the pictures come out in the right combination, people win money - the coins drop into here," he explained, pointing to the money bowl.

"This is for gamblers."

"I didn't know you've heard of gamblers."

"Of course I know what gambling is. We watch CSI. They live in Las Vegas. You know that!" she giggled.

"Right," he grinned at how smart she was. He hadn't realized she was aware of where the show took place and that it was the gambling capital.

"Can I try it, Daddy? If I win, you can keep the money.

Wisdom of the Horse

I know you and Mommy need money."

"It's broken. That's why it's here."

"Are you going to fix slot machines since not enough TV's need fixed?"

"I'm going to try to fix this one, but don't tell mommy about it. It's got to be our secret. Okay?"

Her eyes widened in disbelief. They never kept any secrets from mommy except about eating sweets without her permission. "Our secret?"

"Yes. Do you promise to keep this our secret?"

She bit her lip and thought for a moment. "Okay. I promise." She was excited and scared to have an important secret from her mom.

"Good girl." The last thing he needed was for Cia to find out he had a slot machine. He had promised her he wouldn't go near one again, but now they were beyond desperate for money.

Elizabeth, curious as ever, was fascinated by the machine. "Who owns this?"

"The Cherokee Casino. It's over next to the gas station in town."

Jeffery had been in the Indian owned and operated casino for a cheap lunch when he noticed an employee giving one of the slot machines a swift kick. He approached the old man and asked what was wrong. The handle wouldn't budge. Before Jeffrey gave it a second thought, he approached the casino manager and told him he knew how to repair slot machines and offered to take it back to his shop. He promised he wouldn't charge him if he couldn't fix it. The manager thought it sounded like a better idea than waiting for an authorized service technician. Sometimes they didn't come to hole-in-the-wall places like this for weeks. Every day the machine wasn't operational the casino lost money. When Jeffery finished his blue-plate special, he loaded the slot machine in the back of his truck, took it home, and then waited until Cia was in bed before he took it into the shop and hid it under the canvas.

"Is there money in it now?"

"Probably."

Her eyes widened in excitement. "How much?"

"We won't know until I fix it - if I can fix it."

"I hope we can fix it. Then, maybe we'll get free money. That would be fun!"

"It's not our money to keep. The advantage in fixing it will be that they'll pay me for my services, and maybe I can fix other broken slot machines."

Elizabeth thought about this. "Daddy, do you think there are more broken slot machines than TV's?"

His eyes brightened. He laughed and tousled her hair. "That would be nice, but I doubt it. Maybe you can take a drive with me and go to other casinos. We can ask if they have broken slot machines."

"No. We should just call on the phone. You don't want to waste your time, do you?" she said.

He was impressed. She possessed a sensibility far beyond her years, but he was disappointed that neither he nor Cia could find a hot button to motivate their daughter to willingly go out of the house.

"Should we open it up and see what it looks like inside?"

"Yes, Daddy. I'm so excited. I wanna see inside!"

Jeffrey dreaded what would happen if Cia discovered the slot machine.

Chapter 7

Shin drove Cia to her parents' farm. They turned down a long gravel driveway lined on both sides with horse pastures built of split-rail cedar fencing. Fifty feet from the side deck of the house, a sturdy paddock provided a temporary home for a once healthy and athletic Arabian mare. Her spirit had clearly vanished. It didn't take a knowledgeable horseperson to see the horse was suffering. The mare's withers protruded, as did her hips. Every rib was visible through her dull white coat. The once expressive dark eyes were now sunken and expressionless. The horse hung her head looking as disempowered and defeated about life as Cia usually felt.

"This is Ambra," Shin said, referring to the mare.

"What's wrong with her?"

Shin sighed, her heart melting at the story. "She's one of three horses who survived a tragic barn fire."

Cia leaned on the fence, trying to get the mare's attention with a handful of grass. A blank look of disassociation remained on the mare's face. Ambra wasn't interested in the grass.

"How did the barn catch fire?"

"According to the Fire Marshall, an electric spark from an old extension cord attached to a portable light fixture ignited the shavings bin. The wood barn was well maintained, but the layout was hazardous. The shavings bin was attached to the outside of the barn, and the hay was stored inside. They didn't have stall mats, so there were deep shavings in every stall, and the barn aisle had woodchip footing rather than concrete or dirt."

Cali Canberra

Cia nodded as if she understood the importance of Shin's explanation.

"Anyway, a spark ignited the shavings. The owner's teenage daughter, Jane, and her boyfriend were apparently necking in the barn office with the radio blaring. They didn't hear the commotion of the horses panicking in their stalls. When they smelled the smoke and rushed out of the office they ran to open the stall doors to let the horses out. The first two horses escaped, but two horses were trapped in their stalls because the tractor and manure cart blocked them in. The barn was engulfed with smoke as the fire spread. Jane's boyfriend blindly slid the stallion's door open. The panicked stud couldn't see. He ran the wrong direction toward the solid wall.

"Jane ran for her own horse, Ambra, who was stalled in the back of the barn. She felt her way to the halter and lead rope hanging on the stall door. Blinded by smoke, she haltered her mare by feel and urged Ambra outside.

"Jane's parents saw the blaze and the smoke as they drove up their driveway, returning home from errands. They ran toward the barn not knowing Jane and Brad had been inside. The Martins found Jane unconscious with Ambra nuzzling her stomach. The barn was completely engulfed in flames by the time they carried their daughter further from the disaster. After the fire was extinguished, they found Brad outside the stallion's stall door – apparently trampled. He died from smoke inhalation. Jane's in the burn unit at Parkland Memorial Hospital in Dallas getting skin grafts and recovering from the smoke inhalation. In addition to the health issues Ambra must recover from, she suffers the aftereffects caused by being in the barn fire, the intense medical treatment procedures, and leaving familiar people and surroundings."

Tears formed in the corner of Cia's eyes. Amazed by the story, her heart ached for everyone, including the horses that perished. A black lab puppy ran to her ankles and nuzzled her. "Who's this? He's precious."

"Jane's puppy," Shin said. "He never wanders very far from

Wisdom of the Horse

Ambra. I think he senses the trauma."

"What's his name?" Cia asked, now with the pup in her arms vigorously licking her face, making her smile and giggle in spite of having heard the devastating story.

"We don't know. We call him Heyoka. It's Lakota for clown." Shin climbed over the fence and gradually took a few slow steps toward the center of the paddock. Ambra, with a glazed look in her eyes, ignored Shin, keeping her rump toward the women. She had been affectionate and respectful before the disaster, but now she lost her trust in humans. Shin took a step toward Ambra's shoulder, staying out of kicking distance. She sat on the ground. "She's disconnected now, but in time, she'll gain an awareness of her surroundings. I'm hoping to peak her curiosity. Sitting makes me less threatening," she explained.

Heyoka ran to Shin, leaped into her lap and licked her hands.

"Two horses survived besides Ambra?"

"Fortunately."

Shin told Cia that two competitive trail horses survived unscathed. A neighboring farm took one horse in because he didn't require any special care and was enjoying the season off to rest. Shin took in the second horse, Cabaret, because until the barn fire he was still competing and was in top-notch condition. She couldn't see letting the horse lose his vitality and get soft when she'd have time to keep him in condition. Besides, she liked the idea of being able to ride a heartier horse than her own.

The local veterinarian, Dr. Mark, treated Ambra. She was in his care until ready to leave his hospital. Shin had called Mark to inquire about the mare – the fire was news throughout the county, especially since the Martins were so well respected for their community involvement. Cia recalled that at Jeffrey's urging she had reluctantly scanned the article in the local newspaper and had seen the story on the local news. Given her own problems, she didn't give it much thought at the time.

Dr. Mark told Shin the Martins were in Dallas living in a hotel to be with Jane. They couldn't even think about what to do with the mare, and they didn't have the money for ongoing care.

Cali Canberra

The horses were uninsured and the Martins were depleting their savings to pay bills while they took a leave of absence from their jobs. Grayson Solvan had called Dr. Mark, knowing the family was struggling. He insisted on paying for the best of care for the mare, whatever it took. If he hadn't been in the process of developing the hospice and equine rescue operation, he would have taken Ambra to his farm. When Ambra no longer needed hospitalization, Mark first thought of Shin's parents, knowing they would be able to provide the mare with around-the-clock physical and emotional care.

"Ambra needed to be sedated just to get her on the trailer," Shin said. "Normally, my parents wouldn't have considered such an approach but under the circumstances, there was no alternative. We've had her for about a month now. We need to apply ointment to her burn marks, which were actually pretty incidental considering everything. Her biggest problem is her loss of appetite – probably because the smoke irritated her throat so much it hurt her to eat, and now she's probably afraid it will still hurt. Horses have an exceptionally good memory. At least she's drinking. The stress caused her to founder. That's why she's standing like that," Shin said, pointing to the mare's legs. Her hind legs were tucked under her body to carry as much weight as possible, and her front legs were placed forward of her body with the weight on her heels. Ambra, like most foundered horses, was reluctant to walk and when she turned she did so by leaning back and pivoting on her rear legs.

Cia cocked her head. "I thought she looked like she was standing weird, but I didn't know."

"A foundered horse stands like that to relieve the pressure on their feet. Fortunately, it seems to be a mild case." Shin didn't mention that the horse's hooves were hot and there was a pounding pulse in her digital artery.

Heyoka ran under Ambra's legs. She knew he was there, but didn't feel well enough to care. Cia called the puppy over, worried he might get stepped on. Heyoka waddled to her immediately, wagging his tail as if being with her was the most exciting

Wisdom of the Horse

thing in the world. She picked him up again and cuddled him for as long as she could hold his attention.

Ambra flicked her ears and turned her head a couple of inches, eyeing the women anxiously. She was finally showing some interest. This was a big step, Shin explained. "Horses generally respond to emotion more often than reason. Ambra's wary of our presence because she has unresolved fears. We need to work with that as much, if not more, than her physical issues. Of course, putting weight on her is our first priority, but her diminished appetite is an emotional response."

Cia sensed Ambra felt as vulnerable and tender as an open wound. This very idea seemed to mirror her feelings. In just this short time, she developed a soft spot in her heart for the mare. As she considered this, she looked into Ambra's eyes. Instantly, the mare's eyes softened and relaxed - she lowered her head and licked her lips. An invisible barrier was removed. Cia felt as if she needed to decipher a message from the mare, and when she did, great progress would be made. Already, the horse inspired emotional insights.

Cia took in the beautiful surroundings and fresh air, realizing her own life wasn't so bad in comparison to the tragic story of this horse, Jane, and Jane's parents – and the friends and family of Brad. In retrospect, her problems were minimal. Of course, she could be sent to prison for what she had done. No one else faced that threat. And, she and Jeffrey could not pursue careers earning a comfortable living because they were in hiding and always would be.

Taking a short-cut, Shin and Cia carefully picked their way down the gentle rocky slope toward the residence. Cia didn't know what she had expected, but a lodge style house nestled in the center of colorful picturesque landscaping wasn't it. Shin motioned her through the heavy hand-carved wooden door into a great room with a see-through flagstone fireplace that was accessible to the rustic kitchen. Shin pointed out the master bedroom and the loft where guests stayed. The small yet spectacular house was decorated with a collision of cultures – Asian and American

Indian, but it worked well. Tall windows invited ample natural light, as did the skylight in the kitchen. Slow moving rice paper paddle fans mounted to the ceiling circulated the air in the room with its twenty-foot ceiling.

"My parents designed and built this house and planted the ground cover and flowers. The pond and trees were here, but Dad built the bridge across the creek and he built the gazebo. I helped a little, but I was away at college and graduate school most of the time during construction. My brother helped them quite a bit for a couple of years until he started traveling more often for his business."

"It's beautiful. They must do well financially," she said without thinking.

"They do okay. They have very little interest in money for the sake of money. My father makes Native American drums and sells them at Powwows and to galleries. He gets good prices because of his CDIB."

"CDIB?"

"Certificate of Degree of Indian Blood," she explained. "People with a CDIB can legally label their goods as *'Indian-Made'* rather than *'Hand Crafted'*, which often brings higher prices."

To obtain a CDIB, a person must get on the Dawes Roll by proving they are a descendant with a certain amount of Indian blood. It's like a horse registry. With a CDIB card the person can apply for membership to the tribe and receive tribal benefits. Her father was actually a Commissioner on The Indian Arts and Crafts Board, an agency within the U.S. Department of the Interior, based in Washington, DC. The Board was created by Congress to promote the economic development of American Indians and Alaska Natives through the expansion of the Indian Arts and Crafts Act of 1990, a truth-in-advertising law providing criminal and civil penalties for marketing products as *"Indian-Made"* when such products are not made by Indians, as defined by the Act.

"Well, it looks like he must make a lot of money to have such a nice place and all the horses," Cia said.

Wisdom of the Horse

"It's a decent income. Mom makes a little income here and there, but as you can imagine, there's not much of a clientele out this way."

Cia looked around at the quality of artwork and decorative pieces, and the materials and workmanship in the house. "They must do a lot better than you perceive." The house brought back her longing to pursue her own artistic work, but it would never be possible again.

Shin gazed out the kitchen window toward the pond. "My father did most of the finishing work in the house. He's quite a craftsman in many areas, including woodworking, but his passion is making the traditional drums. My brother helped them financially when they wanted to build this house. For years we all lived in a rustic cabin in the woods by the stream. You can't see it from here, but it's only about a five minute walk through the woods."

"Your brother sounds generous. What's he do for a living?"

"He's very famous in the horse industry. He does horse and rider clinics all over the world and he writes books about relationships between women and horses, and about gentle training using our Native American ways." Feeling dwarfed by her brother's success she didn't mention that she wrote articles for equestrian magazines.

"Do you have horses?"

"I only have one of my own. I keep her here since my parents have the land. She's a rescue horse. My parents and brother healed her physically. I healed her emotionally, and now I'm her companion."

"It sounds like you have a perfect family."

"Our family is very close."

"What's your horse's name?"

"Maya. Her name is Hindu for illusions."

Shin led Cia to the screened-in porch, knowing her mother would be waiting there for them. Shin promptly made introductions, then added, "Where's Dad?"

"Out riding. I imagine he'll be gone for quite a while. He

packed a lunch."

"Do you know if he rode Cabaret?" Shin asked her mother. "When we talked yesterday he said he thought he'd probably ride him this morning."

"Yes. He got up early and was on him at dawn. Your father loves that horse, even though he's an Arabian." In general, Thundering Cloud thought of Arabians as being easily spooked and not very sensible. This horse showed him his assumption was an unjust stereotype. "In fact, he's going to ask Dr. Mark if he thinks the Martins would consider selling him. He'd love to own him."

"I'd love to own him myself – if I had the money. Maya's great, but she doesn't have the heart and the personality Cabaret has."

"We're being inconsiderate of our guest," Mrs. Crow said to her daughter.

"Sorry, Cia. I'm going to make lunch and eat it in Ambra's paddock. Hopefully she'll enjoy the company."

"Try to get her to eat a little hay," Mrs. Crow requested of her daughter.

Ambra was accustomed to sweet feed and alfalfa, neither of which she could eat now that she had foundered. She had little appetite for grass hay. While at his hospital, Dr. Mark discovered the mare had a thyroid problem and wanted to start her on Thyro-L, but it needed to be mixed in with feed or syringe dosed, which the mare wouldn't tolerate.

"I will. I'm going to ride Maya while you do your thing. Call me on my cell when you want me to return. I assume you'll be at least a couple of hours?"

Mrs. Crow made a quick evaluation of Cia's eyes and skin. "Yes. At least a couple of hours."

Chapter 8

Almost three hours later, just as she completed her first session with Cia, Mrs. Crow spotted her husband and Shin cantering the horses toward the house, their long flowing black hair trailing behind.

"Look out there," she said, directing her attention to her family. "What do you see?"

"Pardon?"

"What do you see?"

"Shin and your husband, I assume."

"That's all?"

"Well, they're riding horses in a green field."

"And?"

Cia felt flustered, but overcame it quickly. "I see two people who are bonded and are having fun. What do you see?"

"I see four spirits that are as one," Mrs. Crow said softly.

"I hope I'll learn to see like you do. I need to pay more attention to things."

"And to your spirit guide – your intuition."

"I'm looking forward to it."

Mrs. Crow hung a pendant around Cia's neck – it was an ancient Chinese coin. She said Cia needed the energy over her heart chakra and that she should wear it whenever she wasn't sleeping. Then, Mrs. Crow packed Cia a bag filled with herbal remedies, teas, and a natural liniment.

Cia thanked her and hugged her.

Shin entered the house and almost tripped over Heyoka who wouldn't leave her alone once she approached. Cia picked up the puppy and giggled as he licked her face, her problems, aches, and pains forgotten.

When the women returned to Shin's car to leave, Heyoka ran into the paddock with Ambra and laid down, curling into a fluffy ball for a nap next to the mare's front feet.

"You don't know how long it's been since I've broken my normal routine. This has been so refreshing," Cia told Shin on the drive back home.

"What is your normal routine?"

"I rarely leave home except to buy groceries, and half the time Jeffrey goes to the store for me. Other than that, sometimes I go to Elvin's for fast food, but that's about it. I'm sick of being in the house, but I'm not motivated to go anywhere," she said hopelessly.

"Why are you isolating yourself?"

"I'm not."

"It sounds like you are. Do you stay home by choice?"

"I guess."

"Are you doing things you enjoy at home?"

She turned her face away. "No."

"Why are you afraid to go out into the world?"

Cia swallowed hard. A lump formed in her throat. I'm not."

"I think you are," Shin said bluntly. "The only way to deal with fear is to confront it directly – to stop and look at it."

"I'm not afraid of anything. I'm just so depressed. I have a lot of problems you couldn't understand."

Shin thought about that for a moment. "Problems aren't always negative. Some are just challenges of everyday life. Try to discern the difference between stress and problems. Your answers will often depend upon the way in which you view obstacles."

"How can I not view obstacles as problems that are negative?"

Relating life's lessons to horses was often an easy way to understand things, even for those without a genuine interest in horses. "Picture this. I'm riding a horse on an obstacle course neither of us has ever ridden, and the obstacles are very challenging because we haven't done anything like it before – perhaps we're required to ride through a labyrinth, with many of the areas elevated, and if we skip any part of it or if the horse steps on any part he shouldn't, we must start over and over and over until we ride it perfectly. This is a huge challenge, but when we get it right

Wisdom of the Horse

there is such a sense of accomplishment. And more importantly, now we have a new skill set to use on future obstacle courses – challenges, if you will – and our experience will make the future easier. In fact, perhaps not even a challenge at all. In other words, at one time something can seem impossible, but the exact same thing in the future may be no big deal to experience."

Cia felt hopeful. With Shin's guidance, somehow she would at least overcome her periods of doubt about her ability to overcome her depression. Perhaps she really could at least get past living her life just drifting through her daily routine. Genuine happiness still seemed nearly impossible, but maybe the contentment that eluded her would soon come knocking on her door.

When Cia didn't verbally respond, Shin said, "We have a lot of deep work to do."

"What's the plan?"

Shin smiled. "Can you trust the process and not think about a plan?"

"I don't know. I'll try."

"Please. Try your best to trust the process. For starters, you need to start exploring things that interest you. Mix up your daily routine."

"I want to, in a way, but in another way, I'm too depressed to look forward to doing anything."

"How do you feel right now? Do you feel depressed?"

"Actually, I feel really good right now. Whatever your mother did made me euphoric. It's amazing. I feel so rested I can't believe it."

"She balanced your energy. She usually explains it –"

Cia interrupted. "She started to, but I told her not to bother. I assumed it would be over my head."

"It's a simple concept. There are seven chakras – chakras are energy centers in our bodies that change on their own and can be manipulated, like what my mom did for you. Energy work is fascinating. The chakras are in the sacred teachings of Eastern and Western traditions. In the West, Roman Catholicism offers the same teaching in the form of the seven sacraments. Judaism

Cali Canberra

has the Tree of Life, an energy system used by Kabbalists."

"Seems pretty out-there to me, but I have to admit, I can't remember ever feeling this good in my life, let alone in the past several years. There must be something to it."

"The practice has been around for over 5000 years. Anyway, let's get back to talking about you."

"I don't know what to talk about. Other than right now, I live every day fighting off feelings of wanting to die. My husband treats me fine. I don't know what's wrong with me."

Shin turned on the CD of Native American fluting. "So, you're not having any marriage problems? Your husband hasn't hurt you emotionally or physically?"

"No. Jeffrey's wonderful," she said. It was the truth, except for the part about why they were living in practically the middle of nowhere without friends or family.

"I'm glad he hasn't hurt you in any way. But if you think about it, the real hurt is not what others inflict but what we do to ourselves."

Cia almost laughed. "That's the truth!"

Firmly believing the mind is highly susceptible to the power of suggestion, Shin said, "The herbs my mother gave you will help with a lot of those depressing feelings. Some of what you're feeling may be from a chemical imbalance in your brain. It might take several weeks though, so don't get discouraged."

"I'll tell you one thing - if I could feel like I feel now every day, it would be a dream come true." Almost, she thought. It would almost be a dream comes true.

"You need to get outdoors while the weather is nice. Movement pumps up the immune system and endorphins. Depression and stress inhibit the immune response. Try hiking or something – exercise and being in nature will elevate your mood. And, it's free. Make sure that while you're outdoors you only think and feel in present time. If you allow your mind to be someplace other than where you are, it means the moment is never good enough."

"Okay," she said with little commitment to the agreement. After the idea actually registered, her thinking changed. "When I

Wisdom of the Horse

was single, I used to love to hike and go camping with the guy I was dating – not Jeffrey – an old boyfriend. I haven't done it since we broke up," Cia said, feeling warm inside recalling the fond memory.

"I'm going camping at the end of October with my father and brother and a family friend. We're riding our horses to a place we camp at several times a year. Would you like to join us?"

Cia felt a pang of excitement. "Yes! Except, I don't have a horse to ride."

"You can ride Maya for me and I'll ride Cabaret."

"Is your mom camping?"

"No. Not this time. If she can find someone to stay at the house and take care of Ambra, she'll be at a Wayne Dyer and Deepak Chopra seminar in Dallas."

Cia felt animated for the first time in years. "I'd love to join you."

"You'll have to learn some basics about horsemanship and riding first, but we'll have time. Can you come out here a few days a week? We could combine therapy sessions with horsemanship and riding."

"Sure. I can't wait."

"We do some Native American rituals during the trip, but if you're not interested, you're welcome to go off on your own and walk or read or do whatever."

"It sounds interesting, but I'll bring a book, just in case."

"What kind of reading do you usually do?" Shin asked.

"Actually, I haven't read for pleasure in years."

They drove several miles in silence. Shin was concerned that Cia still hadn't mentioned having a child.

Out of the blue, Shin asked, "What's your family life like?"

"Okay," Cia said, not ready to talk about her daughter.

"For someone who wants help, you're sure evasive."

"I'm sorry. I feel like if I'm numb about my life it won't hurt as much."

"You know that's not the case."

"I know. I know. That's why I finally came to you, but I can't find the words to explain my feelings other than I feel like I'm living in purgatory," Cia reflected, proud she hadn't broken down and cried. For some reason, today, she was experiencing a hint of inner strength. Perhaps from not feeling exhausted, she assumed.

"Cia, you have to stand up inside yourself and change. Only you can do it for yourself. You've heard the saying 'you have to name it to claim it' - it's true. I can help you identify your core issues, and my mother can help you become physically healthy and balanced, which will help your emotions - but you're the key player in this. We can't do it for you."

"I understand."

"You'll never feel peaceful or in harmony with life if you don't live your life in balance – your spirit and your body need to heal."

Shin didn't see Cia roll her eyes.

"One thing at a time. First I need to stop feeling so depressed."

"I'm going to give you an assignment. Take the herbs my mother gave you as she prescribed and spend at least two hours a day in nature - walk everyday until I see you next week. You don't have to walk non-stop. Just go somewhere scenic, breathe deeply, and be aware of your surroundings. Try to find pleasure in every step you take and in each thing you see, hear, feel, smell, and breathe. If a depressing or negative thought comes to mind, picture it as an object - then put the object in an imaginary box and tell yourself you'll get to the problem box when you come back to visit me. If you have a big stack of boxes to deal with when we meet again, so be it. Just tell yourself not to give the unhappy or negative thoughts any energy until later. The problems will still be there later for you. Do this every waking moment until I see you."

"I'll try."

"You can do it. I know you can."

"I don't know where to go."

"Find a place where you can walk in the woods or a field. It won't be hard to find if you actually look - we live in a rural area. Don't you live near the river?"

Wisdom of the Horse

"Yes."

"There are plenty of places all along there. You'll find an entry into the forest that other people have made or that the deer made. If you end up at a dead end, just retrace your steps and keep searching. The point is being out in nature and breaking your routine."

~ ~ ~ ~ ~

That evening over dinner, Cia showed Elizabeth and Jeffrey her new necklace and she explained to her daughter that money from different parts of the world looks different. Elizabeth begged to wear the necklace - she loved it as much as Cia did. Cia then told them about her time at the Crow's farm. She went into detail telling the sad story of Ambra, Jane, and Brad and then lightened things up telling about the silly puppy. Elizabeth was enthralled with the idea of her mother touching a real horse, yet when Cia told her she could join her and pet horses and play with the puppy, Elizabeth tensed up.

"I'll be going there a lot. Why don't you come just once and see if you like it as much as I do?"

Elizabeth frowned. "Why are you going to be there a lot?"

"I'm going to help out with the horses so we don't have to spend money on my therapy with Shin."

"Is therapy what's going to make you happy?"

Cia cupped her daughter's cheeks between her hands. "Yes."

Jeffrey cleared the table and prompted Elizabeth to help him do the dishes. As they settled into the routine of him washing and rinsing, Elizabeth drying, and Cia putting the plates in the cabinet, he took a chance. "I've got an idea," he said to Elizabeth.

"What?"

"How about you and I go in my truck to the horses when Mommy's there, and then if you don't like the horses or Heyoka, we'll leave. You just say the word."

Elizabeth rolled her eyes in exaggeration. "No, thanks."

Chapter 9

The next day Cia woke up feeling refreshed after a full night of sleep. The herbal tea and the capsules must have worked. Even if it was a placebo, she didn't care. She accomplished the immediate goal of feeling rested. For the next three days she followed the recommended diet and took the herbs, but she hadn't mustered up the energy and courage to follow Shin's suggestion to walk and be in nature, let alone for two hours a day.

By the fourth morning she told Jeffery she was ready to leave her private self-protected world. "Can Elizabeth stay with you?" There was no point in trying to get Elizabeth to join her. "I want to walk while I'm motivated. I'm afraid that if I wait until you're finished working…"

Jeffrey didn't let her continue. "Don't worry about us," he said relieved she was willing to work on herself finally.

"Great. She's still asleep. Give her a kiss good morning for me and tell her I'll be with her as soon as I can."

Wisdom of the Horse

"No rush."

Cia desperately wanted to believe that the longer she lived without caffeine, white flour, white rice, and sugar, the sooner her pains would disappear. For the third day in a row at breakfast she ate melon, a hard-boiled egg, a small bowl of plain oatmeal with fresh berries, and a handful of almonds. After her third cup of green tea she was ready to go. Jeffrey told her about a trail opening next to the Glover River Bridge down the street from their house. He didn't know how far the trail went, but it looked wide and like it had good footing from what he could see when he fished from the bridge.

The trail was easy to find. She was astonished she had never noticed it. Apparently, her mind was always preoccupied when she drove down the stretch of road wondering if she would have the strength to return home again.

When she discovered an entire trail system with offshoots heading in several directions, including up a seemingly endless meandering scenic slope, she decided to call her time outdoors a hike rather than a walk. For a long while she was able to cautiously hike along the river until she came to a steep ridge and a cluster of boulders reminiscent of an old western movie. She was drawn to an enormous smooth flat-topped boulder, a perfect place to rest and reflect. In the distance below she spotted a clearing with a fire pit surrounded by stones.

Unable to go any further by the river and granite cliffs, she backtracked until she spotted another trail winding uphill. She challenged herself to make it to the top. A part of her wanted to be like Forest Gump and keep walking, never returning to life as she knew it. 'Put that thought in a box' she said to herself, and did it.

At the top of the hill, she decided to not only call her walk a hike, but to call the hill a small mountain. What was the difference technically between a huge hill and a small mountain? Anyway, Oklahomans claimed this area was the world's highest hill. For now, she hiked energetically and nearly pain-free. Her wrists and fingers had a lingering dull ache, as did her shoulders

Cali Canberra

and lower back, but it wasn't unbearable as it usually was.

She rested on a boulder overlooking a trickling stream. A flock of birds soared overhead just as she spotted a herd of elk in the meadow. The sound of a squirrel scrambling in the dry fallen leaves behind her caught her attention. She thought she heard the whinny of horses. Moments after resuming her hike she discovered a magnificent vista. Standing amidst a grassy knoll on the high ridge, she looked down upon a picturesque horse farm where a dozen horses grazed in a lush pasture. A barn and riding area stood in the distance. The scene was so beautiful that she wished she had binoculars to see the horses closer.

Anxious to make more discoveries, she briskly continued on, ignoring her labored breathing. She hiked the ridgeline and what seemed to be about a half-hour later she spotted an enormous stone and log house with a tennis court and natural rock swimming pool. She had no idea anyone wealthy lived in their town, let alone that there was a spectacular horse farm. Because of the river and the ridgeline it was so close, yet so far - as was her sanity, her will to live, and her freedom.

Chapter 10

One of the first things Cia learned from Shin was how silence on the outside and silence on the inside are different. At home, the chatter in Cia's head drove her mad. With the horses out at the Crow's farm and out hiking in the forest she felt the relief of silence on the inside. Shin told her she must ask herself and her spirit guides the right questions to get answers. She was still struggling for the right questions because so much in her life was wrong - things she didn't feel she could pinpoint and things she could identify but felt helpless to change.

Day by day, she worked on paying attention to her thoughts. She was amazed at how she energized negative thoughts when she forgot to replace them with positive thoughts. In the past, the idea of 'positive thinking' seemed simply to be a catch phrase. Now she was learning that positive thinking really could change someone's life. Shin tried to ingrain the lesson that rather than continuing to build up emotional scar tissue, Cia could choose to see events differently. By doing so, she could get on with her life.

Within ten days, Cia and Shin had six therapy sessions in the paddock with Ambra. Cia was intrigued by the life lessons she absorbed simply by knowing how to just be around the emotionally and physically scarred horse. She learned how understanding life and understanding horses is the practice of acceptance and leaving enough time in the day for something to happen that you didn't expect. In such a short time, her life no longer felt so shallow and incomplete. Now there seemed to be hope for change.

Like some people, some horses need routines and are flustered and thrown off balance when a routine is not followed. Ambra was one of those horses. A routine evolved over the course of several sessions. Shin and Cia entered the paddock together and evaluated Ambra's weight and water intake. There was no choice but to leave her haltered with a short lead rope hanging so she could be caught. With methodical coaxing, Shin struggled to doctor the mare.

While Shin rode Maya, she led Cabaret, keeping up the mileage he was accustomed to covering. Cia remained in the paddock easing toward Ambra. Eventually the mare glanced at her. The first two days it took fifteen minutes, the second two days it took only a couple. The mare held her attention longer each time. When Cia stood, the mare repeatedly walked off. Cia picked clover from outside the paddock to make an offering with an outstretched hand. Eventually, Ambra would reluctantly approach, one short step at a time, stretch her neck out far enough to gently take the clover into her velvety lips and then she'd walk off. This ritual could go on for an hour or more, the mare doling out a tiny bit of trust at a time.

Cia expressed her concern that she hadn't made a lot of progress with Ambra.

"Things done in your own life and things done with horses don't need to be grand, only fitting. Ask yourself what you think the horse is ready for next. Do the same thing in your own life. You'll feel the spark of being on the journey," Shin explained.

"I'm taking one step at a time – now that I've met you. It doesn't feel as overwhelming as I thought it would. Not that I've done anything incredible, but being here around the horses and hiking helps tremendously. Not that I don't have my bad moments," Cia said, her voice trailing off.

"That's progress."

"I came out yesterday and pet Maya and Cabaret and the other horses" Cia said, "and then spent an hour with Ambra. She finally turned her body sideways. I know you said it would be a

Wisdom of the Horse

big step for her if she didn't turn her ass on people."

"You should have brought your daughter," she said casually as if it were an afterthought. In reality she had been waiting for an opportunity to bring up the idea.

Cia was caught off-guard. She thought she had made it clear she didn't want to discuss her family life. "I wanted time alone," she said finally.

"You're welcome to bring your daughter when we're not having a therapy session. She can ride Cabaret. The Martins said he's wonderful with new riders, including kids," Shin goaded.

"Thanks."

Ambra had progressed enough, and so had Cia, for Cia to hold the halter and lead rope today. With Cia rubbing small circles on her forehead, Ambra relaxed just enough to allow Shin to doctor her without it being a dance that she resisted participating in. Her resistance to being touched was diminishing once she was caught.

It finally seemed as though Ambra had a breakthrough – accepting that she wasn't going to get sweet feed or alfalfa anymore, she reluctantly began eating grass on her own. No one could just walk up and pet her yet, but they could approach the mare without her pinning her ears or threatening them by kicking out a back leg and throwing her head in the air. Shin could now tie the mare to a sturdy post to medicate her without Ambra pulling back in distress. Still, they needed to get the mare to the point where a single person could treat her. It had become taxing on Mrs. Crow and Thundering Cloud to coordinate their schedules simply to take a few moments to administer medicine or ointment.

"How many times a day does this need to be done?" Cia asked.

"One thing or another needs to be done five or six times a day."

"And she needs to be hand-fed to get her to eat enough?"

"For now."

Cia stood with her hands on her hips and thought aloud. "We have a fenced area about twice this size at our house. It's overgrown with vegetation, but Jeffrey could mow it and make some repairs. What if we bring Ambra to my house? Between Jeffrey and me she could get everything she needs."

Shin raised her brows and swirled the idea around in her mind. "You are a lot closer to the vet if something happened," she said hesitantly. "Has the fenced area been a horse corral?"

"I don't know. There are four rails, like yours, and sturdy posts. It was there when we moved in."

"We'd have to do a cleansing with sage and a ceremony on the land before we could take a horse there. Would that be okay?"

"Of course. And you can check on us everyday if you want. Your office isn't that far from my house – it's definitely a lot closer than here."

Concerned about Cia having no other experience with horses, Shin was reluctant. "Maybe."

"Give me books to read. I'll do a crash course on horse care. You can test me."

Shin looked to the passing clouds floating in the otherwise crystal clear sky. "You need hands-on experience and she needs to learn to trust people again."

"Please –" Cia pleaded, looking as if she would break into tears.

"I know you want to help, but a teacher and actual experience are important. You could read books, but they are books - words in print. Look at it this way – drawings of food don't satisfy your hunger. A glass of water doesn't satisfy your thirst until you actually take the drink."

Cia had visualized helping Ambra, and that by doing so at her own house, the horse and the puppy would lure Elizabeth outside. Elizabeth loved her toy and model horses and drew pictures of horses and other animals. When they bought her a swing set and slide she was too afraid to go outside to use it – but maybe a horse – a real horse, would be a motivator.

Their physician said they should risk Elizabeth having a panic attack and deal with it if it happened. It would be for everyone's benefit. Cia and Jeffrey weren't willing to take a chance of

Wisdom of the Horse

traumatizing their daughter, especially when they knew they had caused her fear of being outdoors and her fear of strangers. They hadn't thought ahead, and now they were all paying the price.

Heyoka stood on his back legs and pleaded for Cia's attention. "Oh – and the puppy – Ambra is attached to Heyoka. I can take him, too."

This was the first time Shin saw a joyous expression on Cia's face. Part of her wanted to jump at the idea to help Cia and to give her parents a break and the freedom to do what they needed to do, but a horse's well-being was at stake.

"You need more experience, and I'd have to ask my parents. It would be their final decision. I just come here to give them a break and ride Maya and Cabaret. Can you come every day this week?"

Cia smiled from ear to ear at the prospect. "Sure. And Jeffrey and I can start getting the paddock ready. It needed to be cleaned up anyway, but we had no reason to do it. If Ambra and Heyoka don't end up coming, the worst thing that can come of it is that our place looks a little nicer."

"That's a great attitude. Keep it up."

Heyoka loved being with Shin and Cia – Mrs. Crow said the puppy rarely left Ambra unless they were at the farm. The lab learned to keep his distance from the heavy hooves of the horses and discovered that fresh hoof trimmings were yummy to chew on.

During this therapy session at the Crow's farm, Cia learned how to tie the lead rope in a quick-release knot and to groom Cabaret. She picked burrs out of his tail. "Can I start riding? I spent two hours yesterday observing Cabaret, just like *Horse Walk Beside Me* says to do," she said, referring to the book written by Shin's brother about relationships with horses and nature.

Shin picked out Maya's feet. After she sprayed Healing Tree thrush antiseptic treatment on the frogs and soles, she spread Healing Tree hoof moisturizer and strengthener on Maya's hooves. "What did you observe?"

Cali Canberra

Heyoka licked one of Maya's glistening hooves and made a face at the disgusting taste in his mouth. He decided to eat some horse manure to cover the unpleasant taste of hoof conditioner. His delight with the gourmet snack was curtailed when he spotted a rabbit to chase.

Cia brought out a piece of paper from the back pocket of her jeans. She unfolded it and read, "He likes clover better than the other grasses. When I use my fingernails to vigorously scratch his chest he puts his neck in a funny position to show me that's the right spot. When he grazes, he never cocks a foot, but when he's getting groomed or is standing tied he rests his back left foot more often than the right. When he trots or runs he always starts with his front left foot first. He likes apples more than carrots. He doesn't like me pulling those hard rubbery things on the inside of his legs."

"Those are good observations. And, for your information, the hard rubbery things are called chestnuts. The chestnut is what remains in the evolutionary process of horses – it was once like a toe. Anyway, yes. You can start to ride today, but we're only going to walk."

Cia grinned. "That's fine."

Chapter 11

Shin demonstrated how to hold the reins and how to mount a horse bareback from the tree stump. "When you swing your leg over, don't hit his rump – and sit down gently. Center yourself and take a deep breath with a slow exhale."

Cia did as directed. The gelding stood still, having been trained not to take a single step until asked to do so.

"Visualize yourself being at one with him – being in harmony – a melding of body and soul."

Cia closed her eyes for a second to think about her instructions. A sudden disorientation forced her eyes open.

"You felt Cabaret's energy radiate up through your core. That's good," Shin explained.

With a content expression on her face, Cia stroked Cabaret's neck and concentrated on her visualization.

"Horses can feel a fly land on them. That's how sensitive they are to touch. Now, lightly squeeze your legs and kindly say 'walk' – as soon as he takes a step, release all leg pressure and remain centered and balanced over his center. You'll feel it when it's right," Shin said as she rode in a half-circle around them to make sure Cia understood.

Cia smiled at the simplicity and easy response from the horse. She pictured Elizabeth riding behind her, holding her little hands around her waist and giggling. Of course, just getting her daughter outside would be a big start.

"Good. Now, say 'whoa' and gently pull the reins toward you. The moment he responds, take the pressure off of the reins to let him know he did the right thing."

Cia thought she was gentle enough, but apparently she wasn't - the gelding stopped abruptly, throwing Cia forward. She grabbed his thick, silky coal-black mane to keep from falling. She then centered herself and asked for a walk again, this time pulling the reins more gently. The gelding stopped as smooth as could be. A wide grin spread across her face.

"Very good. Now, I want you to create a positive affirmation about riding and put it in the now."

Cia squinted and crinkled her nose as she tried to figure out what Shin meant.

"Tell yourself something like - I AM an intuitive rider. Not, I'm going to be a good rider with practice."

Cia nodded and repeated the positive affirmation to herself.

Shin asked Maya to trot. "You should create positive affirmations in the now with a lot of issues in your life. It's amazing how your thinking will turn into doing."

"One thing at a time. I AM an intuitive rider. I AM an intuitive rider."

"Let's walk around the field and see how you do," Shin said. "Practice stopping and starting."

Cia moved her hips with the horse's movement and stilled her body when she cued the horse to stop. She liked this – it was simple. Her confidence quickly inflated.

Several minutes later Shin directed Maya to walk side by side with Cabaret. "Knowing the cues that cause response allows you to master a level of communication – whether it's with an animal or a person. If you know which action gets which result, you eliminate confusion. If a horse isn't in pain or fearful, he'll do anything he thinks you want him to do. Your responsibility is to eliminate any confusion."

"So be clear and concise?" Cia said more as a statement of understanding rather than as a question. That's how they home-

Wisdom of the Horse

schooled Elizabeth.

"Yes. For everything you want a horse to do, you'll learn the cues. Like with asking for a walk and then a transition to a stop, then transition to a walk. Everything must be done calmly, gently, and precisely with no room for interpretation by the horse."

"I'm trying to stay with the motion. When I do, it feels so natural, like I've been riding all my life."

Shin smiled gently. "You're doing great. Feel the gentle rise and fall of your horse's breath. Breathe with it – stay in sync and the rhythmic breathing will soothe both of you. When you're in the groove, turn your brain off and let your body do the work."

She gave Cia time alone to follow her directions. Once in complete harmony with Cabaret for an extended period of time, a pinkish blush crept over Cia's face. The calmness of her breathing combined with riding bareback, feeling every movement of the horse between her legs, in her pelvis, and throughout her spine had a mildly erotic feel. It was completely outside of her realm of experience. All of her senses rose to the surface. A languid expression formed on her face.

Chapter 12

A couple of days later, after their routine with Ambra, the women rode in silence as the clean scent of pine trees drifted in the air. Cia's festering frustration and grief was forgotten for the time being. Even though this was a leisurely trail ride, she felt a sense of adventure, especially knowing she would be joining Shin and her friends on the riding and camping trip.

"You okay?" Shin asked when Cabaret stepped up the pace and rushed toward Maya.

Cia nodded. "I'm fine. But what if he spooks?"

Shin smiled. "The more balanced your body is, the more likely you are to stay on. You need to learn to manage your impulse to pull back on the reins hard and to manage your impulse to squeeze your legs to hold on."

Cia's eyes widened. "But how would I stop a horse and stay on if they spook or take off running?"

"If you pull backwards hard and abruptly a horse will resist and get mad. If you squeeze your legs to hold on, that's really telling the horse to move faster – squeezing is the speed cue. You need to stay calm to get the horse calm."

Cia took in a deep breath, wondering if she was endangering herself. "But what if the horse takes off running?"

"You'll turn it into a circle. Our horses are all trained to give to the pull of a rein, even in a panic situation. It's ingrained and instinctual for them to follow their nose – if you pull the nose to your knee, you'll effectively stop the horse from running off. It's an early essential lesson in training. The key is keeping yourself calm and balanced."

Wisdom of the Horse

Cia wondered if she could handle a scary situation.

"A masterful person understands the factors that determine behavior. Successfully functioning in any aspect of life - whether you're dealing with people or animals, being able to predict the behavior of others can be almost as powerful as being able to control the behavior of others."

That's profound, Cia thought, and then she realized they had been guiding their horses into a figure eight pattern. Until this moment she wasn't aware that she subconsciously followed what Shin and Maya were doing, her cues so slight they were imperceptible. Cabaret responded with such finesse, it amazed her.

Cia's new experience with the horses, especially trying to get Ambra to eat more and to trust people again was rewarding. And now riding Cabaret who barely knew her and who could run off out of control made Cia hopeful about life. The vision of her soul beginning to grow diminished the anxious darkness of despair she had been living with for years.

"You look like you're having fun," Shin commented.

"I feel better, I can tell you that. At least most of the time. I'm still depressed when I'm at home, but I don't wish I was dead anymore."

Shin nodded. "You're taking action in physical terms and emotional terms. That's what's helping. The consequences of your life's actions and your actions being on or around a horse are the same – a single action can result in a cascade of physical, emotional, and spiritual effects."

Shin headed for a trail. Cia followed, lost in her thoughts. Heyoka joined them a safe distance behind, excitedly alternating between sniffing the ground and running to catch up.

The trail remained wide enough for them to continue riding side by side. Shin was more concerned about a therapy session for Cia rather than a riding lesson. She'd teach her about turning in both directions and backing up another time.

"Having a horse is an agreement to take a journey. Even the commitment of taking care of Ambra, although you wouldn't own her, would be a journey. It will enable you to envision your life in a transformative way. I have a friend, I think I mentioned him – Grayson?"

Cia nodded.

Shin continued. "He helps terminally ill people that want to be around the horses. You wouldn't believe the transformations they make."

"How? I mean, if they're dying, what kind of transformation can they make?"

"Each relationship in your life carries a fragment of your spirit – even relationships with animals. In my experience, clinically depressed and terminally ill people feel it more than most people."

Cia reflected. "If I knew for sure that I was going to die whether I wanted to or not, I think I'd just mope around and feel sorry for myself. I hate to say it, but that's probably what I would do."

Shin had so much to teach this woman. "Eastern cultures and Native Americans believe in a continuum of lifetimes rather than a single life followed by eternal reward or punishment. I believe that's the truth, so I wouldn't feel sorry for myself."

"I guess you're right. We have to believe that, or what's the point? I haven't thought about death in that way in so long. I've only thought about it as the end result of releasing myself from my shitty life."

"When you define your understanding of your life's purpose, you'll feel differently," Shin said.

"I don't know what I'm supposed to be doing. That's part of my problem."

"Your life's purpose is something you're supposed to *be* rather than *do*. Not a role or a career, but who you are being inside and how you are to people and animals and nature."

Cia, thirsty for Shin's wisdom, repeated the statement to herself, wishing she could write it down.

At the creek Shin guided Maya down stream a few horse lengths so Cabaret would have room to find a desirable drinking spot. The horses sniffed the knee-deep water. Maya pawed, splashing water and digging in the wet sand beneath her hooves.

Wisdom of the Horse

Shin spoke casually. "There's a difference between really living and just existing, just as there's a difference between good horsemanship and just being on a horse going along for the ride."

"I want to really live – not just exist. I feel like I've just been existing for years," Cia said, now aching in her heart, facing her feelings and problems, even if only to herself.

"I can see that," Shin said, stroking Maya's neck.

Heyoka discovered he could swim. He made it to the far side of the creek and shook the water off his little body, wagging his tail, proud of his incredible accomplishment. Looking like a giant wet rat, he found a patch of loose, soft soil and rolled on his back and squirmed. The women laughed at him, lightening the moment.

"I've let my life deteriorate before my eyes without realizing it. There's so much I need to change about myself if I'm going to have any kind of future at all."

"Change can only take place in the present. You can't change the past. And in many ways, thinking about the future is useless. You have to be in the now – in the present. Move yourself out of victim consciousness and make the changes you need to make."

Cia's heart sank. Victim consciousness was the perfect description. Her husband's actions and her own actions made her feel like a victim. "You've already helped me so much," she said, tears suddenly cascading down her face. Regretting how she had lived her life, and how much she needed to change, a hard knot formed in her stomach.

"I've only facilitated in you helping yourself. Only you can heal Cia. I can show you the way, but that's all I can do. The journey is yours to take."

Cia cried and twisted a chunk of Cabaret's mane hairs in between her fingers. "A journey, or an adventure, or a life sentence."

"Pardon?"

"Never mind. I'm just talking to myself," she said as the tears burned her cheeks. "I was feeling so good until a minute ago. I don't know what happened."

"You're like a horse."

"What?"

"Horses and people are the same in many ways. Your emotions are as changeable as the weather. That's a warning about being around horses – they can be unpredictable, seeming to be going along just fine, then something triggers an emotion of fear or excitement. Just like us. We're fine, then suddenly scared or exhilarated. Or in your case, sad and depressed. But always remember, you can go back to being fine again."

"Are horses really that temperamental?" Cia asked, a little concerned for her safety.

Shin twisted around and brushed a pesky fly off of Maya's rump. "I wouldn't call it temperamental, although a lot of people do. I see handling horses and riding as an agreement between a person and a horse. You'll always be in a conversation of signals, suggestions, and kind debate. If you allow it, the horse will carry you into moments of grace and teach you bravery."

Cia internalized Shin's perspective. Flittering yellow and black butterflies swarmed the tree limb hanging over the water only a few feet away.

Shin cued Maya to cross the creek toward the far side of the trail. Cabaret and Heyoka eagerly followed. "Lean forward and raise your butt without tensing your legs," Shin called out just before they headed single file up the slope. "Don't grip your legs any harder than needed to maintain your balance."

A few minutes later they arrived at a large patch of tall, blue stem grass. Shin dismounted and stretched. Cia did the same. The horses snatched grass as if they hadn't eaten all day.

"Have you ever fallen?" Cia asked.

Shin laughed animatedly. "Lots of times."

"Do you get mad at your horse when you fall off?"

"No. To me, a fall is a reminder," Shin said without hesitation. "A relationship with a horse is like how we must live – we get up when we fall, and we go on."

"But doesn't it hurt when you fall?"

Shin didn't want her to dwell on the idea. "How's your body

pain? Are you doing better still?"

"Most of the time I'm pretty good. I find that you were right - I notice the pain when I start getting emotional or depressed. The rest of the time, I do pretty well."

Shin shooed a fly from Maya's neck. "Chronic pain can be where emotions are held. When emotions are dealt with, along with the other changes you've made in your life, pain is often released."

"I think you're right."

"Do you still feel like you're just working hard to get from one day to the next?" Shin asked.

"Yeah. But at least now I actually want to get to the next day. I love my family, but knowing that Ambra needs me and that I can help her has made all the difference in the world."

"You've been living the life Ambra is living. Simply existing, but not much more. You're moving out of that stage of your life."

Cia looked to the ground in thought. She picked up a thick blade of grass and chewed it. "You're right. I'm Ambra, but human. It's pitiful. Both of us are pitiful," she said and then broke down in tears, her body trembling.

Cabaret lifted his head and dangled long grass stems from his mouth. His expressive dark eyes stared at his new friend as he wandered over and hung his head into Cia's chest. Cia offered a half-smile and rubbed Cabaret's forehead before reaching her arms around the horse's neck. Cabaret stood, doing his job, being there for someone who needed him. Not speaking, Shin watched Cia cry. It was a positive step and a required release before she could proceed.

Finally, Cia collapsed in exhaustion, lying down in the grass, spreading her arms and legs like she was making a snow angel – just letting the sun absorb her heartache.

Shin sat next to her, stroking her forehead like a mother stroking a child with a fever. "I'm here for you. And so are the spirit guides. One day, you'll catch an updraft you can soar on. I promise."

Cali Canberra

Heyoka crawled onto Cia's stomach and chest to lick her face. She giggled and rolled onto her side. She rubbed the puppy's tummy as he lay on his back, paws in the air. "I'm better now. I guess I just needed a good cry. I never allow myself to let loose like this. It felt good. Thank you."

"It's only natural to need a release."

Cia wiped the tears from her face with her worn flannel shirt and sat up, still petting the puppy. Cabaret nuzzled her hair in between taking bites of grass. "Just being out here is such a release."

"You need to talk more, though. I think you've pushed aside your most serious problems because they're too painful to deal with. For you, it seems easier not to deal with the real issues. In reality, not dealing with them is making things worse."

Cia couldn't tell Shin the crux of her problem. At best, she could get help to deal with the life she and Jeffrey had created. "I'm sure you're right," is all she could say.

"The pain of avoiding dealing with a serious problem is profound. You must feel that in your heart."

"I do. I'm just not ready. You are helping me though, you know."

Shin stood and wiped the grass off her jeans. "I'm not trying to validate my work," she said simply. "Let's ride."

Cia looked around dumbfounded. "How am I going to get back on?"

It was time to lighten the day. Shin ground tied Maya, picked up a four foot long stiff stick, and then approached Cabaret's left side. She tapped the gelding's left knee with the stick. Cabaret bowed. Shin tapped the gelding's right knee and told him to pray. Cabaret kneeled. Cia's eyes opened wide as her mouth hung open.

"Get on!"

Cia grabbed a handful of mane and awkwardly mounted the kneeling bareback horse. Cabaret slowly stood up and then repeatedly raised his head up-and-down wanting a treat. Shin picked a handful of grass and fed him as she stroked his neck. An incredible smile spread across Cia's face. Her tears and heartache

Wisdom of the Horse

was forgotten in an instant. Heyoka ran around in circles as if he knew this was a breakthrough.

A moment later Shin gracefully mounted Maya bareback without the aid of a tree stump or a trick. "Like I said - if a horse understands what you want, and knows they'll be rewarded for doing the right thing, they'll do just about anything for you."

The women rode to the crest of the hill and looked down upon a secluded flatland. Cia didn't know why, but she felt the presence of something she had never experienced before. Her mind searched for a reason behind the pattern of the rocks.

"It's an Indian Medicine Wheel," Shin said before Cia had a chance to question what she saw. "Have you heard of Earth Medicine?"

Cia silently shook her head, in awe of something she knew nothing about.

"Earth Medicine is a system of self-discovery. The Medicine Wheel of Native Americans has a correlation with the Taoist teachings of the East. Earth Medicine can help you discover who and what you are in this world, and your primary purpose in life."

Cia looked at Shin with furrowed brows. "I don't understand how rocks in the pattern of a wheel can do anything, let alone anything so important."

Shin began walking Maya down the slope. Cabaret followed without being prompted. "Would you like to learn about the Medicine Wheel?"

Cia slid forward onto Cabaret's withers. Unable to reposition herself as they rode down the incline, she instinctively turned the gelding and traversed until she could get a better seat position. This didn't go unnoticed by Shin – she was testing Cia's instincts and her ability to control the horse while her thoughts were elsewhere.

When they reached the bottom of the slope, within twenty feet of the rocks, Cia asked exactly what she would get out of it if she learned about the Medicine Wheel. She couldn't believe it could help her discover herself and find her purpose.

Shin explained that Earth Medicine can do many things, but

of primary importance for Cia, it would offer to free her from the feelings of being a victim of circumstance and it would help her become responsible for her own life. "Earth Medicine can transform your Earth Walk," she said in conclusion to the short description. She slid off Maya, stretched her legs, and gave the mare a chance to nibble some grass. Cia did the same.

"What's an Earth Walk?" Cia asked as if she were learning a new language.

"It's being alive in your physical body on earth versus being in the next dimension many call death. It's the way you live your life and express who you are. It's your fears, dreams, and ambitions."

She went on to explain about Earth Medicine, an ancient wisdom, the essence of a knowledge that is shared by many tribes of the world. Its concern is with how our Earth connections can allow us to attain mastery of our own destiny. Most people don't know about the teachings because they have been hidden within the traditions of American Indian Medicine Men and protected by tribal shamans.

"My grandfather and his father before him were tribal shamans," Shin said reminiscently. "Generations ago, elders representing the major tribes met and agreed to preserve the Medicine teachings by orally telling each of the generations, hoping it would be fully practiced forever. They usually use stories to teach and are often known as Storytellers."

Cia, fascinated and curious asked, "How do you decide when you want to follow Eastern spirituality or Native American spirituality?"

"That's a good question, but I don't have to decide. Both cultures, or religions, or philosophies, whatever you want to call it, believe all life – plant, animal, mineral – contains a spiritual essence. A living life force. Most ancient ways stress the importance of human soul growth as the reason for existence."

"That's handy. You don't have to choose mom's way or dad's way," Cia said lightly, recalling her parents, Orthodox Jews, rejected her because she wouldn't be part of their traditions,

Wisdom of the Horse

rituals and strict way of thinking.

Shin smiled, and then seriously added a scientific detail. "DNA in modern Native Americans suggests that North and South American Indians came from one culture in Asia that migrated across the Bering Strait. The link explains the similarities in their philosophies."

"Surely there are differences."

"Of course. There are," she replied. "And there are differences between Indian tribes. Customs and beliefs vary. That's why when you read books about certain ways of performing rituals, it's only a guide and never set in concrete. Even Jewish people are like that. Some Hasidic, some Orthodox, some Reform - and varying degrees of each. It's the same in every culture."

Cia couldn't believe she was out horseback riding and having thought provoking conversation. It wasn't so long ago that the most interesting part of her day was watching Oprah and Dr. Phil. She had forgotten how much she loved learning and expressing her creativity. She envied Shin's freedom to conceptualize her religion in her own individual way. Growing up in her family, it was not tolerated so she walked away thinking she didn't want religion as part of her life. Now she was discovering that spirituality and religion and all that surrounds it are open to interpretation.

"Have you grown up with Earth Medicine or was it taught to you at a certain age, like when Jews start going to Hebrew School for their Bar Mitzvah or Bat Mitzvah?"

"I grew up with Earth Medicine and spirit guides."

Cia tried to make a joke. "Why are all the spirit guides you hear about Indians?"

Shin didn't know the question was meant to be funny. "The reason so many spirit guides have an Indian identity is because we have a way of perceiving and living life in a circular way rather than living in a linear way."

Cia was in awe of all she heard even though she still didn't understand. "I must sound stupid, but I don't get it. What exactly is Earth Medicine?"

79

"Before you can grasp the basic ideas you must first understand what the Medicine Wheel is."

They let the horses loose to graze and then walked right up to the rocks that formed the wheel. "For us," Shin said, referring to North American Indians, "medicine means more than some substance to restore health. 'Medicine' is an energy force inherent in Nature. Your 'medicine' is your power and an expression of your own life-energy system. In Eastern cultures it's called *Chi, Qi,* or *Prana.* Perhaps you've heard of that?"

Cia nodded. She had taken yoga classes years ago and learned about Prana, Yin, and Yang. Not details, but enough to vaguely understand.

Shin continued. She made a gesture meant to encompass all of the rocks. "This Medicine Wheel is a circle of energy that provides knowledge of the energetic power. In essence, 'medicine' is your own personal empowerment. Can you see its importance now?"

Shin began climbing up boulders nearby. Cia followed as she listened.

"Yes. I do. I think I'm starting to understand. Basically, the rocks that make the wheel are a symbol of power?"

"My father teaches that the Medicine Wheel is a spiritual, physical, mental and emotional device that allows us to attune ourselves to Earth influences. The wheel itself is comprised of a set of symbols in the form of an encircled cross."

At the highest point they could safely climb on the boulders, they stopped and looked down on the Medicine Wheel. Cia wondered how the rocks were placed so perfectly to form the circle and the spokes, but she didn't change the subject.

Shin continued. "American Indians and other civilizations around the world use ancient stone circles. They aren't identical, but serve similar purposes. Our American Indian Medicine Wheel is portable, as you can see. It's a symbolic map that can be carried and set up wherever we want."

"What exactly is the symbolism?" Cia asked, enthralled.

"The four spokes are pathways to the center. The center

represents the Creator, but can also represent the Self. The perimeter is marked by eight larger outer stones representing how the powers of man and the powers of the universe can be brought into harmony. The eight stones that make the inner circle represent inner and spiritual realities. The rest of the stones – eight of them, again, form the arms of a cross. See the two stones positioned in each of the four cardinal directions between the inner and outer circles?"

"Yes."

"The four arms are the Four Great Paths – Clarity and Illumination in the East, Introspection and Transformation in the West, Wisdom and Knowledge in the North, and Trust and Love in the South."

Cia, clearly fascinated, sat down, unsure of her equilibrium. Shin remained standing.

"You're so fortunate to have all this knowledge. I grew up in an Orthodox Jewish family and had no interest in it. In fact, my parents were always saying I shouldn't tell people I'm Jewish because gentiles won't treat me the way they should. But at home, everything was about being Jewish. They kept Kosher, and somehow always found a reason to talk about the Holocaust. It wasn't my thing, and I didn't think it made sense not to tell people I'm Jewish. My parents were furious when I married my husband – he's not Jewish, and that wasn't acceptable to them. They wanted me and my husband to follow their specific traditions and wanted Jewish grandchildren."

Shin felt bad for Cia. "Do they accept Jeffrey now?"

"No. They disowned me. Seriously. They disowned me because I didn't marry an Orthodox Jew. They probably would have done the same thing if I had married a Reform Jew – that's how strongly they feel," she said, tears forming in her eyes. She suddenly wondered how she had turned the subject of the Medicine Wheel to her parents disowning her.

Shin hoped Cia would continue talking about her past and her feelings, but nothing more came. There was a long silence, other than the birds flying overhead and the sound of the horses chewing grass. "Sometimes we use a buffalo skull to indicate the Creator in the center of the circle because the buffalo was very symbolic. In my great-grandfather's day, and his family before him, the buffalo was almost everything Indians needed for survival. Flesh for food. Bones for making implements like utensils and weapons. The hide for covering the tipis and for clothing. Parts of the body were even used for making things to hold water and for cooking. The buffalo sinew was the thread for sewing. The skull was a representation of the mind of *Wakan Tanka* - the Great Everything. What some refer to as God."

"I don't see a buffalo skull in the center," Cia observed.

"No. You're right. We don't have one because my father believes it's best to leave the center empty as a reminder of the Void which is the invisible Source of Everything."

"This is very complex."

Shin motioned for Cia to follow. They climbed down the boulders and reclaimed the horses. It was time to start heading back. Shin mounted Maya by leading her up to a fallen tree. Cia gave Cabaret the commands she had learned earlier to get the gelding to kneel.

Chapter 13

Jeffrey was uplifted by his wife and daughter's transformation ever since Cia began therapy and working with the horses. The day that Ambra and Heyoka moved to their property, for the first time in years, it seemed that joy had finally infiltrated their lives. Elizabeth blossomed. Without coaxing, she eagerly ventured to the paddock and bonded with the mare and the puppy.

He too spent time with Ambra, but was fully aware that she was more interested in his wife and daughter. The mare instinctively trusted Elizabeth, probably due to her small size and uninhibited demeanor. Ambra even lowered her head to let Elizabeth halter her and hold her as Cia applied topical medications.

Holding the feed bucket against her tummy, Elizabeth beamed with self-importance and pride each time Ambra eagerly ate her feed and Thyro-L supplement. When they tried hanging the bucket from the fence rail, Ambra reluctantly picked at her ration and didn't finish it.

Elizabeth was playing in the back yard throwing a tennis ball for Heyoka when Cia returned from horseback riding with Shin. Jeffrey greeted her at the picnic table with a bottle of wine and a fruit and cheese platter. She guessed something was up – he had an enthusiastic look on his face. It was an expression she hadn't seen in years.

"Please don't be mad," he started.

She tensed up but didn't respond.

"A while ago, I brought a broken slot machine home from the Cherokee Casino. It was one of those five reel steppers."

She didn't know what a five reel stepper was but she glared at him, took a sip of her wine, and tapped her fingers on the table.

"Elizabeth and I fixed it."

"So?"

"After I fixed it, I couldn't resist investigating how the software operates. I was able to break a portion of the coding, so I contacted…"

She cut him off. "You did what? Are you insane?"

"Cia, you don't understand. I did it for a positive reason, not to rip anyone off."

She stared at him, more furious than she had ever been in her life. "You swore you'd never do anything illegal again."

"It wasn't illegal. Please, hear me out."

"I don't care how shitty our life is, I'm not letting you get involved in anything to do with slot machines."

"You're jumping to conclusions. Let me explain."

She crossed her arms in front of herself and sat rigid. "This better be good. You've just lost all the trust I had in you."

"We can't keep living like this. So, I contacted the CEO of Aristocrat Technologies and told him I was able to crack part of the code for their five reel stepper. At first, he didn't believe me, but I offered to tell him how I did it. He put me in contact with someone in development – I told them exactly how I did it, and they were impressed."

"So?"

"That was the point of the call. To impress them with what I'm capable of. A few days after my initial contact, the CEO, Paul Oneile, contacted me and said they could always use people like me and he already had some things in mind they'd like me to examine and troubleshoot."

She interjected, "But what about your record?"

"I don't have a criminal record."

Cia always forgot that detail because she thought of him as a criminal. A former criminal, at least. But one of the points of the plea bargain was that he wouldn't have a record. The problem with lack of good employment has been about having new identities to be in the witness protection program. Who would hire someone in his field without him having a resume and the educational background? The government couldn't create a new identity that would allow him to work in his chosen field.

He continued. "But I told Paul about my arrest and everything else, including being the top in my class at MIT. He seemed to believe me. Anyway, he offered me freelance consulting work, and it's going to be lucrative."

Cia shook her head, wondering if he was telling her the truth without any editing or sugar-coating or lies of omission. "What's the name of the company?"

"Aristocrat Technologies. They're based in Australia."

She arched her brows. "Australia? Can we even leave the country?"

"I don't know yet. I've got to contact Carl," he said, referring to his lawyer that handled his predicament, a term only he used. "But we wouldn't have to move there. They have offices in Las Vegas and Sparks, Nevada, New Jersey, and Minnesota. If they can't bring me to Australia from time to time, they'll work it out."

"Would we move?"

"That's the main point. We don't just need more money. We need to move somewhere we'd enjoy living."

"How could that happen? We still need to be in hiding."

"Yes, but it's been so long now, I don't think we need to be nearly as careful. We could move now, if we had the money. I'm certain of it."

"How can you be so certain?"

"I just am. As long as we keep using our fabricated names and backgrounds, we'll be fine. Elizabeth is coming around so much that I think with some professional psychological help we could get her into a public school. We could live normal lives."

"I don't know. I'm scared. I'll always be scared."

"Don't be. As long as we keep low key, we'll be fine. It's been so long now."

"You'll make good money?"

"Yes. And after how we've been living, it will feel like we're rolling in money!"

"I love you," she said, then sipped her wine as she tried to find the right words. "But I don't think I can trust you. I'm afraid that if you're around that environment again you'll -"

He gently placed a finger over her lips before she could continue. He ran his fingers through her hair and kissed her long, and deep, and hard – they way they used to kiss before all of their problems began.

"You can trust me. I swear."

"So, where would we live? I can't imagine living in Jersey. And Minnesota's way too cold. That only leaves Vegas – if you even have a choice."

"It is my choice. I told them I'd want to work out of Vegas."

"I can't imagine raising a child there," she said, wanting to change the subject of trust and what he had done to cause half of their problems.

"We could live in the outskirts of Las Vegas. Or if you want, we could get a small farm of our own somewhere out west. It would need to be where I could easily commute from, but it's an option. You can get your own horse if you want. Whatever would make you and Elizabeth happy is fine with me."

Cia hated their rental house and was bored by the town they lived in, but she finally was starting to enjoy life a little bit. She had settled into the routine of taking care of Ambra who she had become so attached to, and she looked forward to her therapy sessions and riding Cabaret. She almost felt like he was her own horse ever since she started riding him three or four days a week.

After a long hesitation she responded. "What you would do is legal?"

Wisdom of the Horse

"Yes. Definitely. There's no hacking involved and I'd never be on a casino floor. I'd be helping improve Aristocrat's products."

"Couldn't you work from here? Maybe just fly to Vegas a couple of times a month? Lots of people work from home using the internet and teleconferencing."

"No. I'd need to be at the regional headquarters several days a week. Besides, you don't even want to live here."

She didn't speak as she watched Ambra eat her hay while Elizabeth stood on double-stacked milk crates, methodically braiding beads and ribbons into the mare's mane and tail. Cia wanted to leave southeast Oklahoma so much, yet she didn't want to leave the horses she had come to care about – the horses that were helping heal her soul. They were now part of the fabric of her life. And the relationship between Ambra and her daughter may not be able to be replaced by another horse. How could she risk it for any of them?

"I don't get it," he said, breaking the awkward silence. "I thought you'd be excited. In fact, I thought you'd be relieved we could get on with our lives and that you could pursue your art again."

"Let me think about it."

She desperately wanted to trust his judgment about being able to let their guard down, but what if he was wrong?

"I don't know what there is to think about."

She ignored his statement. "Is this a new company? Would you have job security?"

"They've been around forever. They're a leading global provider of gaming solutions. I wouldn't worry about job security."

"What's gaming solutions mean?"

"It means they develop world-class software and hardware. They're the ones who came out with the new MKVI platform in 2001, and the High-Demon Hyperlink® and SuperReel Power™ - and they have the Oasis Casino Management System – which is what I'd be involved in at first."

She didn't say so, but she was upset that he must have been

using the internet to keep up with what was happening in the industry. He hadn't mentioned a word about it.

"It's all Greek to me," she said. "You know that. What's the management system do?"

"Oasis is a program that manages the casino's slot accounting, cashless wagering, bonusing, and player loyalty programs. A casino's revenue stream is entirely dependent of the system's ability to provide accounting and reporting on gaming activity as well as linking together casino and hotel revenues."

"It sounds like a great opportunity for you," she said reluctantly. "But the timing is poor. Let me think about it before you decide."

This wasn't the time to tell her that he had already made a commitment to the CEO and the regional manager to be ready to work after Thanksgiving. He'd have some time to convince Cia that this was the right move. For now, he'd let the idea sink in. Let her conjure up all the benefits and possibilities in her mind.

Chapter 14

Two weeks later...

On a crisp October morning, Shin, her father Thundering Cloud, her brother Tate, and Cia trailered the horses and a pack horse to the Ouachita National Forest - 351,000 acres designated for horseback riding and hiking. Four generations of the Crow family had hiked and ridden these mountains and forests. The area was their life support system - they were still in awe of the splendor and the Great Mystery's creation. Kiamachi Country was breathtaking this time of year.

They avoided the tourists by using a little known southeast entry where there was a newly opened section of riding trails. Thundering Cloud had been in the section a half-dozen times, but this was the first time for his daughter and son.

The first horse off the trailer was Tanka, an eight-year-old Appaloosa-Quarter Horse crossbreed pack horse. They brought him to carry the heavy load of water, sleeping bags and warm clothing. In Lakota, *Tanka* means great and big – and the gelding was both, as was his heart.

When they unloaded the other horses, Cabaret was wound up – prancing and snorting and rearing in the air, challenging

Cali Canberra

Shin's authority. When Shin tied him to the trailer to tack him up he anxiously pawed the ground. No one had ever known Cabaret to act like this, but some horses were rambunctious when they were in new surroundings. Once he was tacked up and mounted, he was perfectly behaved, although clearly anxious to cover ground. Tanka, a faithful companion, calmly trailed behind Cabaret and Maya.

Cia rode Maya next to Thundering Cloud, drawn to his radiant, energetic aura. Because of Shin's influence, Cia was now eager for a different form of higher education. She yearned to develop relationships with people who possessed a secret knowledge and wisdom that would dispel her disillusionment and bewilderment about life. Hopefully, on this trip they would help her assemble the things she had learned, so her insights would be more than a mosaic of knowledge – she wanted a clear picture with all the blanks filled in. Then, maybe her spirit would understand the meaning of life.

When Cia first locked eyes with Thundering Cloud, the Native American's authentic presence cast a calm that rippled through her in a way she never imagined possible. She envisioned him bringing brightness to a dim room. Thundering Cloud, in spite of his face being etched with lines, was the quintessential picture of health. He looked sanguine riding his Paint horse, Zunta, bareback. Anyone could see in his expression the enjoyment he felt in every stride. *Zunta*, in Lakota means honest. Cia was sure the name described the man as much as the horse.

Tate rode *Shunke Canku* bareback. In Lakota, Tate's name means the wind, and his horse's name means iron horse. The pair went ahead of everyone, Tate needing personal space for a few hours. The hectic pace of putting on clinics throughout the world, going to powwows, and writing his books had caught up with him. He had been craving a reunion with nature for months. This was his time to discharge his battery. Canku, quick to sense his leader's mood, responded with swift precision to Tate's every cue. After too many miles driving his truck and trailer and flying all over the world, Tate relished the freshness of the crisp, clean air

Wisdom of the Horse

on his skin. With the group behind him, he stifled the impulse to gallop - until he spotted a bald eagle soaring through the clear, blue sky in the distance. He gently squeezed Canku with his legs, inclined his head toward the horse's silky mane, and let the horse stretch his neck as he sprang into a gallop that felt like they were floating on air.

Approaching a small glistening lake they smoothly transitioned to a trot and then a relaxed walk. Canku's flanks were heaving from the mammoth effort to keep up with the eagle. Tate's eyes sparkled as he walked his trusted companion along the water's edge. On the surface of the crystal clear water he watched the reflection of the trees and light above, and the reflection of himself on his horse. The picture was as beautiful as the photos taken of him by Gabrielle Boiselle for his first book on Native American horsemanship.

Since they were so far ahead of everyone else, Tate dismounted and sat on a large flat rock, warm from the sun. Canku nibbled the three foot tall Little Bluestem grass, which had once been the forage supply of the great herds of buffalo, deer, and elk. A pale light reflected in the pine trees. With the sun lowering in the sky, the orange leaves on the red oak trees contrasted with the beauty of the dark purple leaves on the black tupelo.

In the mean time, Thundering Cloud and his daughter enjoyed a riding rhythm of capable riders with finesse. Shin had given the lead rope of Tanka, the pack horse, over to Cia because even after a few miles Cabaret was anxious to move out and Tanka couldn't even keep up with his walking pace. As an advanced level competitive trail horse, Cabaret wasn't used to slow leisurely rides – the pace they had been riding to accommodate Cia and the pack horse didn't suit his high-energy personality and level of conditioning. Ever since mounting, Shin needed to lightly bump him back to keep him at a walk. When they approached a large clearing with good footing Shin excused herself and allowed Cabaret to enjoy an extended trot and then a rhythmic canter. He was the smoothest and proudest horse she had ever ridden. Now she knew why so many people preferred Arabians for distance work.

Cia repeatedly readjusted Tanka's long lead rope as Thundering Cloud described the various wilderness areas of Kiamichi Country and the strong culture of thriving Native Americans living in Oklahoma. His grandfather and father passed along to him their talent to be great horsemen and great storytellers - he entertained Cia with a few personal stories of wilderness survival trips on their *sunka wakan*, the Lakota word for a powerful dog, which is a horse. Terror squirmed in Cia's chest as she visualized some of the threats they had faced over the generations. She silently reevaluated her own fantasy of a wilderness survival trip. Turning over various scenarios in her mind, her confidence vaporized one moment, and then the next moment she felt a gut-level sense of destiny to challenge herself.

"I'd like this trip to help me gain a new perception of nature and horses," Cia said.

"When I am riding," Thundering Cloud explained, "it seems as though colors become sharper and more vibrant and all of my senses are refined. We enter the wilderness with all of our senses to know the wilderness is here to humble us."

Enthralled, she hung on his every word and his subtle gestures. The elder energized her and inspired her to focus. Her gaze traveled up to a flock of sparrows. "I have a feeling this trip is going to be an incredible experience. I can tell already."

"Having experiences is not enough. Having experiences you learn something from is the only experience of value."

"I understand what you mean, but I like to have experiences I can tell other people about," she said, temporarily forgetting she didn't have friends anymore now that they lived in Oklahoma.

He offered a faint smile. "You need the approval of others?"

"No. Not really. But I like being interesting."

"That's a form of needing approval. And, I assume you feel good when people compliment you. That's a form of approval."

Cia laughed. "Everyone's like that!"

Thundering Cloud noticed Cia struggling to hold her own reins while trying to lead Tanka. He took Tanka's lead rope and

Wisdom of the Horse

told her he'd take care of him, and then guided Zunta and Tanka to a large patch of grass and let them relax and nibble. "When you don't seek or need external approval, you are at your most powerful. This security can give you a liberated feeling that's practically euphoric."

Shin galloped back to join her father and Cia. "That felt great," she said, her face a tad red from the adrenaline rush. Cabaret halted and tried to turn his haunches to Zunta. She verbally reprimanded him.

"We were just discussing the concept of people wanting approval from others," Cia said to Shin.

Shin nodded. She and her father had debated the subject over the years. She had mixed feelings about the practicality of not caring what others thought. To her father she said, "You're not lecturing, are you?"

"No. We were talking and the subject came up."

Cia interjected, "He's not lecturing me. It's just that I think it's human nature to want approval about certain things."

"You don't need it," Thundering Cloud said assertively.

Shin loved these healthy debates. "I think you're right in most circumstances, but in regards to the idea of me writing Lynn Andrews style fiction -"

Cia interrupted. "Lynn Andrews style fiction?"

Thundering Cloud answered for his daughter. "She's a wealthy white woman from Beverly Hills who befriended a couple of old Indian women in Canada. She wrote a series of novels about the things she learned from them. Now, she's got a huge following."

"Would you still be a spiritual psychologist if you wrote novels?" Cia asked Shin, wondering how the woman could juggle so many things. She knew Shin well enough to know she'd never give up her time with horses.

"Sure. But I wouldn't see nearly as many people," Shin answered.

Cia was relieved. Shin had become her lifeline. "Then you should try to write a novel."

"Actually, I'm almost finished writing the first one. I just don't know if I can put myself out there for approval – or rejection. Or, as Dad says, just put myself out there and honestly not care what anyone thinks either way."

"You've never told me about any of this," Cia said. "Knowing what I do about you, I'll bet you can achieve anything you set your mind to."

"Right," Shin said. "Anyway, if I try to do what Lynn Andrews does, if people don't enjoy reading what I write, I've got no audience. I need their approval or I won't succeed." She hesitated, and then added, "The magazine articles I write don't fulfill me. I love the idea of writing to educate and entertain people."

"I'm sure you do," Thundering Cloud said, speaking frankly as if Cia wasn't there. "I've sensed for a long time that you haven't been writing what you would really like to write about. From what you've told me, I think that by writing for magazines you took the easy way out, and now you're not satisfied."

"Initially, I was satisfied, and I was proud of my articles, but now, I'd like to write more from my heart. I want to serve others both as a means to my own awareness and an expression of it."

"Then do it," Cia said. She was glad to know Shin had her own issues to deal with. She supposed everyone did, no matter what their level of education and experience in helping others.

"I'm afraid of the criticism I might get," Shin said honestly as she tied her black hair into a knot to get it off her shoulders.

"You must have so many good stories," Cia said encouragingly.

"She does," Thundering Cloud said. "And there are always stories within other stories. Nothing that ever happens does so in a vacuum. Everyone has their stories – it's a matter of how interesting they are and the way in which they are told."

Thundering Cloud edged closer to his daughter and looked into her soul. "You're an artist in search of yourself. Your early writing was only important because of what it can lead to. You, too, are a storyteller. You must tell the stories that you want to and forget about what others may think."

Shin agreed, but suddenly she felt the wariness that haunted her when she slipped into her insecure moods.

"I guess you're right. But sometimes I don't even feel like I'm a writer. Not in the way that Tate is. It's strange. But then again, I don't feel like I should have or want or need a title like 'writer'."

He looked deep into her. "It's good you feel that way. You know, I've taught you that titles inhibit growth."

"Pardon?" Cia said.

"Titles inhibit growth. A title is stifling. It's meant to define who you are and no one is one thing or has one way of being or doing. For instance, if a woman thinks of herself and introduces herself as Mrs., she is defining herself in terms of her husband."

They began riding again. Thundering Cloud proudly watched Shin's erect yet relaxed posture that matched Cabaret's. "To be honest," he said to his daughter, "I think you feel as if your writing is a competition for success with your brother. You shouldn't feel that way."

"Sometimes I can't help feeling that way! I'm a hypocrite. I'll admit it," Shin said, breaking into a smile.

"No. You're not," Thundering Cloud said. "But when you're personally invested in something you just don't pay attention to the nuances of thoughts, feelings, actions, and what the Creator has in mind for you."

Not knowing how to respond, Shin pursed her lips in frustration. Cia didn't know this side of Shin. It was interesting.

"You can't live for prolonged periods of time within the polarity of being true to yourself and needing the approval of others," he said, sensing the internal trauma she attempted to hide.

"You don't understand. I have to write what readers like or I won't have an audience."

"They like Lynn Andrews – they'll like you. And even if they don't, so what! Compromising who you are to gain the approval of another is a way of giving away a piece of your spirit. Don't do it. You'll never feel at peace with yourself. You'll never truly approve of your own being."

Shin thought of his words as she felt him looking into her – looking through her. The pure blackness of his eyes radiated calmness. Her father emanated wisdom and a powerful presence that gave her the confidence no one else could.

After a long silence without a response, Thundering Cloud decided to change the subject. He turned to Cia and said, "Don't tell me your answer, but when you were first out of high school, what did you dream your life would be like? Just think about it, Cia."

"I know what my main dream was, outside of having a healthy and happy family."

"Think about what your dream is now."

That was part of Cia's problem. She didn't want to think about the future, to have dreams, to have goals. What was the point? Nothing turned out the way she anticipated anyway. "Okay. I know my dream," she said halfheartedly.

"I think you scaled down your dreams as you inflated the size of your fears."

She was stunned. How would he know? Did she have such a worn down look about her? Could he see into her soul? See her cynicism about the world and what it had done to her? Could he see her worry that hope for an exciting future was tainted by her past mistakes? Didn't he know she was leading a new life? That's why she was on the trip – it was integral to her journey in gaining inner peace, in soul searching, in finding the depths of her spirit, in finding new wings so she could soar. That's what he should sense if he was trying to read her. He dug up emotions in her core she didn't know existed. Speechless, she stroked Maya and waited to see if he would continue talking.

"You're always looking, but not always seeing – is that correct?" he asked.

"What are you? A psychic?" Cia said sarcastically.

He ignored her disrespect. "You think you see, but you are blind. You have sight, but no vision," he said, knowing she would understand he was referring to the spiritual world. "Do you know

Wisdom of the Horse

what I mean by vision?"

"A goal for the future?" she asked hesitantly.

"No," he said. "Vision is the capacity to believe in what your heart sees - what others can't see. Vision is seeing positive possibilities where others only see negative probabilities."

Shin interjected. "I have vision. What I don't have is the trust that what I envision will really happen. That's what I'm searching for. The trust," she realized.

He smiled at his daughter. All he wanted was for her to put it into words. He lifted Zunta's head with a light signal from his hands. Tanka, Cabaret, and Maya followed. They briskly returned to the trail.

"Sometimes I wish I never had to return to civilization," Shin said, a tight hard lump forming in her throat.

Thundering Cloud smiled, more to himself than outwardly. "That is because in the wilderness there is no competition with others. We only struggle with our own limitations and those of our horses. In this way, we feel a greater triumph and accomplishment."

Shin smiled. He told her this every time they rode together on long trips. "We should spend time talking like this more often. You give me so much courage, Dad."

He winked at her and said, "Courage is like muscle; it gets stronger with practice."

Cia felt grateful to have met Shin and her father. They offered her reassurance about life. Everything they said was inscribed with a truth and certainty. Hopefully, they would help her gain more access to the spiritual world.

Chapter 15

Just as he turned down a fork on the trail, Thundering Cloud brought Tanka up by his right knee and quickly told Cia to turn Maya back in the direction they had come from and stay away until he called for her or came and got her. Trusting his instincts and sensing there was no time to question him, Cia promptly did as instructed. Nearing the cascading stream, Cabaret stopped dead in his tracks, arched his neck, and grew edgy. A brownish grey bobcat with mottling dispersed over its thick fur cast enormous shadows as it crawled up the boulders in front of them. Huge, dark green cat eyes peered at the horses and riders. Shin stroked Cabaret's neck and relaxed her body so he would sense her lack of tension. The bobcat hung his head and slithered a few steps in their direction. Cabaret, looking google-eyed, instinctively backed up, shying away.

"Keep calm. You're doing fine. The cat's no threat. He's playing a game with us," Thundering Cloud assured her. Zunta stood relaxed paying attention. Tanka stared out into space, not seeming to notice the bobcat.

Testing her ability to read the horse, Shin ignored the chill shooting up her spine and lightly tugged the left rein turning

Wisdom of the Horse

Cabaret into a circle to get his feet moving and his mind thinking of something other than the bobcat. After two circles created swirls of dust at his feet, he caught on. The cat growled and showed his teeth. Cabaret, head now high and the whites of his eyes showing, flared his scarlet nostrils. Shin leaned her body back slightly and inhaled a deep, calming breath. "It's okay. You're a warrior," she told him dismissively knowing he would be paying attention to her demeanor and would likely take her cue and follow along.

Cabaret's fear evaporated. He let out a couple of loud snorts in the bobcat's direction – the cat whirled about and ran off. The game was over.

Thundering Cloud and Shin jogged off to join Cia. They told her about the confrontation with the bobcat. Cia's insecurity and nerves surfaced, worried about such an encounter happening to her and not knowing how to handle it.

"His bravery is equal to that of a lion, and so is his heart," Shin told Cia as she worked hard to slow Cabaret's pace to a walk.

Cia arched her brows. "You're brave, too."

Thundering Cloud patted his daughter on the shoulder. "Wilderness challenges are empowering for people and horses. You both did well. We'll see what happens when we come upon a two-hundred pound black bear."

Cia chuckled, unconvinced that he was serious. They continued on their journey. "Is that your family?" she asked, pointing to the crows perched in a tree ahead.

"*Hunkapi.* I am related to everyone," he said. "Have you not read my son's book?"

She stifled a laugh. She was only teasing, but he didn't get the joke. They rode in a subdued silence, listening to the birds and other sounds of nature.

Shin felt Cabaret getting antsy. "I need to let him work off some energy again. You don't mind if I go ahead, do you?"

Her father nodded. "Not a problem. Just keep heading northwest. No matter which trails you take, you'll end up at our destination if you make sure to head northwest."

"The trails are easy to see?" Shin asked.

"Yes. But – I have to warn you – from here, do not take the third trail that will let you turn left. Stay straight."

"Why?" she asked, temporarily forgetting that she hadn't ridden this new section of the forest before.

"Just don't."

Shin cantered away on Cabaret, moving with the rhythm of his stride. It was her own form of meditation and she knew he was dying to expend some pent-up energy after having faced down the bobcat. She had no idea if he had ever seen one before. After about a half-mile she slowed him down to a trot, then a cooling down walk. She had forgotten her father's warning and turned down the pine needle covered trail to see what she could see by getting off the main trail.

Within a few minutes they approached the view of a breathtaking shallow valley of rolling grassland dotted with huge oak trees glistening in the sun. At the peak, an extraordinary feeling overcame her. It felt morbid, but she couldn't explain it. Cabaret looked like he was going to jump out of his skin as he danced on his hind legs in the midst of what felt like chaos. She could feel his heart pounding against his ribs. Seconds ticked by. On impulse she dismounted and held the reins. He threw his head in the air and pinned his ears to his head. Every muscle in his body tensed as he pawed the ground. Trying not to get stepped on, she stroked his neck attempting to calm him down. For the life of her she didn't know what either of them was reacting to. Experiencing a sense of vertigo, she had never had such a deep sinking feeling in the pit of her stomach for no reason whatsoever.

When Cabaret calmed down enough for her to mount, she did so and then tried to get him to continue on the trail toward the beautiful valley floor. He wouldn't go forward. Terror filled his eyes. She gave him a stronger leg to urge him forward but he refused. Instead, he lowered his head, rounded out his back, reached his hocks under himself and backed up as quickly as he

Wisdom of the Horse

could. She reprimanded him with her heels and a firm voice. In response, he repeatedly bucked and twisted his body in mid-air. Shin stayed on and gave him his head until he kept all four hooves planted to the pine needle covered ground.

Once again, she asked him to walk forward. This time he tried a new tactic - rearing in the air, snorting, and striking out with his front feet. Before she had a chance to try another method to bring him under control he did a hundred and eighty degree turn and raced off as fast as he could run. When she tried to slow him down he tossed his head in the air and kicked up his hind legs to let her know she had no control over him. To no avail, she attempted to pull his nose around to her leg, but he braced against the pressure. At a full out gallop with his neck stretched out even with his withers and his flaring nostrils pointed in the air, he headed back to the main trail. The most Shin could do was stay balanced over him so she wouldn't fall off.

Approaching the main trail Cabaret slowed to a jog and turned toward their destination.

Following the winding trail, not more than a minute later, her father stood on the ground holding Zunta by his reins and Tanka by the long lead rope. He stepped out onto the trail, blocking the path and startling the pair. Cia remained astride Maya.

"Whoa," Shin said to Cabaret. White foamy lather dripped from his chest and between his back legs. His entire body was drenched with sweat.

"You went down the trail I told you in no uncertain terms not to go down," Thundering Cloud said. He made no attempt to hide his irritation just because Cia was with them.

"I wasn't paying attention. What's the big deal, anyway?" she said, trying to hide the trauma she and Cabaret had felt.

Thundering Cloud mounted Zunta but did not ride off. His daughter must have had a scare. He could tell by her pallid skin. "I told you it was forbidden."

She looked at him blankly. Not meaning any disrespect she said, "You didn't use the word forbidden."

"Forget it," he said, still agitated. "At least you're okay."

Cali Canberra

"We're okay, but it was really odd," she said, and then explained all she felt and how Cabaret had responded.

"That's why I told you not to go. You're lucky nothing else happened. Horses have been known to throw their riders in a panic and take off running. Some have been lost forever in these rugged mountains."

"Lost horses or people?" Cia asked, in one way disbelieving and in another way she simply wanted clarification.

"Lost horses," he replied. "But most people leave carrying some trauma. I'm surprised you're all right. You must have some power."

"What are you talking about?" Shin asked.

Finally, he turned Zunta and Tanka and headed down the trail with Shin and Cia riding beside him. "Do you really want to know?"

"Of course. That's why I asked."

"Fine," said the storyteller. "In 1825, a 16-year-old white man by the name of Smith Paul ran away from his home in North Carolina and was adopted into the Chickasaw tribe. He traveled the infamous Trail of Tears to Indian Territory with his adopted family and his Chickasaw bride. Years later, he rediscovered this rich, pristine valley between two rivers he had encountered years before as a scout. In the raw wilderness Smith Paul vowed that whites, Indians, and blacks would be treated equally. He was a pillar of strength and courage. In August of 1838 when whites were settling this land, stealing this land from my people, Smith Paul was riding his horse as he approached the lip of the shallow valley – just about where you went." He paused for added drama.

"And?" she asked impatiently.

Thundering Cloud continued the story. "An extraordinary sight met his eyes. He couldn't make sense of the image. The valley below was speckled with dozens of large, dark blotches, standing still as stones. Smith felt certain that they were some kind of large animal, but whatever they were, they weren't alive. Finally, he was able to tell that there were twenty or thirty horses, mired helplessly in the bottom of the mud – all dead, and left behind, no doubt, by an earlier party of emigrants that had been caught during the heavy rains on the boggiest portion of the trail.

"A group of elders joined Smith and the others along the lip of the basin. They spoke among themselves in low tones, gesturing now and again to the grisly panorama below them. They needed to ride through the valley but they could not ask the people to endure such a thing. Smith ached for the people. He had not lived among them all these years without gaining an understanding of what horses meant to them. They would part with their most cherished possessions before they would give up their ponies. Finally, a senior war chief said that they would, in fact, cross the valley.

"They started down the incline. Up close, Smith could see that the animals had once been fine Chickasaw ponies: handsome paints, sorrels, and buckskins. But now they stood in the stiffening mud up to their knees, tongues lolling hideously, their flanks spangled with the gray-brown mud they'd kicked up in their efforts to free themselves. Their eyes were long gone, devoured by vultures and crows. Smith shuddered at the empty, sightless eye sockets. Here and there a pony stood in so lifelike a position that Smith half expected it to toss its head and whinny at the men's approach. But the valley was deathly silent, except for the faint wind whispering through dozens of mud-caked manes and tails.

"Darkness had fallen by the time the group struggled up the basin's western edge, but nobody had the slightest desire to camp anywhere near that horrible place. They kept moving mournfully into the twilight, until at last the piercing stench of the place blew away on the evening breeze.

"Now, as far as what I can tell, horses are very sensitive to the spirits of those dead horses. And people in touch with their psychic power, their inner voice, also sense the horror of what happened there. That is why I told you not to go."

Chapter 16

When they approached the hardwoods, Thundering Cloud halted Zunta and looked to the sky. Cia caught sight of his expression and looked at him questioningly. He inhaled deeply and announced that rain might come later in the night. It had not been in the weather forecast when they left their farm.

"I have a rain poncho," she told him. "As long as there's no hail, I'm fine."

"We only get hail in the summer," Shin said.

"It's so breathtaking out here no matter what the weather. Thank you for inviting me," Cia said to Thundering Cloud as if he had invited her along.

They gazed at the pristine lake ahead. From their vantage point the water reflected the sky and the shadows of the tall pines lining the water's edge on the south side. The silhouettes of purple martin swallows, unmistakable with their sharply pointed, angled wings and forked tails, flew over the lake darting swiftly across the sky, catching insects in midair.

"I'm so grateful to be cut-off from the outside world right

Wisdom of the Horse

now. I know we're very different," Cia said, "but I think we have something in common besides loving horses and nature."

"What would that be?"

"The conventional world doesn't interest me, and I sense you feel the same." She recalled her long-ago career, artistic painting. She would get so wrapped up in a project she forgot the rest of the world existed.

Thundering Cloud simply nodded in agreement.

Cia had met Shin with an ache inside that was now turning into hope for a purposeful future. With Shin's help, and being around the horses, she was learning to see the world anew – like a shift of light on the landscape. "Do you think the birds see us?"

Thundering Cloud surveyed her with affection and remarked with a grin. "Nature is indifferent to the human realm and to human concerns. When enduring the wilderness, we can relinquish our own egos thus minimizing the importance of our selves. This is called self-forgetting and is extolled in almost all spiritual traditions."

Cia's eyes sparkled as she thought about the things Shin and this wise old man had taught her. "I love the wilderness."

"It's beautiful," he said. "But the wilderness can be a dangerous and scary place. Storms and the great predators demand respect. You must learn to not allow yourself to edge easily into fear."

Kicking up dust, Shin cantered Cabaret to the shore of the lake and slid to a halt. A few minutes later, with Tanka trailing behind, her father and Cia joined her. They let the horses drink as schools of tiny fish swam nearby. Silently, they remained absolutely still as the afternoon light sneaked through the trees. Thundering Cloud listened, as if to a faint whisper. Suddenly, he smiled before Shin and Cia saw or heard anything. Canku came galloping around the bend. Tate spotted them through the cluster of yellow-leafed elm trees.

For the next hour there was a loud clattering of hooves on hard-packed ground as they rode head to tail on a narrow trail through the dense forest.

Cali Canberra

Shortly after faint streaks of orange appeared on the distant horizon, they came upon the wide river crossing. There was only one place to cross the water between the vast boulders. A steep and short sandy trail led to large flat rocks buried on the river bottom. This was the safest place to cross. The river depth was almost chest high to the horses causing the riders to raise their feet in order to stay dry. Cia rode Maya in the middle of the group so she wouldn't need to urge the horse forward. Zunta was first up the deep sandy incline leading to an intimate grassy oval clearing about the size of a tennis court. In the middle of the clearing was a fire pit with a large stack of dry broken tree limbs. The clearing was surrounded by dense vegetation except for the west side, which had been cleared for the horses. To the north was a steep and rocky mountainside; in the east, a sheer drop off on the far side of a cluster of trees; on the south side, the flowing river. The sole way in and out of the area was through the river.

Dark birds were silhouetted against a still, clear sky while the trees began swaying and rustling with the light wind. Thundering Cloud and Tate tied picket lines around the trees for the horses as the women removed their tack. The clan settled at their destination. When the long shadows cast by the afternoon sun disappeared, they started the campfire and awaited Grayson's arrival.

Dusk contrasted against a roaring blaze from the loud, crackling fire when Grayson and Chief arrived. After greeting his friend, Thundering Cloud looked past him, cleared his throat and loudly inquired about where the tents and sleeping bags were.

Grayson's voice faltered as he dismounted Chief. "Roy must have forgotten. He was supposed to bring out everything before he left town today. He's going to that rodeo in Oklahoma City. I guess he was too preoccupied with the thought of winning the big jackpot tomorrow. He thinks he's got a great shot at it."

"I guess we'll be roughin' it then. I'll let you tell the women," Thundering Cloud said, his face neutral.

Thundering Cloud and Grayson had planned this all along – no tents or sleeping bags for the night. They assumed the women

Wisdom of the Horse

would never have agreed to test their hardiness to such an extent. This way, they'd see what they were really made of.

Grayson shrugged and walked off to switch out his bridle for a rope halter and attach Chief to the picket line to graze. Thundering Cloud followed and took the saddle and saddle packs off Chief. The wind began to moan just as Grayson greeted Shin and Tate.

Cia wandered out of the pine trees hoping her shoes didn't smell – she hadn't thought about what direction the hot, yellow liquid would drain when she pulled her jeans down with her ass facing up the slope as her toes pointed down the slope.

Being a gentleman, Grayson reached out a hand in greeting as Cia approached. Her intense look of a victim struck him. This obviously lost soul almost brought him to his knees with the emptiness behind her eyes. He sensed that secrets tormented her and that she yearned for a release. He knew the feeling. They looked into each other's eyes as she introduced herself. When he shook her hand a burst of heat expanded in his solar plexus. He was strangely moved by this woman who wasn't remarkable in any certain way.

Everyone sat on bales of straw around the campfire.

Shin broke the binding spell. "Cia recently started therapy with me, and we've become friends. She's giving my parents a break by taking care of Ambra and Heyoka at her house. The vet's closer and the mare's making some progress," Shin explained.

Cia beamed with pride. "My husband's taking care of Ambra while I'm on this camping trip." She felt a little more hopeful about life as she thought of how Elizabeth excitedly stared out the windows, watching the horse when they brought her to their property. The third day, she wandered onto the deck for a closer look. Heyoka remained at the mare's side twenty-four hours a day, and Elizabeth was eager to play with the puppy and pet the mare. Still, her fear kept her from satisfying her curiosity. A few days later, Elizabeth couldn't resist venturing outside to the paddock. It was close to a miracle.

"That's helpful," Grayson said, not realizing Cia had no prior

Cali Canberra

experience with horses.

Cia kept talking. "The progress really all started at the fence line when my daughter picked up a handful of grass and held it out for Ambra. She slowly walked over and grabbed the grass and stayed, waiting for more."

She assumed Grayson would recognize this as a milestone. This was the first time the mare had done anything like a normal horse since her trauma. Heyoka rolled on the ground next to Elizabeth and begged for her to play. She ran in the house, got a ball, and ran back out to the paddock where Heyoka had returned to Ambra's feet. Elizabeth threw the ball to the far side of the paddock and the puppy eagerly retrieved it. For anyone else, this wouldn't have been a celebration, but as Jeffrey and Cia watched, they were thrilled. Before the horse and puppy arrived, Elizabeth nearly went into a hysterical panic mode every time they tried to get her to leave the house – refusing to go any further than the back deck. She wouldn't even go on the front porch.

Hollowed gourds of tea were refilled and a new one poured for Grayson.

Tate interjected, "Shin wanted Dad and me to get to know Cia since she'll be around. She's never handled horses before ours, so we're all going to teach her."

"Great," Grayson said as he scanned her clothes and shoes. Not affluent, he thought. "So, you'll work with their animals on your days off from your job?" he asked Cia. He trusted the Crow family's judgment when they allowed the traumatized, burned, and foundered mare to move to Cia's property.

"I don't work," Cia said, slightly embarrassed.

"Are you looking for work?" he responded.

"Not really. Not now, at least. Maybe…"

Grayson sensed that he made her uncomfortable and it pained him. "We could always use more help at our farm. Give me a call – if you want to, I mean."

"You live in the beautiful log and stone house with the pool and tennis court and barns?"

"Yes. That's it."

Wisdom of the Horse

"I envy you," Cia said whimsically.

"It is a spectacular home," Thundering Cloud interjected. "If you want to live like white man."

"Your place is really fabulous too," Cia told Thundering Cloud. "Especially with all of your Asian and Native American artifacts and décor. I love your sense of style."

Grayson nodded. "We have something in common, Cia. I'm into the Eastern and Native American cultures, too – the history, the customs, spirituality, healing, and the arts and crafts."

Thundering Cloud laughed. "He's a wannabe."

"A wannabe? What's that?" Cia asked, her brows furrowed.

"He wannabe an Indian instead of a *wasichu*!"

Cia smiled. "I know what a *wasichu* is. It's a white person."

"Right," Thundering Cloud said. "Many Native Americans of today wannabe white. Many of my brothers and sisters of the Nations are havetabes – not wannabes. But Grayson, he's a wannabe Indian because he thinks it's romantic. It's special."

"I wannabe an Indian, Dad," Tate boasted in the voice of a young warrior boy.

"I know. You wannabe because you found a way to make a good living and lead a rewarding and exciting life as an Indian. Not many can do that. You're smart. You're my son," Thundering Cloud said proudly.

Tate's eyes conveyed a sense of pride in his heritage, but in his heart he felt a hint of guilt – childhood friends had often accused him of capitalizing on his ethnicity.

Everyone waited for a verbal response from Tate, but none came. To diffuse the awkwardness, Shin poked at the fire until it crackled.

Cia broke the silence and spoke to Grayson. "I understand you work with terminally ill people. That must be an emotional strain."

"It can be," Grayson admitted. "But I like being of service. Dying people not only teach us about the process of dying, but also what we can learn about how to live life in such a way that we have no unfinished business. I personally had a near-death experience when I was in a car accident with my daughter, and it led me to my vocation."

Cia nodded. "Shin said you're in the business of buying the life insurance policies from terminally ill people. How do you make money doing that?"

"If a viator, the person dying, has a $250,000 life insurance policy, our company buys the policy for $150,000 cash so he can have the money while he's still alive. The vast majority of terminally ill people lose their life insurance policies because they can't afford to continue paying the premiums on the policies since they usually can't work. Plus, they often need the money for living expenses and to pay medical expenses not covered by health insurance - or any number of things. It's a blessing to the viator to have the money when they need it most, rather than when they pass on. It's very profitable and it's humanitarian."

"Wow," Cia replied. "I've never heard of anything like that. Shin said you help them spiritually and encourage them to be around your horses. That's so kind of you."

Shin explained to Grayson what she had told Cia. "I told her about how you and Dad help the viators accept and cherish their remaining life as it is and that you prepare them for meeting the Creator."

Thundering Cloud's face softened, reflecting great wisdom and strength. "It is a sacred day when a soul, the spirit, is released and returns to its home. That is when virtual liberation is achieved. Grayson and I teach his viators valuable lessons passed on by my people. We share the teachings of Black Elk with healthy people and the sick. Black Elk has said that it is good to have a reminder of death before us, for it helps us to understand the impermanence of life on this earth, and this understanding may aid us in preparing for our own death. He who is well prepared is he who knows that he is nothing compared with *Wakan Tanka*, the Great Spirit, the Creator, who is everything; then he knows that world which is real."

Grayson looked to the heavens, then to Cia. "We share the knowledge of how to walk the path of life in a sacred way."

Wisdom of the Horse

"It is not without reason," Thundering Cloud said, "that we humans are two-legged along with the winged; for you see the birds leave the earth with their wings, and we humans may also leave this world, not with wings, but in spirit. This will help you understand why Native Americans regard all created beings as sacred and important, for everything has a *wochangi*, an influence, which can be given to us, through which we may gain a little more understanding if we are attentive."

"What exactly do the viators learn?" Cia asked.

Grayson wondered if she was truly interested or just making conversation. "You must be a yang person."

Should she feel complimented or criticized? "Why do you say that?" Cia asked.

"Because," Grayson replied. "A yang person likes to take things apart and analyze them to see how they work. A yang person is enterprising and involved in practical activities and work."

Cia didn't think that sounded like her. She couldn't help but wonder why he jumped to the conclusion. "What are the characteristics of a yin person?"

"A yin person likes to bring things into harmony. They're introspective and individualistic and very concerned with personal development and very concerned with ideas," Grayson said.

Cia held her tongue, desperately wanting to assert that she was much more yin than yang. For some reason she didn't feel it was appropriate to make an issue, but his assumption disturbed her.

Thundering Cloud quickly told Cia, "We all have both yin and yang. There are times in life or situations where we are more one than the other, but essentially we strive to have the balance."

"What exactly do you teach the terminally ill?" Cia asked since Grayson didn't answer the first time.

Grayson didn't really want to talk about it, but he needed to at least tell her a little something. "One thing we teach is that the body is a temporary repository for the spirit within. And we help the viators live the rest of their lives in a way that enables them to

Cali Canberra

experience deeper levels of truth and that takes away their fear of death."

From the tone of his voice, Cia sensed he had no intentions of going into depth. "I didn't mean to pry or overstep my boundaries. I'm just curious," she said as Shin refilled her tea. "I assume that since you deal with terminally ill people you implement Eastern and Native American healing practices also?"

An awesome silence lingered. Cia could not read their eyes. It was as if time was frozen. A vague sensation – a mixture of fear and expectation swept over her. She felt as though she had inquired about a forbidden subject. Everyone else calmly averted their eyes and concentrated on the flames before them. A sudden blast of cool air mysteriously chilled them as it kicked up the fire. She could have sworn that for several moments the fire changed its shape into a gigantic buffalo. Beads of sweat gathered on her forehead as she felt sure they had used a special power to transform the shape. She had recently read about shape shifters. At the edge of her vision she saw Grayson and Thundering Cloud exchanging glances.

An uneasy feeling grew in the pit of her stomach when the realization came to her. Grayson and his investors only made a profit when people died. Grayson must not do anything to try to heal them. Her emotions were amplified. A wave of nausea swept over her. Blood rushed to her head as her mind registered the bizarre circumstances. Grayson was obviously a kind and generous man with a good heart, but then again, he made no attempt to help people heal – it was unsettling, to say the least.

Still, no one broke the silence. Grayson finally stood up, rigid, his face expressionless. Not knowing what to say or do next, he turned his face away.

By now, the full moon had risen in the sky, accentuating the brilliant contrast between dark and light. The dancing flames of fire silhouetted the silent, diversified group. Loud nickering began when a flock of birds soared from the ground to the moonlit sky. Shortly after, Shin and Cia excused themselves to check on the horses and to offer them water buckets that had been filled

Wisdom of the Horse

from the river.

After Cia's question, a restless feeling grew in Grayson. As he thought about how no one can escape the cycle of life and death, he silently wandered away to the hammock hanging between the tall pine trees near the cascading river. Stretched out, he considered taking his boots off, but decided against it. Mesmerized by the full moon, the black velvet sky, and the crackling stars lighting the universe, his eyes turned heavy and carried him into sleep as he surrendered himself to the depths of his imagination:

By private invitation, people from all over the country pulled into an empty pasture with their horse trailers. They had each been invited to the *Circle* by Tate with a simple, compelling explanation sent by e-mail. Tate wrote, "I respect you as a horseman who has not had the opportunity to learn about *The Way of the Spirit*. Please accept my invitation to find out if you want to have a personal transformation and learn to follow a luminescent path of truth with your most treasured horse. Should you accept my invitation to the *Circle* for one night to hear a message, and then you decide to stay, please be prepared to stay for at least a week. If you stay, you choose to be initiated into a knowledge as old as time. You can choose to be blind, or you can follow your destiny and join the *Circle*."

Within moments of parking, each person groomed and tacked up their horse in time to be ready to ride. When the attendees saw each other, as instructed, they did not speak among themselves although most of them recognized each other due to their fame in the horse industry.

The riders mounted their horses and took their places and touched toe to toe next to each other, forming something akin to a cavalry line. A gun fired, signaling the start of the race. Following markers that not only indicated the way to their ultimate destination, but also the gait in which they should be riding, they rode their horses across rolling hills for two miles until they came to the trail heads. One trail led to an incline shortening the distance to their destination, but took much more of a toll on their horses. The alternate trail was an easier climb, but longer distance. It was up to each rider to choose the trail they felt suited their horse's ability and condition. Both trails had good footing and water crossings where horses could drink. Eventually, the trails

Cali Canberra

took them to the same open range where they galloped to the finish line as the sun set in front of them with vibrant oranges, pinks, and reds illuminating the crystal clear sky.

Three hours after the race began, Thundering Cloud spotted the cloud of dust in the distance. Within moments thundering hooves galloped toward him. He whistled to signal the camp. Running Bear heard him, then stoked the kindling in the fire pit and added more dry wood. Many of the large stones surrounding the pit were hand painted with drawings and symbols. Ten feet away from the campfire bales of straw were positioned around the fire and thick flakes of grass hay were placed a few feet behind each bale.

Following instructions, the first rider to arrive at the finish line backed their horse fifty steps in a straight line, then trotted in a perfect serpentine pattern, and then flawlessly cantered a figure eight pattern performing flying lead changes in each direction proving their horse was sound. A nod and a smile from Thundering Cloud were all that the winner needed before they walked their horse out to cool him down. Moments later, one by one, the other horse and rider teams arrived at the finish line. Once the horses' pulses and respirations were stabilized, they silently rode deep into the woods on a narrow tree-lined trail covered with pine needles, hickory nuts, and acorns. *The Circle of Initiation* was hidden away in a clearing next to the river.

Thundering Cloud, dressed in fancy regalia, welcomed the riders and directed them to take their places on the straw bales. Each rider was asked to sit down, holding the lead rope of their horse behind them, letting their horse eat the hay. He placed a long beaded necklace over the winner's head and chanted as he painted the winner's face with symbols that matched his own. Next, he offered the winner a deerskin pouch with five stones inside and then stood in front of the fire and threw gun powder into the flames – not moving an inch when the flames roared in all directions for a moment, nearly reaching his face. He simply grinned and thanked the Great Mystery for protecting him.

"Welcome to the *Circle*," he announced as he looked around the group of especially talented and dedicated horsemen and women. "As you know, you are the first chosen ones. I will explain why you have been invited here, but first, you must each agree to keep an open mind and heart."

He looked around the *Circle* and with his dark piercing eyes acknowl-

Wisdom of the Horse

edged each person's nod of agreement.

Thundering Cloud continued. "Whether or not you are initiated into the *Circle*, you can never talk of our gatherings unless you are specifically told to do so to a particular person. Each of you has been selected because of your intimate knowledge of horses and your kindness to them. Also, because you are ambassadors of the horse - and because of the strong public following you have developed as leaders in the horse world. We know all of you practice *Waonspekiye*, - teaching with patience. Each of you has been successful writing books and many of you have instructional videos and teach at your own clinics and at large events like the Equine Affaire. After you leave here, you are asked to share with all that will listen, the *Woksapa* - the wisdom - which will be imparted to you, but do not speak of our gatherings. The Spirit Guides have honored each of you and given you the awareness of your talents and of your divine relationship with the *Suktanka* – the glorious horse. You will dishonor the Spirit Guides, the *Suktanka*, and everyone here if you speak of the existence of our *Circle*. You will honor us all when you share your *Suktanka Woksapa* with the world and with your own followers. That is our purpose. To spread the *Suktanka Woksapa* – Wisdom of the Horse."

"*Suktanka Woksapa*," Tate stood and said to the sky.

Spontaneously, the flattered clan stood, keeping one hand on their lead ropes, and repeated together, "*Suktanka Woksapa!*" without really knowing why.

A collective smile spread around the *Circle* as everyone looked up at Thundering Cloud who was now illuminated by the fire and the full moon and cloudless night that filled the sky with bright shining stars.

Thundering Cloud walked back to the winner of the race and placed his hand on the winner's shoulder as he spoke. "So, Ms. Canberra, you have won the race and your horse remained sound. It is an honor to win such a race."

"Thank you for the opportunity," she replied.

"My daughter Shin, and Running Bear are serving you a very special tea that we'd like everyone to sip slowly. Drink it all, but drink it in sips only or you will become ill."

David O'Conner took the first sip and reflexively spit it out. "I'm not really a tea drinker. I don't even drink coffee."

Thundering Cloud saw him and smiled. "Yes. Many *wasichu* don't like the unusual taste! But you must drink it to experience the journey."

Groaning, O'Conner took another sip and swallowed this time, despite the nauseated look on his face. His wife, Karen, a coffee and tea connoisseur, liked the aroma and didn't mind the taste.

"It'll put hair on your chest!" Pat Parelli moaned after he tasted his tea and wondered what the dark-skinned man meant by 'experience the journey'.

Linda Parelli said, "I don't want hair on my chest. I'll pass."

John Lyons laughed, "I've had worse."

Lynn Palm wouldn't try her tea. Monty Roberts faked sipping his.

"I like it, Mate!" Clinton Anderson said with his crisp Aussie accent. "I'd drink this in my lounge room after a ride on Mindy."

"This isn't as bad as Vegemite," Linda Tellington-Jones said playfully to Clinton.

A moment later, Tate rocked the hammock, waking Grayson. "What's Vegemite?"

"Pardon?" he said, confused. They were barely illuminated by the waning moon. He adjusted his eyes to what little light there was.

"You've been talking in your sleep saying, 'This isn't as bad as Vegemite' and laughing hysterically."

He looked at him curiously. "Seriously?"

"Yeah. You were dreaming."

Grayson tried to sit up, but his ribs ached from laughing so hard. Branches swayed in the soft breeze as he debated whether to tell him about his dream that was surely induced by the Vision Blend tea.

Chapter 17

The fire crackled with expectancy of more dried wood as Grayson used a set of antlers to maneuver hot coals to the east side of the pit. Looking into the fire he recalled the first time he drank Vision Blend tea. Thundering Cloud easily enticed him to try it so that he could experience clarity and deep introspection. The elder warned him not to try peyote so early in his journey. A weak mind could not handle the separation of realities. Thundering Cloud guided him into a meditation after drinking two cups of the tea. In deep meditation he began to discover his true spirit. He didn't want to return to his own reality – making a living in the high pressure business world, being a white family man, fitting into white man's society. Now he struggled to balance between the white world and the world of Native American customs and wisdom. He had grown so much with the help of Thundering Cloud and his family and he looked forward to the lessons he would learn on his pathway when his time came.

Eventually, Grayson began sharing his own near-death and out-of-body experience. His insights helped the viators on their paths to the sacred world. He showed them the way to leave behind all impure thoughts and all ignorance about death of the body. He taught them lessons from Black Elk - light destroys darkness, just as wisdom drives away ignorance. Death of the body gives the soul and the spirit light.

Switching his mind to present time, Grayson observed Cia's fascination of Shin and her father describing the emotional and physical changes in Shin's mare, Maya. While owned by someone else, the mare was abused by her trainer and when the owner of the mare got her back she was vicious. The owner couldn't deal with the mare and ended up taking her to an auction known for selling horses that would be slaughtered for horse meat. Shin had heard about the mare and went to the auction with the intention of buying her no matter what condition she was in.

Grayson hadn't heard any details until now. "You've done a great job building a relationship with Maya. I'd never suspect she had any negative history, seeing her now."

Shin smiled. "It only took a few days to get her to trust me." She didn't tell how she never left Maya's presence in those few days. Her parents brought her food and beverages and she slept on a cot in the small pasture where horse and owner learned to respect each other and got to know each other.

Tate elaborated, directing his words to Cia. "We burned sage to cleanse the mare and the pasture holding the negativity. Then we had a renaming ceremony. Shin had to retrain Maya to respond to gentle touches and not to fear punishment when she did something wrong or when she didn't understand what Shin asked."

Cia nodded in understanding. She wondered if Tate knew she had read his book.

"Do you have any interest in working with abused horses, Cia?" Grayson asked her.

Wisdom of the Horse

Cia's eyes brightened. "I don't want to work with mean horses, but difficult horses would be fine if I can learn more first. It's been rewarding working with Ambra. If anyone ever told me I would develop a relationship with a horse at all, let alone a scared burn victim, I would have told them they were nuts. Now, it's practically what I get out of bed for every day."

"We have rescue horses," Grayson told Cia. "They haven't been physically abused, but they need to gain a lot of weight, get their feet back in good condition, and get their coats healthy. They have skin problems like rain rot and scratches – it's very painful for them and clearing it up is going to irritate their skin in the beginning, so they may not want to be caught or touched. It won't be easy, but it won't be dangerous like Maya was for Shin. Would you be available to work with them? I'd pay you."

"Sure. I'd love to try to help them, and any extra money I can make would sure help," she said, feeling humiliated that the small amount of money would even make a difference in her life. That is, unless she agreed with Jeffrey that he should take advantage of his new career opportunity in Las Vegas.

She planned on spending part of this camping trip alone to think out some things. Jeffrey wanted her to make a final decision about them pursuing another radical change – and taking a risk with their lives - their freedom. It weighed on her that if she didn't support his idea for a career and the move to Vegas, he might find a casino here and go behind her back to get extra money. If she could earn a little something, perhaps he wouldn't be tempted.

She and Jeffrey once lived a life of relative luxury with plenty of discretionary money. Now they barely paid their bills and their lifestyle was going radically downhill. She knew her husband was just as frustrated as she was about their current lifestyle.

Thundering Cloud cleared his throat. "By the time you get the first group of PMU horses, Cia will be ready to work with them." On the drive they talked about the PMU horses and the fact that Grayson and Laura were rescuing them.

Grayson nodded. "The more help the better. The faster they come along, the sooner we can sell them."

Shin's eyes widened in disbelief. She was speechless for a few moments. "Why would you sell them?"

"We can't feed saleable horses forever," Grayson said reasonably. "If we did that we wouldn't be able to take in other horses to rehabilitate and sell, let alone other horses that will never find another home. If these horses simply need compassion, time, and money for handling and health, we'll give it to them and then make sure they go to good homes when they're ready."

Shin almost began to weep. "You have so much land. Why can't you keep them all so we're sure no one else will harm them again?"

"We can't keep all the horses we rescue. The idea is to get them to a point where other people who will take good care of them will buy them and give them good homes. That'll make room for more horses. I don't intend to make lifelong homes for horses that can go elsewhere."

Thundering Cloud assured his daughter that Grayson and Laura would make the farm a retirement home for any horses that couldn't be placed elsewhere. Some of the horses would surely be too sick, permanently injured, or too old for anyone else to want.

Cia put her hand on Shin's thigh for a moment. "It makes sense. More horses will be helped this way."

Shin finally nodded in resignation.

"I would love to be involved," Cia said euphorically. "Shin said I need to be in nature and feel the presence of other living creatures that can't judge me and that I can't disappoint. She was right. I know I've got a long way to go, but since I've been working with Ambra and learning to ride, I've changed so much in such a short period of time."

Shin smiled. "There's more for you to learn, but you'll find a lot of what you do around a scared or insecure horse is instinctual now that you know safety and how to think like a horse. You'll become very attached to certain horses – like you have with Ambra."

"That's what I'm afraid of," Cia admitted. "Getting attached, and then the horse sells."

Grayson looked deep into her eyes and felt her sincerity. "I'll tell you what. You learn what you need to learn and then work with the horses. Whenever you're ready, choose one for yourself. Let that be the one you bond with the most – the one that will be yours, that will become a part of you. The rest we'll sell."

"I can't afford to keep a horse. That's part of my problem – money! I'm not rich like you," she said to Grayson.

"You won't have to pay for the horse. It will be a gift, including the expenses to keep up the horse," he assured her.

"You don't even know me. Why are you being so generous?" Cia asked him as tears clouded her eyes.

Tate answered before Grayson had a chance. "He's a rich *wasichu*. He wastes more money every month than any of us will ever earn in a month. It's all relative, Cia. When someone offers you something from their heart, accept it graciously knowing that for them, their reward comes from the giving. Grayson is very generous with his time, his land and his money."

Thundering Cloud wished his son had let Grayson answer for himself, but he couldn't argue with the words that flowed. He looked at Tate and nodded.

Shin hadn't talked to her father or brother about it, but she thought she'd throw out an idea. "Would you consider letting me be in private practice on your new property? I could use one of the mobile homes, and offer an integrated therapy program for people like Cia to be around animals – not just horses, but barn dogs and cats."

"Aren't you busy at the clinic in town?"

"They're shutting it down. It loses money and they don't have the funds to operate it."

"Really?" Cia asked, holding back tears, afraid of losing access to Shin if she had to move to the city. She temporarily forgot that there was a chance she'd be leaving the area herself.

"Yes. The doors are closing on the first of the month. I have no idea how I could pay for overhead to practice anywhere and…"

Grayson put his hand up as if to tell her to stop talking. "You can practice there if you think people will drive that much further to see you. If you want to let your patients be with the animals, just have them sign a liability waiver. I'll have my lawyer draw up an agreement."

"What percentage of my fee would you want? And how would we handle clients like Cia that don't have the ability to pay?"

Cia was embarrassed, but she noticed the others didn't seem to care that she didn't have money.

"You keep it all. I don't need your money. I just need my lawyers to write an agreement to protect me if your clients try to come after me for anything," Grayson said without thinking twice.

Wasichu! Thundering Cloud, Tate, and Shin all thought at the same time. *Wasichu* look for trouble instead of harmony.

"As always, your kindness and generosity are appreciated and will be rewarded," Thundering Cloud told his friend.

"Doing what I can is reward enough," Grayson replied.

"*Wasichu* life has been good to you," Thundering Cloud said. "Yet, you are not always happy. You must get back to having fun for the pure pleasure of having a good time. The Spirits know what you need. Let them guide you into personal happiness. You can have many friends with varying interests. You do not need to be so generous to have us care for you. We are your brothers and sisters, even if you do not give so much. You are the son of Mother Earth and Father Sky. You are one with the Creator – the Great Mystery. Your generosity is appreciated and accepted, but it is not conditional."

Grayson nodded. "I know. That's why it's easy to help. That's why it's easy to help horses – to be around horses. As long as we don't hurt them, they accept us and all of our flaws, and many choose to be with us. If we don't hurt them, they make no judgments. You and your family are the same. I am grateful to be in your world."

"Our world. We are one," Tate reminded him.

The clan sat quietly, appreciating each other and the serenity of the night. Eventually, Tate suggested they start setting up the tents. Grayson explained there were no tents. Tate and Shin laughed

Wisdom of the Horse

aloud wondering if Cia could handle sleeping under the stars. Cia said she was fine about it.

The women remained at the fire as the men checked the horses. There was silence for quite some time. Shin inhaled the pine scented cooling air while concentrating on the soothing sounds of water babbling over the smooth rocks in the river. She felt her soul being caressed by the Spirit Guides.

Grasshoppers chirped loudly and coyotes howled in the distance.

A few minutes later the men returned. Out of nowhere Shin said, "I think I'd better go on a vision quest."

"Good idea," Thundering Cloud said. A vision quest would be the best way for her to make a final decision about what direction to take her writing career.

"What's a vision quest?" Cia asked.

Tate answered simply. "It's a personal transformation in the wilderness."

"I don't understand," Cia said.

"It's different for different people," Grayson said. "The first time I went, all I knew was that I was searching for something I had lost in myself. For a revelation. I wanted to be face-to-face with my fears and desires."

Thundering Cloud elaborated. "When you do a vision quest you reap the fruit of death without physically dying. You reenter the womb of the world severed from old limitations. This is self-transformation."

Grayson was struck by Cia's intense interest. "The experience will mark the beginning of change in Shin's life."

Shin said, "Vision quests and other wilderness fasts have been a part of human culture for thousands of years as a way to celebrate or confirm a life passage. It's not always done out of pain or in wanting answers. In many cultures, without passage rites, individuals could not have been capable of assuming the responsibilities and privileges given by their new station in life."

Cia was frustrated. "What exactly do you do? That's what I don't get."

"You fast alone in the wilderness for three or four days," Thundering Cloud said. "You must be very clear with yourself about why you want to be alone and hungry upon the Earth. You shed your old skin and become a new person. In the wilderness there is nothing but a circle drawn in the dust, an empty form filled by your perceptions and values. It becomes a mirror where you will see your true self reflected. You gain priceless information about self-understanding and seeing your relationship to Mother Nature.

"The time you spend can symbolically represent your passage through a transition or crisis in your life. You'll see that like being with horses, there are no judgments in the natural world – there are only consequences for your actions or lack of action. No one is there to impose their perceptions on you. If you have any negative feelings about your vision quest, you'll understand that it is only because of your own way of looking at your experience. In the isolation you'll have the opportunity to fight your personal demons and tap your own power. You'll come out with a sense of personal power - your own voice - your own connection to the Creator. When you return to your normal life you'll have a clearer understanding of yourself, of nature, and of the other people in your life."

Shin made it simple. "It's a way to try to get from one phase of your life to another."

"It sounds so scary, in an exciting way," Cia said.

"Remember," Thundering Cloud explained, "fear is a sign of courage."

Grayson spoke up again. "Fear is also a sign of the onset of power. During a vision quest you must force yourself to eliminate your pretenses and pride and to be stripped down to the bare bones of your will. You must respect and accept your own way of being with your fear. Fear, if you let it, will always teach you self-respect and self-awareness."

"I'm afraid I would be too lonely," Cia said.

"I need to do this," Shin said with determination. She was tired of feeling powerless and incapable of influencing the

direction of her own life when it came to her writing.
Thundering Cloud smiled and nodded.
"Aren't you scared?" Cia asked Shin.
"I'm not worried about my physical safety," Shin told her.

Chapter 18

The atmosphere changed abruptly. A bone chilling gust of wind blew in, startling everyone. The campfire flickered and darted ten more feet into the sky. Gray smoke swirled north and then abruptly shifted west. The temperature dropped. Nimbus clouds blocked the moon and stars. Tree branches snapped from every direction in the distance, one after another, scaring the horses. A flash of lightening lit the sky. Grayson's horse, Chief, snorted, threw his head in the air, and stomped his rear legs. Cabaret arched his neck and anxiously pawed the ground restraining his urge to flee. Maya and Zunta were acutely alert, but remained still except for their ears perking in the direction of the wind. Tate's horse pulled back and broke loose from his picket line but didn't run. The pack horse, Tanka, wasn't tied since he normally would never leave the other horses, but now he startled and quickly trotted off about twenty feet before he stopped and looked back and saw the other horses weren't following. Horses and humans froze in contemplation, instinctively concerned about the ominous clouds and the crashing of thunder.

    Seconds later, the angry sky punctuated the night with a bolt of lightening, explosive and deafening, which sheared a tree limb from a red oak. It crashed to the ground, a branch grazing Chief's flank. A unified, short audible gasp erupted from the group as Chief, scared for his life, broke loose from his picket line, whirled around and tore off running through the river and toward the trail.

Wisdom of the Horse

In the darkness no one could tell if he stopped, afraid to leave everyone, or if they no longer heard his thundering hooves pounding the ground because he was too far away. Everyone rushed to untie their own horse from the picket line, hoping to avoid a mass panic.

The awesome roar of the storm intensified. Earsplitting sounds of thunder, cracking wood, and branches tumbling to the ground were so loud no one could even hear the horses nickering to each other. The wind gathered more strength and blew the flames of the campfire sideways. Holding the scared horses by their lead ropes, everyone began throwing and kicking anything that looked remotely flammable as far away from the blaze as they could. Then they began dousing the fire.

"Stay with your back to the wind," Thundering Cloud yelled in between the eerie sounds of the storm. If Chief's heading home he'll be able to see better than we can in the dark. Hopefully, lightening will illuminate the sky when he needs light to find his way. He'll be fine if he's sensible. Tate and I will search for him."

With only the moon shining through the trees to light the area, Thundering Cloud removed Zunta's halter and replaced it with a bosel and mecate. Like a young warrior, he deftly swung his body onto his horse. He looked up. Rain was threatening to arrive any minute. There was no point in making torches to light their way.

Adrenaline rushing through his veins, Tate walked briskly toward Canku. "Shin - Cia – stay away from the river. There might be a flash flood," he yelled as he swiftly swung his leg over Canku to ride bareback in a rope halter with a long lead line.

Grayson was ashen, making no attempt to hide his spontaneous display of vulnerability over being fearful for Chief's safety. "I'll go with you," he said hesitantly, concerned to leave the women alone in the wilderness while the winds continued to gather force. Wondering if the women would panic if things turned for the worse, he piled their belongings at the trunk of a red cedar tree for protection.

Thundering Cloud yelled to Grayson, "You should stay with

the women. Is there shelter anywhere you can get to? A cave or anything?"

"No. There's nothing."

The women carefully led their horses toward the mountainside. Cia was calm and composed, adeptly handling Maya as if she were experienced. Of course, the horse wasn't hard to handle, but still, Cia's confidence under the circumstances was commendable.

Thundering Cloud and Tate cantered off through the river and toward the trail.

Suddenly, Cia tripped over a rock and stumbled down the slope they had just begun to climb. The lead rope ripped through Shin's fingers when Cabaret startled in reaction to Cia's stumble. His flailing hooves kicked up sand as he tore off running between Cia and Maya, separating the two. The moment Maya realized she had a chance to follow Cabaret, just as she contemplated her choice, a bolt of radiant lightening hit the hundred-year-old white oak tree next to the mare. A huge branch fell, the crash shaking the ground. Instinctively, Maya fled and followed Cabaret who was crossing the river, heading for the trail they came in on. Once through the rushing water, Maya challenged Cabaret for the lead position.

In the dim moonlight, as if in slow motion, the women watched Tanka cut through a cluster of trees to reluctantly follow Cabaret and Maya. The inherently lazy pack horse stepped into a wide deep sink hole with both front legs. He squealed and his face contorted from the pain. "Taaankaaaa," Cia screamed, her voice shaking with primordial fear. Tanka couldn't pull his front legs out of the hole. With his flailing hindquarters in the air, he twisted his head and neck as if it numbed the grueling pain.

Moments later, rain pelted the ground. The unmistakable look of resignation swept over Shin's face. She slid the hood from her water-resistant Boink riding jacket over her head. Cia hadn't had a chance to retrieve her rain slicker. When Grayson spotted Tanka he rushed toward the suffering horse as he zipped up his all-weather jacket. Within twenty feet he tripped over thick exposed

Wisdom of the Horse

tree roots and fell, hitting his head on a boulder. The women gasped as they witnessed the accident. The rain drowned out all other sound except for an abrupt wailing radiating from Grayson's throat. Cia's chest hammered erratically – she didn't think she could withstand any more traumas on a trip meant to be relaxing and enlightening.

Before the women could get to Grayson, a torrential downpour drenched the earth. With the blinding rain, there was no point in moving until they could see.

The fury of the storm faded as quickly as it came. The rain turned to a light drizzle giving Shin the chance to help her friend. She took cautious precise steps through the mud and reached Grayson's unconscious body draped over a boulder. Cia hopped toward them.

"He's breathing. Take his pulse!" Cia told Shin, looking toward the ground in an attempt to keep the rain out of her eyes.

"I am. It's weak," Shin announced as she assessed her options.

"I can't believe this," Cia complained. "There's no cellular coverage here. We don't have a way to contact anyone and we can't get him out of here. Even with horses to ride in good weather and daylight it's a four hour ride back."

"Calm down and apply pressure to the wound," Shin said quietly. She placed one hand over Grayson's heart and one hand reached for the sky, her thumb and index finger forming a circle.

Cia did as asked, the agitation showing on her face. "What are you doing?"

"Please. Be quiet. I'm praying to the Creator."

"Are you crazy? He needs a paramedic - not a healing prayer," Cia said in a smug condescending tone, her wet hair sticking to her face.

"I'm doing energy healing on him."

"He's got a low pulse and blood gushing from his head. Energy work is not going to fix this," Cia said, her tone sharper than usual. She had a flashback from childhood - memories of walking in on her father chanting while in deep trance-like states.

He chanted at the synagogue, too. He spoke Hebrew and never explained to her what he was saying. For some reason all the chanting and words she did not understand frightened her. She remembered being scared her father was evil even though she knew people adored him and respected him. She didn't understand why he wore the things he wore, and when she was young and scared and confused, no one told her why. Even when he spoke English he would say words she didn't understand. She recalled thinking he was talking in code because he was saying something bad. Why didn't her mother want her to tell her public school friends she was a Jew? Was being Jewish evil, she wondered as a child. Other kids seemed so proud of whatever they were - especially the Christians.

Shin methodically passed her hands an inch or two over Grayson's body from head to toe, transmitting healing energy.

"Look at the blood. I can't believe this. What if he dies?"

Shin ignored her. She wasn't concerned about the blood at this point - the head has more blood vessels than any other part of the body, so it bleeds more, and the bleeding can stop quickly when pressure is applied.

Putting aside her memories, Cia willed herself to calm down. She inhaled a deep breath and glanced at the backpacks at the base of the nearby tree. "We must have a first aid kit and flares."

Shin had to respond. "Find the first aid box, but don't bother with flares. The trees are too dense to use them."

Cia wiped Grayson's blood onto her soaking wet jeans and trudged through the mud toward the backpacks. She pierced the air with a scream. "A snake!" she said, drawing out the word, her chin quivering. She hobbled backward a few steps, her heavy and stiff jeans irritating her legs and waistline.

"Calm down!" Shin insisted, her face devoid of fear as the snake slithered toward her direction. "It's a Blue Racer. It's not poisonous. We may have to eat him if he sticks around, though."

Thunder argued back-and-forth like surround sound. Lightening bolts brightened the sky. The rain reduced to a mist. The once blazing fire was now reduced to hot coals radiating steam and billowy puffs of smoke. The temperature continued to drop. Their clothes were soaked. There was no dry wood to put on the hot coals which were sure to burn out if the drizzle continued or the rain started up again.

Shin resumed chanting, now with both hands over Grayson's heart. His head stopped bleeding and, miraculously, his facial muscles moved and he opened his eyes. Shin put her hands on his shoulders and helped him steady himself. Grayson took a couple of deep breaths. Other than slight disorientation, he was fine.

"Where are the horses?" Grayson asked the women.

Cia looked disconcerted. "They took off, except Tanka – he's badly hurt."

"We'll see if there's anything we can do," Grayson said as he stood up and regained his equilibrium.

Grayson, Shin, and Cia walked carefully on the slick, fallen leaves and through mud puddles to Tanka. They were devastated to find that not only were both front legs stuck in the wide, deep sink hole, but a broken and splintered small tree stump was impaled through his chest. The gelding's legs jerked spastically. He was in shock. Tremors shook his body. The excruciating pain in his eyes was unmistakable.

Overcome with remorse, Grayson forced himself to push fear and regret into the recesses of his mind. His face tightened. He took a deep breath of crisp air and pulled a razor sharp Case bowie knife from his ankle sheath. His eyes never wavered as he deftly put the horse out of its misery with a single deep slash of the jugular. A collective exhalation of breath pierced the stillness. Time stood still. The gelding's eyes had a vacant stare – his stiffening lips showed his stained teeth. A hush fell over the gruesome scene. Finally, Grayson stood motionless, eyes now averted. A faint odor of acrid blood drifted through the breeze.

Watching Grayson, Cia's knees weakened as nausea rolled through her stomach. Anguished tears drenched her already wet face.

Shin looked at the horrific scene and then to Cia she said, "In the trauma is a revelation."

Chapter 19

A slate-gray sky was the backdrop for sheets of rain drenching father and son, making their ride to gather the loose horses slow and challenging. When the unrelenting rain finally let up, Thundering Cloud and Tate navigated the tree-lined mountain trail allowing the horses to follow their instincts as to direction and pace. Each time lightening brightened the sky they scanned the area for the other horses. Coyotes howled in the distance from time to time.

Canku abruptly stopped in pitch blackness. "Shhh," Tate whispered. They listened intently. Canku snorted and began backing up, causing Zunta to back also. "There's a diamondback rattler," Tate whispered. "Hear it?"

Thundering Cloud answered by turning Zunta around. Tate followed. The black clouds floated away from the moon allowing enough light to navigate. They picked up the pace where the trail widened enough for the horses to walk side by side without prompting. Usually Canku was eager to lead, but tonight was different. He sensed trouble. The men tried not to talk in an effort to hear the loose horses. It was difficult now that the ground was wet – horses walking on dry leaves and sticks were loud. They approached a flat area where the trees thinned, the trail rocky and riddled with long deep crevices. Canku pushed his way in front, carefully picking his way through the path. Occasionally, he stopped to regain his balance.

Wisdom of the Horse

Bolts of lightening electrified the sky like daylight, allowing the men to see a few yards ahead, an exceptionally narrow trail on the edge of a steep cliff dropping down to rushing water rapids.

Tate gave a speculative look to his father. "Should we turn around?"

"Hold him." Thundering Cloud dismounted and tossed Tate his hand-braided macate reins. He took one cautious step at a time, feeling his way to the primitive trail. He stopped, waiting for more lightening. When the sky lit up, it was evident the terrain was treacherous. The trail was beaten down by deer and elk and it was improbable a horse had ever ventured on this ground.

Zunta grew anxious. He pawed the ground and threw his head in the air repeatedly, trying to persuade his leader to continue. Canku imitated him.

"What's the verdict?" Tate asked as he bumped the nose pieces down to calm the horses.

"It's slippery and unstable footing. Narrow. Very narrow. But the horses seem anxious to go this way. I think we'll follow their instincts."

"I'm game," Tate said with a boyish grin, young and naïve enough to be excited for the adventure. "How far down do you think the river is?"

"At least a hundred feet."

"That's what I was thinking."

The men carefully mounted their horses. Another bolt of lighting scattered across the sky followed by thunder grumbling like a hungry bear. Canku startled and lost his footing, letting his hind right leg slip down the cliff. He caught himself quickly and scooted tighter into the mountainside. Tate stroked Canku on the neck, thankful for his sensibility.

"Do you hear something?"

"Whoa," Tate told Canku quietly. The horses halted immediately. The men strained to hear. Thunder shook the heavens and earth once again. In reply, a horse nickered repeatedly and the sound came closer to them.

"*He-aya-hee-ee!*" A call to the Great Spirit. "*Suktanka!*"

Thundering Cloud called out.

"*Suktanka!*" Tate repeated even louder.

A loud whinny pierced through the other nocturnal noises of the wilderness.

Suddenly, Canku was nose to nose with Cabaret.

"Are you alone, boy?"

Cabaret nickered as he nuzzled Canku's neck.

A tidal wave of relief. "Thank you, Creator," Thundering Cloud muttered to himself.

Once again, gusting wind kicked up and a sprinkle of rain fell from the sky. The sense of relief was suddenly lost. If a downpour started again, the precarious trail footing would become even more treacherous. As it was, there was no margin for error.

Beneath his normal veneer of confidence in difficult situations, Tate's heart missed a beat. "How are we going to turn him around? This trail is too narrow and we can't back out of here. It's too dangerous."

"Cabaret must have found an open area up ahead. It's the only way he could have turned around to get to us. Maybe we can try to ride forward and see if he'll back up – hopefully it's not too far," Thundering Cloud suggested.

"One wrong step backward and he's off the ledge."

The trees swayed as the wind moaned. Suddenly, rain fell in cascading sheets at an angle. The men cautiously sat astride their mounts praying for a miraculous solution. Before they had a chance to come up with an idea, the thunder roared again as the downpour engulfed them.

Father and son silently prayed to the Creator and concentrated on keeping their bodies relaxed so as not to cause tension in their horses. Thundering Cloud had never been a coward. He thought of his father and his grandfather and all those before him who had bravely died many moons ago. He wondered if he would be joining his elders. He didn't pursue death or fear death. *Whatever happens happens.*

Once again, the rain left as quickly as it had come.

Tate's heart was ready to jump out of his chest as his neck

Wisdom of the Horse

had a prickly feeling. "What's that sound?"

A bolt of lightening flashed a brief image. They looked up and watched hundreds of huge rocks begin tumbling down from the mountain like an avalanche. The ground began to crumble beneath them.

Chapter 20

At the same time the Crow family and Cia set out on their wilderness journey, Laura Solvan, along with her son and daughter, were at the U.S. Arabian Nationals in Louisville, Kentucky.

As always, the competition was invigorating and stressful. But, that's what Laura and her kids lived for – the adrenaline rush of showing their horses in the highest levels of competition. Heather was so committed to riding and competing that she graduated from high school in Dallas a year early and then studied at Palm Beach Atlantic University, a Christian school, just to be immersed in the circle of wealthy Wellington, Florida equestrians. When Heather turned nineteen, Laura's father bought her family a membership in the Palm Beach Polo & Equestrian Club and a $2.9 million dollar house on thirteen acres in Palm Beach Pointe, an equestrian paradise, so Heather could easily compete while majoring in Applied Communication. For her nineteenth birthday, she selected two stellar mounts - a 16.3 hand chestnut Hanoverian mare by Wallstreet Kid, and a 16.3 hand black Oldenburg gelding who was schooling at second and third level dressage with world renowned trainer Bill Warren at Pineland

Wisdom of the Horse

Farms. Her formal riding instruction also came from Klaus Balkenhol, the U.S. Dressage Team Coach. For Heather's age, she had been one of the most prepared riders in Palm Beach for the Winter Equestrian Festival, the most prestigious dressage and show jumping spectacular in the United States. She even went so far as to have sessions with the highly acclaimed Sport Psychologist, Ann S. Reilly, Ph.D.

Laura and Heather competed at Rolex, Devon, and Wellington - another world compared to the Arabian circuit. The Arabians were prettier than most event horses or hunters, but Laura and Heather didn't see Arabians as being nearly as athletic. Heather rode hunt seat on her horse competing in hunter/jumper classes when she was young, until she went to Rolex with her mother for the first time. That's all it took to hook her on the much more challenging discipline. Ever since, they teased Brett about his being head over heels in love with Arabians. Brett playfully argued with them, defending the breed - emphasizing that Arabians were more intelligent, versatile, kinder, and beautiful – claiming these attributes were more important than the qualities of their horses.

None of them could give Grayson flack about his Quarter Horses who consistently won in reining, cutting, and stock horse classes. He had a great eye for undeveloped talent and he had the ability to bring out the best in any horse he worked with. Chief's sire, the historic Quarter Horse stallion, Hollywood Dun It, is the only NRHA All-Time Leading Sire of Reining Horses with offspring earnings in excess of $4 million dollars. Grayson, with high hopes and a keen eye, bought Chief as a weanling and turned him into a champion show horse. Laura, Heather, and Brett didn't quite understand how he could give up the glory, the ribbons, the trophies, and the publicity of competing at upper echelon shows just so he could trail ride and have a better relationship with his horses using natural horsemanship methods. Laura hoped he'd at least start competitive trail riding if he really was completely giving up the show ring.

Laura and Heather had only been to the U.S. Arabian Nationals for the past two years to cheer Brett on. Before that,

Cali Canberra

Brett's biological father, Drew, flew in to meet him at all of the Arabian shows, making it clear to Laura that his new wife would be uncomfortable if Laura was there also. Laura thought it was ridiculous, but she stayed away since Brett didn't seem to mind either way.

Brett hadn't been interested in the horses until he was in high school – which was when Drew had left Laura to marry an assistant trainer he worked with years before. He had gotten the young woman pregnant. Drew left Laura with the clothes on his back and in his closet and a half-million dollars paid by Laura's father, in accordance with their prenuptial agreement. Laura's father wasn't going to let any man touch a dime of their money except for the half-million agreed upon. When Drew met Laura at an opening day hunt, he was a trainer dabbling in a variety of breeds and moved from farm to farm. She hired him and then married him. Laura's father said he only proposed to her so he wouldn't have to keep looking for work every time he had a dispute with a farm owner.

Drew spent the half-million dollars he 'earned' from being married to Laura on buying a bankrupt Arabian farm in Texas that included a dozen of the horses. Drew let Brett pick three horses as his own to take to Oklahoma. Brett chose a mare, Campala, and two geldings, Casino and Accomplice. For a few years, one of the horses Drew acquired when he bought the farm turned out to be a nice stud that was able to support the farm and the horses they bred and showed. Then, two years ago, they discovered the stud was a CID (Combined Immune Deficiency) carrier – which could be compared to a horse having AIDS. News traveled fast and it bankrupted Drew. The new wife immediately left him, taking off to Brazil with a wealthy businessman who breeds and shows Arabians as a hobby. Drew was left to raise their young daughter on his own.

Drew, now working as a used car salesman, was too embarrassed to show his face in the Arabian crowd again. He told Laura she could watch her son compete and she needed to pay for it, too.

Wisdom of the Horse

Now, at the U.S. Nationals, Laura, Heather, and Brett killed time walking around the commercial exhibitor area. Heather stopped at a booth displaying a type of horse blanket she had never seen.

"Look at these, Mom," Heather said as if it was one of the most exciting inventions in the world.

"We have plenty of blankets," Laura told her.

"But look – these have elastic at the neckline. That's ingenious. I can't believe no one has come up with that before."

Laura was interested now. "That is smart. They would fit some of the horses a lot better."

A sales rep at the booth overheard the women and approached them. "They're selling like hot cakes. These are Turtle Neck turn-out blankets. They're waterproof and breathable with a Teflon® coating."

Laura looked at the price and thought they were quite reasonable, especially for the quality of material and workmanship. She reached into her wallet, pulled out a full color and gold-foiled embossed business card and handed it to the sales rep. "Give my farm manager a call next week to get an order. He'll have the measurements for all the horses. I'll let him know you'll be contacting him."

"Great. Could you write his name on the back?"

"Sure," Laura said, and then jotted down Bruce's name using her Montblanc. "Is there a discount for buying quantities?"

"How many would you be buying?"

"Around twenty or so," Laura said.

"I don't think so. We get a considerable amount of sales for a lot more than that at a time, and the customers don't expect a discount."

"That's trainers spending their client's money though, isn't it?" Heather said.

"Sometimes. But the breeders and other people have gone wild for these blankets, so they're selling almost as fast as they can produce them. I'll talk to my manager, though."

"Fine," Laura said. "See what you can do."

Brett was embarrassed when his mom always tried to get a better price for something, but he didn't dare say a word to her about it. They continued walking around, shopping as if they were required to.

They strolled down another wide aisle, passing tack stores, equine artists and sculptors, gift shops, jewelers, barn designers, barn manufacturers, real estate companies, and an array of anything you could think of for horses, riders, and their farms.

When they reached the junk food vendor area, Brett spotted Greg Bordeaux.

"Mom – it's Greg. Let me see if he can talk to you now," Brett said.

"I'm not in the mood to discuss business right now," Laura replied.

Brett bounced like a young boy excited to see Mickey Mouse. "Please?"

Laura hated it when Brett acted so immature. "Calm down. Play it cool or he'll think you're anxious to do business with him."

"I am calm, but he's Greg Bordeaux. He used to be very famous, Mom. You don't understand..." his voice trailed off as he looked longingly in Greg's direction.

"Grayson's having him investigated and we don't have a report back yet. We're not making a commitment this weekend no matter what he proposes."

Brett raised his brows. "Investigated? Why?"

"We would feel better if we knew details about his background. Especially under the circumstances," Laura said.

"What circumstances?"

"Nothing in particular. We're just cautious about who we do business with."

"Why do you let Grayson tell you what to do?" Brett spouted the way he did as a rebellious teen.

Heather stepped in. "She doesn't. And you know it. Mom wouldn't do business with anyone without doing her homework first. It's just not smart, whether it's about horses or not."

"Fine," Brett said, and then stomped away in a huff.

Wisdom of the Horse

Heather and Laura looked at each other and rolled their eyes. Brett had always been immature, slightly socially inept, and a bit effeminate. Whenever he was around the Arabian crowd his effeminate side surfaced even more. The family had never discussed it with Brett, but everyone assumed he was gay and would eventually come out of the closet. They never made him feel like there was anything wrong with homosexuality and had always tried to let him know he should feel free to be himself. But no one had the nerve to just come out and ask him if he was gay or bisexual. It was implied that if he was, it didn't matter – they all loved him and accepted him no matter what.

Later in the afternoon they went to the stalls of Brett's trainer that coached him for showing. They found Brett inside the stall hugging his mare with tears running down his face. He was shaking from crying so hard.

Laura slid the stall door open. "What's wrong, honey?"

Brett looked toward his mother and then pointed down at the leg wrap on Campala's front left leg. He was so upset he couldn't talk.

"What happened?" Heather asked. She stroked Campala's neck. Her coat felt smooth as silk under her delicate fingers.

"She's hurt, obviously," Laura replied.

Brett cried so hard he was unable to utter a word.

Laura hugged her son. "Calm down and tell us what happened," she said softly.

Brett just cried harder and hugged his mare harder.

Heather darted off to ask the trainer what had happened. She came back and reported to her mother. "Michael says she was lame when they took her out to school her earlier. They didn't call the vet. They just put liniment on and wrapped her leg. He scratched her from the class."

"He can't put liniment under a leg wrap!" Laura said furiously. She started to bend down to remove the wrap herself.

"Stop, Mom," Heather said.

"I'm taking this off," Laura exclaimed, wondering how a reputable trainer could be so stupid.

"It's Sore-No-More. Vets approve it being used under leg wraps. It's all natural and it's safe under leg wraps. Everyone's using it now," Heather assured her.

Laura looked at her daughter questioningly.

"I'm serious. I've even used it on sore backs under a saddle and pad. Grayson uses it on Chief, too. Trust me," Heather said.

"She's right," Brett said, finally calming down enough to say two words.

Laura relented, believing they must be correct. She used it on her own horses, but she hadn't known it could be used under wraps.

"Have you walked her?" Heather asked her brother.

"No. I don't want to aggravate her leg."

Laura said, "That's ridiculous. Let's see her move. I want to see for myself if she's lame. If a vet hasn't even looked at her and Michael scratched her…"

"She's right, Brett," Heather concurred. "We're going to take her out. A few steps aren't going to make it any worse."

Laura put Campala's leather halter on and led her out of the stall. She walked backwards, facing the mare in order to evaluate the extent of the lameness. She walked her past six or seven stalls.

"I don't see anything wrong," Laura said.

"Me neither," Heather agreed.

"Get a longe line and a longe whip. I'm going to longe her. She's fine at a walk," Laura said.

Brett didn't speak. He simply followed his mother, sister, and his horse.

Campala remained sound at a walk all the way out to the arena. Laura took the wrap off, threw it aside, and then asked the mare to walk on the longe line. The mare immediately raised her tail and trotted off.

"Slow down. Walk, girl," Laura told the mare.

Campala picked up a strong trot, folded her tail over her back, threw up her head and began snorting as she animatedly went around in circles, tugging on the longe line.

"She's sound as can be," Laura announced.

Wisdom of the Horse

Heather nodded in agreement. "Reverse her direction. Maybe she's off when on the opposite lead?"

Laura reversed the mare. She trotted higher and faster with greater extension and impulsion. Campala was feeling good and proud of herself.

Brett was thrilled to see his horse sound, but upset his trainer said she wasn't. Not one to distrust people, he said, "Ask her to canter. Maybe it's at the canter she's not sound."

"If she's not off or head bobbing at the trot in either direction, she'll be fine at a canter, too," Laura said. Brett knew better and his response aggravated her.

"Please. Just canter her," Brett whined.

"Fine."

Laura barely flicked the longe whip toward Campala's tail. She eagerly cantered, pulling harder against the longe line, causing Laura to have to make the circle bigger and bigger – which was bad manners for the horse and bad manners for the human to do in a practice area where other people were working their horses.

"You need to teach this horse some respect. She's going to pull my arm out!" Laura told Brett.

"Reverse directions," he said, ignoring her comment. Campala usually had such good manners that he spent most of his time working with his geldings, Casino and Accomplice. Accomplice, a reining horse, had been placing top ten at the regional level and at the Scottsdale show, but a week before he was supposed to leave for the U.S. Nationals he had a serious episode of colic. At the vet hospital they diagnosed an impaction and treated it by tubing him with mineral oil and giving muscle relaxants. The vet advised against putting him in stressful or excitable environments for at least of couple of months. After three years of intensive training and successful showing, the powerful and athletic nine-year-old gelding had a chance at the title of U.S. National Reining Horse Champion. Now, he couldn't compete. Accomplice already suffered from ulcers over the years and Brett refused to subject him to anything else.

Cali Canberra

Laura tugged the line and walked in toward Campala's head, pointing the longe whip to the front of her nose. The mare did a quick 180 degree turn, spinning perfectly on her hocks and landing her front feet smoothly. She didn't miss a beat transitioning into the left lead canter.

"See? She's perfectly sound," Laura said. "Of course, I'm glad she's fine, but I'm going to kill that trainer of yours."

Laura took Campala to the corner of the arena so she wouldn't be in anyone else's way and continued exercising the horse – she had a lot of pent-up energy.

Brett was relieved and deflated. "Why would Michael do this?" he asked no one in particular.

A bystander approached Brett and Heather. "You have a professional trainer?"

"Yes," Heather answered without giving her brother a chance. "Why?"

"It figures. I've heard rumors that a lot of big-time trainers tell clients their horse isn't sound so they can take a different client's horse into a class," the stranger said.

"I've only heard good things about our trainer. He's always been good to me and my horse," Brett told the man.

"Well, like I said, I've heard rumors."

"Why would he do anything like that?" Brett asked.

"So he could get the training money and show fees. And you probably paid for advertising publicizing his name, right?"

"What good would that do him?" Brett asked.

"Oh, Brett," Heather said. "It's the oldest trick in the book. He's having you pay to get his name out there. How many ads do you think he's ever paid for out of his own pocket?"

"I never thought about it," Brett admitted.

"Well, the guy's a jerk," Heather said.

"But he's not showing her. I'm showing her in open classes and amateur owner to ride classes. I don't know why he would have done this."

"You're showing her?" the stranger asked.

"In all the classes she's entered into. Michael's just been

training her and coaching me. He has no reason to say she's lame when she's not," Brett explained.

The stranger was suddenly embarrassed he had spoken up. "I don't know, in that case. I guess you should go ask him. Anyway, I'm sorry I brought it up. I hope everything works out."

Brett and Heather returned to the practice ring.

"Brett," Heather said, "you really do need to go talk to Michael and straighten this out. You've worked your ass off all year to get to the Nationals. You can't just give up."

"I don't know what to say to him. I can't confront him."

"Then I'll go." Heather told him.

"Will you? I'd appreciate it," Brett said boyishly.

Heather briskly walked to the barn and informed Michael that Campala was sound at all gaits on both leads. A few minutes later, by the time she returned to the arena, Brett left the area, hand walking the mare to cool her down.

"Michael feels terrible," she told Laura. "Apparently one of his Mexican grooms told him Campala was lame. Michael trusted him and instructed him to put on the Sore-No-More and wrap the leg. He didn't check her himself. He feels awful. It turns out another white mare was the one that's lame."

"That idiot!" Laura said.

"Mom. Mistakes can happen. Michael's going to the show office to try to clear this up."

"It's going to break your brother's heart if he can't compete, especially after not being able to bring Accomplice."

Chapter 21

Shin chanted over Tanka, releasing his soul to the Great Mystery. A light rain started up again, washing away most of the blood draining from the horse's jugular. Grayson cut a chunk of mane and tail hair from the gelding and stuffed it into his drenched blue jeans pocket. Shin did the same.

When the time seemed right, they returned to the campfire to warm up, but dying embers were all that survived their dousing and the downpour. Shivering in wet clothes, except for where her Boink jacket covered her, Shin attempted to rekindle the fire. Grayson took over when she gave up hope. He tirelessly fanned the embers and created a flicker of flames.

"We need to find a way to get help," Cia said, her teeth chattering.

"My dad and brother are getting the horses. We'll be fine," Shin replied, unconcerned.

"What if something happened to them?"

"My brother and father know how to survive in the wilderness. They've done it dozens of times together and Tate has done

Wisdom of the Horse

it several times alone, including on his own vision quests. My father and grandfather went into the wilderness alone for weeks at a time all of my father's life. When we were growing up he was always telling us about their adventures. Tate and I were fascinated and thought father and grandfather were so brave. They were true warriors," Shin said confidently thinking about her father being a great storyteller.

"Still, things can happen," Cia said in frustration.

"Don't think negatively," Grayson said.

The rain, thunder, and lightening stopped. They grew hopeful the night would be easier to cope with. The clouds disappeared, allowing the full moon and the star filled night to shine on the earth. Not wanting to jinx it, no one commented.

"Tanka's dead, the horses ran off, you hurt your head," Cia fired back to Grayson.

Grayson smiled as if the list she spieled off was inconsequential. "Shit happens."

Coyotes started a conversation of yips and yodels.

"Look over there," Cia pointed across the river, upstream in a narrower section.

Shin saw the faint glow outlining the shape of a raft. "Do you think I could get to it?"

"I guess it's worth a try," Cia said hesitantly.

Grayson looked at her as if she were crazy. "The water's going to be damn cold and you shouldn't risk being in a flash flood."

"Where does the river go?" Shin responded, unconcerned about his comments.

He looked at his muddy boots. "What do you mean?"

"If you raft down from here, where do you end up?"

"Sorry. I don't have a clue," he lied as he combed his hands through the wet hair plastered to his skull. "Besides, you can already see the water's rising. You can't risk it."

Shin smiled, obviously not taking his warnings seriously. "I did white water rafting at summer camp in Canada when I was in high school. We went on some pretty rough waters. I think I can handle this river."

"I don't think you should risk it," Cia said.

"Do you have any idea how deep the water is now?" Shin asked Grayson, ignoring Cia. They had ridden the horses through the water to get to this clearing. She couldn't imagine it could have risen that much just from one rainstorm.

"I don't think it would be too deep yet, but like I said, a flash flood's always a possibility. I don't think you should take a chance," Grayson said.

Cia couldn't believe what she was hearing. "Even if you could get to the raft, you don't know where the river's going to take you or where you can even get off the river."

"I'll figure it out. There's a full moon and lots of stars. The sky is clear now," Shin said.

"And the water reflects light," Grayson added even though he didn't think she should leave.

Cia rolled her eyes. "You don't even know if there are paddles with the raft."

"I'll find something to use if there aren't," Shin told her, now with more determination than ever.

Grayson was impressed by Shin's bravery. Cia thought she was being reckless.

"What's the worse that could happen?" Shin said playfully, excited by the adventure.

Regretting how she had been acting, Cia decided to lighten things up. "Why don't I go with you? You could push me off the raft and leave me to drown. Nobody would know you murdered a crazy woman."

They all laughed as Shin wrung out her hair and tied it into a knot.

Although the water level looked to be above Shin's waistline, Grayson wasn't aware of any deep drop-offs. His worry was about flash flooding and how fast the river flowed. As a safety measure, Grayson suggested Shin take one of the picket ropes to use as a lifeline, and then he directed her at the river's edge, pointing to where she should cross, hoping she wouldn't get pulled down river so far that she'd wind up completely lost.

Wisdom of the Horse

Cia and Grayson tied the lifeline around an old oak tree as Shin tied it around her waist. It was a challenge to stay in control of her footing and ignore how cold the water was, but she made her way across the river. The risk paid off. The flat wooden raft was in good condition and there was a cooler on top. She opened it and found a twelve pack of Budweiser™. Exhilarated and filled with animation, she pulled a can out and lifted it high into the air showing Cia and Grayson her discovery. On the shore, she found four paddles in good condition. She held the paddles high in the air for them to see.

Cia furrowed her brows. "If there's a raft and paddles and beer, someone put it there. Maybe someone lives back in the woods. What if there's a house close? Someone left the raft there."

"You're brilliant. We need to stop Shin. We'll cross the river and all go investigate together," he said. A split second before Shin pushed the raft around the large rocks in the water he yelled, "Don't go! Wait for us!"

Shin couldn't hear him over the rushing water. She and the raft disappeared downstream before their eyes.

Chapter 22

Everything happened quickly as a rumble of distant thunder groaned in the dark. Less than twenty feet from where Thundering Cloud and Tate had entered the trail, rocks of every size tumbled down the mountain into the river below. The deafening crash echoed. At the same time, the narrow slippery trail began to give way beneath Cabaret. His ears cocked as if listening to a far away sound. Quick to sense the danger, Cabaret's heart pounded in his broad chest - he reared up and spun around without missing a step.

    The dark bay snorted, tossing his head in the air as he made his way back in the direction he had come from. Canku and Zunta followed with their passengers hanging on for dear life as the ground washed away below them. Still tossing his head, Cabaret trotted on down the sharply descending trail, his sturdy hooves slipping in the mud. Just as he entered a small clearing, a tree limb came crashing down right in front of him. He squealed, flinched, and flattened his ears. Without hesitation, he bravely continued on. By the time they were on safer footing and away

Wisdom of the Horse

from falling tree limbs, the rain, thunder, lightening, and clouds disappeared as if they had never been there. The full moon announced itself and introduced a bright sky laced with stars.

Cabaret walked proudly with exuberance as he led them nearly a mile down the gradually widening trail. Soon they were in an open field where Canku and Zunta immediately dove down to eat the tall grass. A spectacular shooting star fell from the sky. Cabaret's wide nostrils flared in excitement. He pranced and pawed the ground as if signaling Canku and Zunta for action. Canku and Zunta abruptly lifted their heads and stopped chewing, keeping mouthfuls of long grass hanging from their lips. It was as if they were reasoning out something Cabaret was telling them.

Cabaret suddenly sprinted and whinnied louder than before. Canku and Zunta forgot about the grass and followed their leader. In the distance, horses whinnied and the communication went back-and-forth as the horses galloped through the wide expanse now lit by moonlight. Moments later Chief and Maya came barreling toward them, snorting with exhilaration, kicking up their heels, mud flying out behind. With the exception of Tanka, the horses were reunited.

Thundering Cloud and Tate dismounted, letting the horses greet each other by nuzzling noses and withers and rearing up on their hind legs. When they calmed down Cabaret stood at Tate's side blowing warm air from his nostrils into Tate's ear. The gelding followed Tate's every move. Maya stayed close watching Chief, Cabaret, Zunta, and Canku ravenously attack the lush green grass as if they'd never have a chance to eat again. The men checked Chief and Maya for injury. Chief had bite marks on his neck and shoulder and scraped hocks, but nothing serious. Chief and Cabaret probably fought over who the alpha horse would be. Apparently, Cabaret won.

Chapter 23

Brett still hadn't heard from Michael about the status of Campala's eligibility to compete now that she had been scratched due to injury. After a heated debate with his mother and sister about what they should do, Brett reluctantly joined the strong-headed women and bustled to the show office. They found Michael pleading with an older man behind the counter. The man's tone offered no encouragement. Fortunately, Joyce, the supervisor, returned from a bathroom break and greeted Michael by name. Immediately, she wondered what kind of a special favor he needed this time. In a matter of minutes Joyce cured the dilemma. She covered up Michael's mistake, following the unwritten code: help the big-time trainers any way possible, as long as they didn't break any clear-cut and strict rules. Without the high-profile trainers and their clients, there wouldn't be enough entries to hold the shows. Over the last several years, entries on a nationwide basis had dwindled in response to the economy, rising costs of showing, and accusations of political motivations of judges and trainers (often the same people) involved in showing high-level Arabians

Wisdom of the Horse

and Half-Arabians.

Laura and her kids scrambled out of the show office, anxious to return to the stall, tack up, and have Brett warm up the mare. In his peripheral vision, Brett spotted Greg Bordeaux leaning on the fence of one of the practice rings. Greg noticed Brett and the women – they were the only people moving at such a pace. He waved them over. His voice took on a tone of confidence as he introduced himself to Laura and Heather.

Heather looked him over in a coldly appraising manner. "We're actually busy. We'll call you when we know we've got ample time to meet," she said, rather stiffly.

Laura's radiant face issued her practiced smile, exposing a row of perfectly white and straight teeth, identical to Brett and Heather. She leaned forward as if to impart a secret. "We've had a little complication, but it's straightened out now."

Brett consulted his watch and excused himself. To Heather's dismay, Laura told Greg what had happened with Campala being scratched and invited him to their sky box to watch Brett show. Having time to spare, they strolled toward a practice arena. Greg's stride was forcibly relaxed as he shaded his eyes against the glow of the sun. He had broken his $275 Fendi sunglasses and couldn't spare the money to replace them right now. Walking, he looked to the ground, as he always did, even before his misfortune. Heather couldn't help but notice the scrutinizing looks a number of people had given him.

At the practice ring, Greg analyzed the horses being worked, wishing he were in the limelight astride the next National Champion Park Horse or Open English Pleasure Horse. He struggled to stop replaying scenes in his mind that rekindled the glory of winning countless U.S. National Arabian Championships, the prestigious Scottsdale All-Arabian Shows, and the Buckeye shows. He tried not to agonize over his memories of the good ole' days and of his lucrative auctions that generated millions of dollars a year. Now, all he wanted was to keep what little he and Elaine had started developing. Was that asking too much? It seemed as if no one wanted to give him a second chance. Too many people were

Cali Canberra

unforgiving, making it impossible to walk out of his history of having been a master at glossing over the truth when his problems began. Sure, he made some mistakes, but he didn't think they were things he should serve a life sentence for. In his opinion, the people in the Arabian breed held him to an unrealistic standard they themselves could not have embraced if they were in his position.

People seemed to think he was only involved in the horse business for the money, but that wasn't the case at all. His interest and passion for horses had always bordered on the obsessive. He loved the horses and the competition, and even the little things - like the feel of quality leather tack and the smell of saddle soap and metal polish. And he cherished the scent of a sweaty horse and new cedar shavings. He appreciated riding in an arena with freshly groomed sand and seeing the faint impressions of hoof prints – ideally in a straight line or a perfect circle.

In the 1970's and a good part of the 1980's, Greg was the dynamo of the Arabian business, trading paper right and left, ruling a dynasty. He had masterminded an effective system to control the high-end of the market by capturing the imaginations of people with seemingly unlimited capital. Sure, his father, brother, and Nick Cordonelli were in the business with him, but he alone was the powerhouse, the driving force that usurped the prestige of Vintage Arabians.

Vintage Arabians and their subsidiary auction company had been the most profitable Arabian breeding and training operation in the world. Then, The Tax Reform Act of 1986 put into law a limitation on the deduction of losses from any business activity in which the taxpayer did not "materially participate," turning the losses into passive losses. The Arabian market crashed and never recovered. He lost everything he owned. He lost his wife, his respectability, his good credit rating, and even worse - the admiration of those who had never done business with him and a few naïve people who had.

Over the past fifteen years, in many ways Greg had moved on as well as could be expected - considering he didn't even have

Wisdom of the Horse

an exit strategy when he saw his world crumbling around him. He remarried yet another younger woman, making her his third wife. The onetime egotistical control freak relinquished control of everything important to him. From the outset of their marriage, he and Elaine put everything they began acquiring in Elaine's name, including their new horse business. The public wondered if it was for asset protection or to prove to his wife how much he trusted her. He gave up his overpowering need for international notoriety and the reputation for having the most expensive horses in the breed. In his heyday he lived in Scottsdale, Arizona and in LaGrange, Kentucky.

After losing everything, he moved to Texas, then California, then Montana, desperate to find a place where he could start fresh. His problems followed him everywhere. His past haunted him regardless of where he lived.

Mixed with the nightmares of his life, he held onto fond memories of the Kentucky Bluegrass country - the land he left behind, along with his dreams. For reasons most couldn't fathom, after being unable to settle anywhere else, he was drawn back to L'Equest, the upscale equestrian development in Kentucky he started from raw land and built into an incredible community, and then lost to Japanese businessmen. He hoped that once he returned to L'Equest his spark and flair would return and he'd find the inspiration to succeed again. He and Elaine found a way to move back to L'Equest and take another road in the horse industry. Together, they began importing Dutch Harness Horses in an attempt to ignite another profitable trend in the horse industry. Now, they were on the verge of losing the horses and the farm because of business conflicts with their only major client. They needed to be bailed out, and needed it quick.

Greg wanted to be in Laura and Heather's presence but planned to avoid discussing his proposition until Brett was available. In the skybox he hoped that any conversation with the women would be about the horses being shown – he'd be happy to give them his professional opinions. If they hadn't even heard of him, they definitely didn't know the Arabian market. That was a good thing. It would be much easier to get money out of people who didn't know the Arab business. Unfortunately, like most things in life, the stark inevitability was that it took money to finance his plans, and lots of it.

Mixing a drink in the skybox with no one around to put him on a pedestal, Greg began feeling out of place. Resentment radiated beneath his surface as he fought back his instinct to sulk.

"Brett says you're anxious to sell some horses," Heather said, her voice charged with authority, her eyes filled with suspicion.

The comment made his dark brown slicked-back hair bristle. Desperate to sell is more like it, he thought. "You get to the point," he said evenly.

"That's how I am," Heather continued, looking out the skybox window toward the arena where tractors drug the green shavings creating a smooth surface for the next class of horses. "Brett says you need cash quick. Sounds like you're in a weak position."

The disturbing words rattled around in his mind. He tried to keep his face from becoming taut with anger. "You're not afraid to speak your mind."

"Business is business," she replied coolly. She couldn't put her finger on what made her leery of the man other than the looks she had witnessed at least a dozen people give him. He had barely spoken and she didn't know a thing about him, his past, or his reputation.

"That's not quite how the horse business works," he said true to form with the hint of a smirk, intending a tone meant to soften her up. From her expression, it did the opposite.

"Like I said, business is business."

Greg hid his emotions as best he could under the circumstances. "I've got some incredible horses. Sure, I'm in a cash-flow bind and can use some help, but the opportunity for Brett to be financially involved in my business is something he shouldn't pass up. I'm willing to take in a silent partner. Brett could own an interest in all of my horses for a fair price if the timing helps me out of my bind."

Heather snickered. "The value of any horse is subjective. From

Wisdom of the Horse

what Brett said, there's absolutely no established market value for the horses you're trying to breed and sell," she said with an edge to her voice and her face set hard.

Amused at the wet bar, Laura casually poured Courvoisier XO Imperial into a Riedel Vinum tulip-shaped glass that was purposefully chosen to fully harmonize the aroma and taste of the cognac while emphasizing the bouquet. Laura never went to a show without her own stemware and alcohol.

Greg felt a surge of annoyance at the implied criticism, but unfortunately, after his life imploded in the eighties, he was well practiced at calmly responding to criticism. His expression was placid. Even after all he had been through in the horse business, he was still unable to tell the unvarnished truth to prospective clients. "That's the beauty of what the opportunity is. I'm in a position to establish the market values of Dutch Harness Horses in the United States. And Brett can be a part of the growing popularity and the future profitability."

Laura was definitely intrigued but his remark spawned a smug condescending look from Heather. He acted as if he hadn't noticed.

Heather quickly decided to play naïve to test Greg's personality. "Excuse me. I didn't mean to be offensive. I shouldn't even have spoken up. This is between you and my parents."

Greg's voice quavered. "Actually, it's Brett I'd do business with."

Heather couldn't control herself. "Brett doesn't have a dime. Other than working on our farm, he hasn't worked a day in his life. It would be my parents making the decision," she said, thinking of Grayson as her father in these types of circumstances, and in most circumstances. She surprised herself at the depth of negative feelings she had about the man whom she had barely spent time with.

Laura looked at Greg with mild curiosity. Without even knowing the man, she could read the wounded pride on his face. She felt bad for what her daughter was putting him through.

Greg dreaded continuing. By now, his mouth tensed, his face

Cali Canberra

looked drawn, and there was an uneasy wariness in his posture. After a few moments of silence he cleared his throat and looked to Laura. "Brett and I were talking one day, and we thought you might consider loaning him the money to invest so he can start his own venture buying Dutch Harness Horses that I sell him and advise him on."

Heather laughed out loud, but didn't say a word. Here the man stood, acting as if he and Brett were buddies. She knew Brett and Greg weren't really friends. Brett was simply one of the hundreds of people Greg ran into in the show world. That's how it was in all breeds and riding disciplines.

Laura interjected, trying not to sound insulting. "We're always being approached about buying. What's so unique about your horses?"

"These are very special horses. Dutch Harness Horses, or Tuigpaard, as they are called in their native country, came from the Netherlands over 100 years ago, tracing back to Dutch Warmbloods." Without asking if they were interested, he opened his photo album and showed them pictures of a horse bursting into the show ring with a proud and distinctive self-carriage. The chestnut moved with its neck upright and arched, tail high, elegantly trotting high off both ends with its hocks providing incredible drive and height that allowed the horse to fully engage its shoulders and lift its forelegs in a high-and-open motion. "You can't tell from still pictures, but at the highest point of movement there's a distinct moment of suspension that's so remarkable it will take your breath away."

Not wanting to appear overly impressed Laura casually said, "This horse does radiate power and authority, and I've always admired Dutch Warmbloods."

Greg took her comment as another strong sign of interest. "My name and experience in the horse world behind these horses will be an asset for Brett. He would be on the ground floor of a relatively new type of show horse in the United States. We can create an entire segment of the industry with the nucleus of horses I've personally selected. And I have access to more horses."

Wisdom of the Horse

Heather noticed he only referred to his experience, not his reputation. She wondered why and she thought his answer sounded like a feeble attempt to convince them of his self-importance. "You're pretty full of yourself. Of course you have access to more horses. There's a glut of horses on the market. We all have access."

Laura's expression suggested she didn't like Heather's tone. Irritation lurked in her eyes. She imagined Heather's words hit Greg like a stake through his heart.

It galled Greg to answer to Heather and Laura – he planned to do business with Brett. Fragments of his father's warnings to get out of the horse business all together haunted him. One memory after another surfaced of his glory days and the endless days with lawyers and packing up his belongings without his second wife, Marcie, at his side.

"My horses are superior to most that are on the market," he replied.

"Right," Heather said mockingly.

After a strained silence, he set his glass down on the wet bar. With smoldering eyes he looked away and started toward the door as he swore under his breath.

Laura grew more annoyed at Heather's attitude. She thought of Brett and abruptly stepped toward Greg and took him by the forearm. Her manner of speaking became crisp and precise. "Listen, she shouldn't speak to you that way. Please accept my apology."

Greg stopped in his tracks, enormously relieved Laura made the effort. The past twenty years of his life had become such an ordeal. Every detail of his hardships had been etched into his brain. He was determined to find a way to keep treading water until he could be on top again – he needed Brett.

"I'm sorry," Heather said without an ounce of sincerity. She sat on a bar stool and stared toward the arena.

"Apologies accepted. Let's start over. My point is that Brett and I would like to work on this project together. He's a college graduate now and ready to go out on his own. I have the opportunity of a lifetime and he can be instrumental in making this venture a huge success."

Laura returned his sincere gaze. "I don't mean this to sound disrespectful, but why don't you have a current client help you out? A client you already have a history with?"

Greg blushed and became tongue-tied. "To be honest, I unintentionally burned a few bridges in the Arabian industry before it crashed. People in the Arabian breed love to spread rumors, and I was the one they went after when everything went to hell. I made some mistakes that I've since learned from and I need an opportunity to start fresh."

Laura was impressed with his honesty. "We all come with a learning history. A past. I'm glad you're not letting your past keep you from moving forward in your life, but I'm not sure Brett is ready to delve into something like this."

Greg felt painted into a corner. "You don't even know what the proposal is. You can't know if he's ready or not."

"Tell me about it," Laura said. There was something she liked about the man, and her son sounded so zealous to have her consider the opportunity.

"I would prefer to wait until Brett's here so we can all discuss this together."

"It's my money. I'd prefer to hear about it now," Laura insisted, especially since she also wanted to get into the horse business, but still hadn't thought about what aspect or how she'd do it.

Greg was reluctant to continue, but Laura did seem interested and they were his only prospect. He couldn't go to any old-timers in the Arabian breed after burning all his bridges. His only hope was to lure in people who didn't know details about his past so that he could put his own spin on describing his experience in the horse business. Buying time, he poured himself Cutty on the rocks. "I can certainly appreciate your position, but if we do this, it will be you loaning the money to Brett – or giving it to him as a gift – so he can…"

Laura cut him off. How dare he dictate the use of her money?

Wisdom of the Horse

She edged closer to him, implying he was treading water now. "Why are you avoiding telling me about this without Brett here?"

Completely out of character, Greg stuttered and answered weakly. "I'm not."

"Yes, you are," Heather jumped in.

"I'm sorry," Greg said, feeling a vague sense of alarm. He might have totally blown an opportunity. A lump gathered in his throat. "I didn't intend to. It's just that when I was visible and active in the horse business it started out as a small family business. When I was younger I was never treated with the respect I should have been because everyone thought my father was the leader...which he was, until I was old enough and mature enough...but, anyway, I just didn't want to leave Brett out of anything. If we did, I'd know how he feels, and it's not a good feeling. In fact, it's demeaning."

What happened to Greg and his family, and to the Arabian horse industry in the late 1980's, shook the foundation upon which his world had been built. Every instinct he had for horses, and the horse business, and every friendship and business relationship he forged had been turned upside down. To this day, the injustice haunted him.

Laura considered Greg's sincerity. A soft smile materialized. "I suppose you're right. We need to treat him like the adult he is. Thank you for bringing it to my attention. As his mother, I'm used to being his protector."

His lips parted in amazement. His explanation actually worked. It was the truth, but under the dire circumstances he was shocked that he had held his composure enough to make her understand.

"Mom, Brett's class is starting," Heather said, feeling a sense of anticipation for her brother.

They left the sky box and went to their front row seats to watch the Open English Pleasure Championship class.

Brett entered the ring at the far side of the arena and dissolved into a unity of motion with his mount. On the exterior, he displayed confidence - an icy calm. But inside, his heart was

Cali Canberra

pounding in anticipation of a ride close to perfection.

As Brett approached, Laura and Heather repeatedly screamed out at the top of their lungs, "Slip through the veil!"

Brett, feeling the electricity in the air, gave a slight nod, acknowledging he had heard them and that he would in fact slip through the veil.

Greg smiled. "What's that mean?"

Laura continued watching Brett and Campala's every move as she explained to Greg, "My husband was a competitive swimmer – of course, many years ago. His coach taught the team members a lot about the mind, body, and spirit connection, and he taught them a process he had learned from a doctor friend of his, Michael Samuels. It's called Slip through the Veil. It's a shift in consciousness - the place where you go in your inner world, your spiritual world, the world of your visionary space - inside your intuition – the world of your power. When you slip through the veil those things become as large as the outer world. You enter the Power. Slipping through the veil isn't just theoretical – it's a real experience. Your body tingles and you become electrified. Energy rises. You're going into a place where you're dealing with body, mind, and spirit. Slipping through the veil is the veil into Spirit. We know when it happens to us."

Laura had met Grayson at the pool at the Stonebridge Ranch Country Club in McKinney, Texas, a suburb of Dallas. She was on her last lap when he strolled up in his red Speedo™. Her perfect form in doing the breast stroke did not go without his notice. He struck up a conversation with her, telling her about his interest in swimming – he swam at Duke University in Durham, North Carolina. He quit the team in his junior year because he couldn't handle his academic career along with the incredible schedule for swim practice and dry land training, and the time away at meets. He loved to swim, but it wasn't a burning passion.

Explaining further about slipping through the veil, Heather added, "Of course, you have to let your mind do it – to give up thinking about every physical movement and let your body do what it knows to do – let your body use its cellular memory. The

Wisdom of the Horse

trick is actually letting go of all the normal thoughts and fears and jitters."

Neither Laura nor Heather was ever able to do it when they were under the pressure of competition, but Grayson was always able to when he competed on his horses and when he competed in swimming.

Greg nodded as they all watched Brett. "Interesting way to describe it. I've had that feeling of where everything feels perfect and in harmony, a certain peacefulness while there's great energy. I assume that's what you're talking about."

"Right. But you can control your mind to go there," Laura said.

Brett approached their side of the arena again and looked absolutely perfect. They hadn't seen a mistake yet.

"Competitive class," Greg said once the gate closed and all fifteen horses trotted the circumference of the show ring.

Heather nodded, not particularly impressed by a group of pretty horses trotting. She and her mother agreed that a bona fide equine athlete was a hunt horse in the field, a show jumper, an event horse, or high-level dressage horse. Even Grayson's reining, roping, and cutting horses were athletes – not of the caliber of her horses, but still, certainly more than what Brett's horse was. A pretty Arabian or Half-Arabian walking, trotting, and cantering in a ring was no big deal to her. To simply judge a horse on manners, performance, attitude, quality, and conformation seemed absurd. Certainly, halter was laughable, as were the Native Costume classes. But if Brett loved his Arabians, they accepted it. Her brother was a gentle and kind soul and she loved him, no matter what.

"What do you think of Brett's trainer?" Laura asked Greg.

"He's been around for years. He's got a loyal and growing clientele," Greg said diplomatically.

"That's evasive," Heather said for her mother.

Greg smiled. "Michael's fine."

"Would you recommend him?" Laura asked.

"For halter classes, yes. For performance, not necessarily,"

Cali Canberra

Greg said honestly. "He knows what he's doing, but doesn't really have enough experience in performance, if that makes any sense."

Laura and Heather nodded. No need to ask more. That was his opinion and he was entitled to it. As Grayson always said, if opinions were worth money, everyone involved in horses would be rich.

The riders followed the instructions called out by the announcer. "They sure don't ask much from the horses, do they?" Heather said.

"It's harder than you think to keep the horses at the right speed in the proper cadence and never breaking their gait. These horses are generally outstanding athletes. But I understand what you're saying in one sense, and that's why I've gotten away from purebred Arabians and into Sport horses – and the Dutch Harness Horses in particular."

Heather grabbed her mother by the arm. "Look! Someone's motioning to Brett."

"Who is that?"

"The USEF steward called him in. It looks like Campala lost her shoe," Greg explained. The United States Equestrian Federation had their own steward, the 'keeper of the rules' – a point of contention with many competitors because the shows were put on by the Arabian Horse Association and they had their own stewards.

A few minutes passed while Brett and Campala stood near center ring. The steward and a couple of other show officials talked and went in and out of the ring. Brett exited the arena as the class continued.

The announcer stated that Brett's horse had thrown a shoe and would not be returning. It could only mean one thing.

"What's happening?" Laura asked Greg.

"He was excused from the class. We should go meet him at the stall," Greg suggested.

Heather was incensed. How dare this stranger impose himself on their family?

Wisdom of the Horse

"You don't need to come," Laura said nicely to Greg as she grabbed her Coach purse and Prada jacket and quickly walked away without looking back.

Heather followed Laura.

"Good luck," Greg called out. "Call me when we can all get together. Brett has my cell phone number."

Back at the stall Brett was crouched in the corner, his head in his hands, holding back tears. His mare nuzzled his hair trying to comfort him.

Laura opened the stall door. "What happened?"

Brett's tears exploded. When he was able to pull himself together he explained. Campala lost her shoe and they automatically had a certified farrier weigh it. It turned out the shoe and pad combined were almost two ounces over the 14 ounce limit. They disqualified him. The Open English Pleasure class was the event he trained so hard to win and set his goal to win. The other classes were simply entered into for the purpose of winning the high-point award.

"Brett, I'm so sorry, honey," Laura said.

"I can't believe this. Joe knows what he's doing. He knows the shoeing standards. How could this have happened to me?"

Heather put her arm around him. "It's a tough break, but you'll get a new set of shoes put on her and ride the class you're scheduled for in the morning. It's better than her being lame."

"I'm fed up with this. I want to go home. I'm so sick of all this show ring bullshit," Brett said angrily.

"You're overreacting Brett. Things happen. We've all got our stories," Laura said.

"First Michael scratches her, then we go through hell to get it straightened out only to get disqualified once I'm in the ring. Campala was going great. Like Grayson would say – the Universe is sending me a message and I need to listen."

Laura smiled at the thought of Grayson and his wisdom.

"Maybe you're right," Heather concurred. "You've been talking about getting into competitive trail riding for a couple of years now. You had a great time when you went on conditioning rides with Grayson."

"I know," Brett said. "But I like the ribbons and trophies."

"We all do," Laura admitted, thinking about how they liked being in the magazines, too.

"Grayson doesn't care about ribbons and trophies anymore," Heather said.

"He just got two Reserve Championships at Quarter Horse Congress," Laura reminded her.

"I know, but you saw his heart wasn't in it. He loves trail riding and camping out with Chief and Stetson. You never see him enthusiastic about shows anymore," Heather said.

"You're right. He cancelled going to the World Championships, and everybody said he was the most likely winner for reining and cutting," Brett said.

"The more Grayson learns from Thundering Cloud and Tate, he's completely different about the horses. You've seen it, Brett. You said you learned a lot of relationship training things from Grayson, based on what they taught him," Heather said.

"I did," Brett admitted.

"You guys really started bonding when you began learning about natural horsemanship and Native American ways," Laura reminded him.

"I know. You're right. Maybe this is my sign to get out of the show world and enjoy my horse for what she is – a companion," Brett said, no longer upset with the situation.

"That's what Grayson does," Laura said.

For several minutes the family stood silently petting Campala, thinking about their relationships with their horses.

"I hope you'll loan me the money to go into business with Greg. I've got to start working," Brett said for the first time in his life.

"How much capital do you need to get involved with him?" Laura asked.

Brett assumed Greg must have made a good impression on his mother. "Ideally, $500,000."

"What's the minimum he could get by with to help him out

of his jam?"

"$200,000 would solve his financial issue, but what's equally important is that there's capital available to buy and import more mares to breed to his stallion - and for marketing and promotion of the program. I ran the numbers he gave me, and they look realistic. It's not like anyone's going to get rich, but it's profitable enough to be worthwhile. Plus, there's always a chance of us being able to do what he did with the Arabians in the late seventies and early eighties. If that happens, it would be a goldmine and I'd be in on the ground level. Of course, I'm not counting on that scenario coming to fruition, but it's always nice to know that there's a possibility of something big."

Laura and Heather were startled and speechless. Brett followed them out the stall and slid the door closed. Heather hooked the latch, and still speechless looked at her mother who raised her brows and smiled.

Stunned and practically speechless at her mother's response, Heather excused herself to find a bathroom and to get soft drinks for each of them.

"Okay," Laura said. "Call Greg and tell him to draw up a contract and that you'll have his money in a few days. I'll call my banker and have him liquidate some stock."

Brett beamed, temporarily forgetting about Campala being scratched. He hugged his mother and said, "Thank you so much! I'm so excited."

He walked away from the stabling area for privacy and used the speed dial on his cell phone. Greg answered on the second ring. The conversation was brief due to the difficulty of Greg hearing over the noise from the spectators at the show ring. Brett returned to the stalls and told his mother how Greg was obviously grateful and pleased that everything's working out. Greg had his laptop with him and could draft a formal agreement. He wondered if Laura could issue a $20,000 check for good-faith earnest money. Laura agreed.

"Great. I told him I thought you would. We're going to meet him at the steak house across the street at eight for dinner. We'll hash out the details, and of course, we'll celebrate!"

Laura was thrilled to see her son so happy. "Sounds good."

Heather returned with their beverages, and with a new and positive attitude. If this is what made her brother happy, it was none of her business if Greg didn't impress her as much as he had her mother and brother.

"Let's call Grayson and tell him my exiting news, and about Campala," Brett suggested. "I want to tell him the Universe sent me a message and I got it."

"We can't reach him," Laura reminded him. "I'm buying him a satellite phone. I know he says he won't use it, but I hate not being able to reach him."

Heather zipped up her jacket. "I don't understand why he doesn't want one. He used to buy every high-tech electronic thing he could."

"It's not the same wilderness experience if you can make and get phone calls," Brett said in his stepfather's defense. Each time they had gone on long trail rides together one of the first things Grayson would say is how nice it was to have peace and quiet and no interruptions.

"I understand. But what if he got hurt?" Laura said.

"Or got stranded out in the middle of nowhere?" Heather added.

"He wouldn't," Brett said confidently. "He knows what he's doing. Hell, by now he's half Indian, all the time he's spent with Thundering Cloud and Tate, and studying the Native American ways. I'm surprised he didn't pay for a blood transfusion to get their Indian blood!"

Chapter 24

Grayson miraculously brought the campfire back to life. They decided to get some relief from the cold, to warm up a little bit before making a final decision about whether they should cross the river and explore what was on the other side.

"You look deep in thought," Cia said.

"When I was in the hammock earlier I had a vivid dream."

"What did you dream?"

"I don't know if I should say. What if telling jinx's it?"

"Telling dreams doesn't jinx anything. Only telling wishes!" she said playfully.

Grayson told Cia his dream about all the famous clinician/trainers racing to the camp. In spite of all that had happened, he found himself thinking more about the dream, and what to him was the most important message – he should spread *Suktanka Woksapa* – Wisdom of the Horse.

Cia grinned from ear to ear. There was something innocent

and childlike in the way he spoke. "I like it. Did you tell the Crows about this?"

"No. I was going to later. Not about the competition part of the dream, but about *Suktanka Woksapa*."

"You should get shirts made with that on it – and coffee mugs," she suggested.

He sensed her enthusiasm was sincere. "I feel like the dream was a message."

"I believe you received an important message."

The fire radiated welcome warmth as a long silence bound them. The illuminated moon and constellation of stars continued shining brightly allowing them to see the river had risen significantly - most of the big boulders were nearly covered by fast running water.

"I'll try to find another trail upstream," Grayson said after a long silence. "Maybe there's another place we can try to cross that's not so deep." He didn't need to remind her that the way they had come into the clearing was by crossing the water on horseback, and it would be the only way out also.

Ghostlike, Grayson's image vanished from sight into the relative darkness. Cia shivered from the chill of the night and fought against a rising panic. At first she dwelled on the mishaps of the trip. Moments later she decided to fully surrender to her experience in the wilderness. After all, that's why she had come.

As Grayson wandered around, he inhaled deep yoga breaths, relishing the tranquility and crisp clean air. The melodious sound of running water over the boulders in the river somehow calmed him. His senses seemed heightened as he listened to owls hooting back-and-forth across the river as coyotes howled in the distance. Shrill cries of wildlife echoed in the night. The air filled with the rasping of insects and crickets chirping. Moments like this made him realize how only the weather and the animals can express the purity of nature.

Cia returned to the campfire and visualized Shin safely floating down the river, anxious to discover signs of civilization. For a moment she worried about her drowning in rough waters and

Wisdom of the Horse

wondered if she really had a death wish since she had no fear of death. Grayson and Thundering Cloud claimed death was not something to fear, since death of the body was not death of the soul or the spirit. All living things, including humans, had souls and spirits before bodies, and when this time is over, the soul and spirit will continue on to other dimensions.

Grayson's voice brought her back to the present moment. "I found a path," he announced loudly, heading back to her.

"Great. It's good to know I'm a genius. Most people don't believe me. You're my first witness," she yelled.

Grayson laughed. "Do you think I should cross?"

"If you do, I want to come with you."

"If we can make it over the boulders without falling into the water and we make it to the other side, from that point it looks like the path goes up hill. But I don't know how far."

"You're rich as shit from what I've heard. I can't believe you don't have a GPS system, a satellite phone, and a helicopter on stand-by in case you call," she said seriously.

He laughed. "Rich as shit? Is that what the Crows said?"

Her heart sank. For once, she was at a loss for words. No one had actually described him that way, but they had said enough to give her the distinct idea that Grayson was very wealthy.

"I didn't mean that the way it came out."

"Seriously. What did they say?"

"I don't recall. But no one used the term 'rich as shit' though, if that's what you're disturbed about. What they mostly told me about was your generosity, and how you make your living helping terminally ill people – and that it was lucrative. They really didn't say much. It's just that I'm so broke, most people are 'rich as shit' compared to me," she said, trying to lighten up.

"I can't imagine you're worse off than most people. There's a lot of financial suffering in this world. In this country. You know that."

"Can we talk about this later? We need to make a decision – do we go across or not?"

They sat quietly a moment to weigh the risks.

"Did you hear that?" Grayson asked.

"What?"

"Quiet. Listen," he said in a hush. He silenced her with a quick wave of his hand. Minutes went by before he heard the faraway call again. He smiled from ear to ear. "It's Thundering Cloud."

The fire began to dwindle again and the smell of smoke lingered in the air. They decided to wait for Thundering Cloud and Tate before going anywhere. Their waterproof boots were heavy and wet, increasing a chance for blisters, and their feet were numb. The cold spread throughout their bodies. Grayson used his shirt to fan the campfire, bringing it back life. Small flames darted into the air providing enough warmth to attempt to dry their clothes.

Hooting and howling from Thundering Cloud and Tate grew louder as the Crows urged the horses through the river which had risen so much that it was a necessity for the horses to hold their noses high in the air as they half-walked and half-swam across.

"Cabaret!" Cia yelled as loud as she could when the horses approached.

Cabaret whinnied and took off ahead of the rest of the horses determined to get to Cia. Due to sheer momentum he literally slipped into a slide stop right in front of her. When he regained his balance he rested his chin on her shoulder and she hugged him and patted him as steam rose over his back.

Leading Maya, Zunta and Thundering Cloud trotted to Grayson who had trudged through the mud and the puddles, anxious to see if his horse was all right. Grayson scratched Chief on the withers (his favorite spot) and led him as close to the campfire as he could for better lighting. He inspected him for injuries. Other than abrasions, he gratefully found none. The instant Cia saw Grayson carefully eying Chief, she realized that just because Cabaret had run to her, it didn't mean he hadn't been in harms way. She stood back to study him as if she knew what to look for.

Miraculously, by the light of the campfire no one saw anything wrong with any of the horses. Tate slid off his horse and told

Wisdom of the Horse

the story of them being stranded on the cliff in the pitch-black darkness with the ground crumbling beneath them and the rocks tumbling down and what Cabaret had done to become their hero.

"Cabaret saved us and took us to the other horses. He's got a lot of wisdom," Thundering Cloud told Cia and Grayson.

Cia's breathing quickened as she listened to their story. "He could have been killed."

"They all could have been killed," Grayson reminded her.

She swallowed hard. "You're right. I'm sorry. It's just that I love Cabaret so much. He's the first horse I've ever ridden and I groom him and feed him when I'm at your house," she said, directing the last of her comments to Thundering Cloud.

Thundering Cloud was reminded of the unique bond between women and horses.

No one spoke for some time.

Cia pictured all Tate had described about their grueling task to return with the horses. "What a story," she said to no one in particular.

Thundering Cloud put his arm around her shoulder in a fatherly fashion. "This is exactly the type of thing I told Shin about on the trail. Remember when I said that you don't get to choose your stories? They choose you and you must surrender to them."

"It sounds like Cabaret's the hero. *Suktanka Woksapa*," Grayson said quietly to Cia.

Cia smiled.

Thundering Cloud stepped away from her and furrowed his brows. "You know *Suktanka Woksapa*? Wisdom of the Horse?"

Grayson nodded. "It came to me in a dream," he said simply.

"Follow that dream." He didn't care to know the dream and hoped his son would not ask either. "*Suktanka Woksapa* is the name of the poem my grandfather wrote my grandmother when he was deciding which woman to marry. He says he let his horse pick his wife – my grandmother. I don't even know if I ever told Tate or Shin that story. How did you know *Suktanka Woksapa*?"

Before he could answer, Shin yelled, "Hey, everybody. I'm back!"

Cali Canberra

"Where were you?" Tate asked as the wind kicked up.

The clan huddled near the hot embers of the rekindling fire.

Shin's teeth chattered and the wind blew her damp hair as she explained why she thought it would be a good idea to raft to a place where she might be able to get help. "There were so many huge boulders and pointy rocks I could barely keep the raft going. It didn't take long to decide to just get off and hike back. It's a relief to see that everyone's fine."

"Except Tanka," Grayson said with a languid expression across his face. His nearly dry shirt billowed in the wind revealing the horse hairs sticking out of his jeans pocket. He told Thundering Cloud and Tate what had happened, including the ceremony to release Tanka's soul to the Creator.

The men were regretful, but at peace that the horse had returned to the spirit world. In this natural world of law and order, of cause and effect, and the circle of life and death and rebirth, they paused and momentarily looked to the heavens, grateful the horse's suffering ended as quickly as it did.

Sitting around the fire, Tate retold the story in detail about their nocturnal excursion. He started by reminding them that unlike now where the sky was clear and the moon and stars bright, while they were gone, the full moon had been hidden by dark clouds. He described the details of how they tried to recall landmarks in the dark with only the lightening brightening their trail from time to time – and he told how the rain washed away the hoof prints, and how Canku paused at the fork in the trail and why they took the treacherous path they did – and finally he emphasized the nightmarish reality of how they came so close to losing their lives on the cliff. In recounting the story, his heart pounded like a trapped feral cat, almost as much as when he heard the cascading rocks falling toward them. He told them of the exact moment when a violent nausea overcame him – and the moment later when he felt something primeval take over his very being. The will to survive against all odds. Finally, he smiled, a half-nostalgic smile, knowing he'd never forget this trip and his time with his brave horse Canku and his wise father.

Wisdom of the Horse

Grayson was struck by Tate's intensity as he recounted the events. He could tell by Thundering Cloud's reactions to his son's storytelling that everything Tate said was inscribed with truth and certainty. Father and son were both able to speak in such a way that their words held power and reassurance about the existence of the Creator and the soul. They had obviously gained access to the spiritual world and it served them well. Others would not have survived the ordeal.

"You should write a story about the experience," Grayson told Tate, unaware Shin was working on her own novel.

"It's not the kind of writing I've done, but thanks for the suggestion," he said appreciatively. His books were exclusively about Native American horsemanship, training techniques and women and horses.

Thundering Cloud looked deep into Shin's eyes, straight through to her core. He leaned in toward her and spoke. "Stories have the power to transform, not so much in the reading or hearing of the story, but in telling and retelling the story. You should remember this."

At that moment, with her father's piercing eyes looking into her awestruck face, she was reminded that there are some things that can't be explained. They must be either felt or observed. Such was the feeling she got from this man who had taught her so much throughout her life. She exhaled a pent-up breath. What had she been missing out on all of these years by not writing the kinds of things she wanted to write about?

Cia swiveled around to see Grayson, who hadn't spoken. "You're sure quiet all of a sudden."

The atmosphere palpably changed when he responded. "I shouldn't admit this, but right now I'd just like to be home sprawled out on the sofa and listening to some good music with a nice cold sweaty bottle of beer."

"Sounds good to me," Tate replied.

Before anyone else added to the new conversation, Cia asked, "Do we really have to fast tonight?"

Grayson's stomach growled. "To tell you the truth, I'm

famished. We thought we were just going to be sitting around the campfire talking all evening – not being stressed and burning calories – especially the rest of you. Cia and I did the least, as far as exertion goes."

"I'm starving," Thundering Cloud said, surprising everyone else.

"Do you think we could go to Grayson's?" Cia asked.

Thundering Cloud returned Grayson's subtle glance and winked. He wondered which route Grayson would choose to return home.

"Fine with me," Grayson eagerly answered. He was tempted to take the most direct way back, which was only a half-hour ride, but he didn't want Cia to know how close they were to safety. In the wilderness, fear, uncertainty, stamina, and the will to survive were only fragments of lessons to learn. Cia needed to return home with more confidence than she had left with – and with a tale of adventure to expand her spirits.

Chapter 25

The fight against the rising, rushing river water made it difficult for the horses to cross back over to the trail. Initially, Maya refused because Cia wasn't experienced or confident enough to be assertive with the mare. Thundering Cloud and Shin turned around midway through the river to get back to solid ground with Cia. Thundering Cloud hoisted Cia up onto Zunta with him and he led Cabaret behind them across the river. Shin, now riding Maya, intentionally remained behind for a moment so Maya would be anxious to join the other horses on the far side of the river. Once the pair finally crossed, Shin got back on Cabaret and Cia got back on Maya.

When they crossed the river, the first part of the trail was slow going, pitch-black from the dense tall trees. The sensation gave Cia a sense of vertigo. Fortunately, after about ten minutes, the trail widened and the trees thinned out, allowing the full moon and crystal clear sky to give them safe, albeit slippery, passage. Cia noticed that they took a different trail than they had come in on. If they had ridden to the parking lot in the National Forest where the trucks and trailers were, they would have ridden at least five hours, given the night sky and the wet ground, and then another hour's drive to Grayson's.

The three hour journey culminated when they approached the spectacularly illuminated back of Grayson's one-of-a-kind, authentic lodge-style home. The modified horseshoe shape was evident. A clear midnight-blue sky and bright stars served as a theatrical backdrop to the wall of windows, the massive stone pillars, and imposing bronze light fixtures highlighting the rich wood tones of the hand-peeled and hand-notched logs. This side was surrounded with decks, porches, and patios so family and guests could enjoy the view of one of the picturesque pastures. Rather than riding all the way to the barn, they rode the horses to the six-car garage and carried in the saddles to dry out overnight.

Next, they settled the horses in the closest pasture to the house. Chief, being a stallion and knowing he was in his own domain, at first pranced around the front split-rail fence line and then staked a claim in the corner of his pasture. Once he relaxed, they let the other horses loose and watched to make sure that Chief wouldn't become aggressive. As soon as Cabaret's bridle was removed he walked directly in Chief's direction as if he wanted to challenge the stallion to a confrontation on his own turf. Chief snorted, keeping a close eye on each of the horses. He remained still until Cabaret reached a certain point. As Cabaret crossed an invisible line, Chief turned his haunches and pinned his ears back as if to give him formal notification that he shouldn't come any closer. Zunta, Maya, and Canku studied the situation and walked away in the opposite direction. Cabaret lowered his head and calmly walked off to join the other horses.

There was an abundance of green grass in the pasture and the water tub was sufficiently full, so the group finally returned to the house and went in through the keeping room. Everyone took off their boots and socks, except for Tate who was embarrassed

Wisdom of the Horse

by the shape of his long thin toes.

The kitchen entry was through a leaded-paned door and provided a view of the great room that was separated from the kitchen by two enormous stone archways. In the kitchen, a massive log truss spanned and defined the areas. In keeping with the grand scope of the space, an iron range hood trimmed with logs dropped from the ceiling over the industrial grade stainless steel Viking™ stove. Granite countertops, solid cherry wood cabinetry, and high-end appliances were the only hint of a modern touch to the clearly Old West architecture and decor.

Grayson invited everyone to make themselves at home. Thundering Cloud pulled food out of the stainless steel Thermador™ refrigerator and rummaged through the walk-in pantry for snack foods. Grayson expertly built a sandwich to die for, stacking two-inches of paper-thin pastrami on deli rye slathered with spicy mustard, topped off with thin sliced Bermuda onion, tomato, and romaine.

Thundering Cloud admired Grayson's work as he grabbed two frosty, ice cold bottles of beer and twisted the top off one. Without restraint or embarrassment, he slugged down almost half, dripping some down his chin onto his filthy, damp denim shirt.

"I'll give you a beer for half of your sandwich," he proposed to Grayson, then proudly let out a long slow burp.

The group roared in laughter at his crudeness. It was completely out of character.

"I'll give you the whole sandwich if you'll agree not to do that again," Grayson replied without hesitation.

Shin laughed at Grayson's spontaneity – she had never heard him be funny before. "Damn! You made me laugh so hard I just peed in my jeans!"

The idea of the normally reserved Shin peeing in her jeans and announcing it set everyone into a belly laugh. Cia laughed so hard she just about choked on her dill pickle. She hadn't recalled having this much fun since college.

Grayson laughed far longer than the situation warranted.

Cali Canberra

Thundering Cloud supposed it was because there wasn't nearly enough unabashed laughter in his life anymore. They had talked a few times about how fulfilled and content Grayson felt now that he had changed the way he lived – having horses for pure pleasure rather than for competition and ego – and for being in touch with his spirit and doing so many worthwhile and purposeful things with his life. The only thing he missed about his old lifestyle was the laughter and silliness, times when he let loose and wasn't so serious. He was aware of his need to strike a balance but hadn't taken the initiative to integrate fun into his life. There were so many important things to accomplish he didn't know how he'd find the time and energy.

When everyone calmed down, Grayson made a second sandwich as he cradled the cordless phone between his ear and neck to check his voice mail. One of the messages was from the private investigator letting him know he had faxed a report about Greg Bordeaux to both his business office in Dallas and to his home office in Oklahoma. The investigator suggested Grayson call him for more details if he wanted to know more than what the brief report offered. Grayson licked the mustard from the knife, grabbed a bag of sour cream and onion potato chips, and excused himself. He climbed up the most distinctive element of the home – a 7,000 pound log around which the carved staircase winds. Upstairs in the loft he used as a home office, scattered all over the floor in front of the fax machine, there were a dozen pages from the investigator. Grayson scanned the information, noting Greg's impressive accomplishments. He decided to wait until he was rested to read it in detail.

Knowing Laura powered off her cell phone when she slept, Grayson called and left her a voice mail telling her everything was fine, but some complications arose and they had returned from their camping trip. He said he'd call during the day to tell her more, and then he returned to his friends downstairs.

The thud of Tate's boot heels on the plank floor reverberated as he left the kitchen. He took a bottle of spring water and a bag of pretzels to the massive great room towering upward to a crown of

Wisdom of the Horse

interlaced log trusses that were highlighted by a faceted wall of windows. Tate had always admired the tumbled river rock fireplace which stood nearly nineteen feet to the peak. Resting on the hearth were bronze sculptures of buffalo, elk, and other wildlife in addition to a cowboy on a bucking horse – all by famous artists, including an original by Fredric Remington. Tate sat down heavily, sinking into the buckskin chair, the exhaustion of the adventure and the hilarity in the kitchen catching up with him. He had eaten in this astounding room many times but had never been this grateful for food.

Thundering Cloud piled food into his arms from the center island in the kitchen - a basket of fruit, a roll of salami, two wheels of imported Brie on a cheese board, and a box of crackers under his arm. He placed his goodies on the battered antique coffee table handmade of old barn wood and rusted hinges. Next, he returned from the kitchen with a handful of plates, knives, forks, and napkins. Sitting on the floor cross-legged – he didn't like to call it Indian style – he dug into the food as if it were his own.

Shin rummaged through the refrigerator once more. "Can I eat these left-over baby back ribs?" she called out to Grayson.

"Help yourself. I think there's potato salad and slaw, too. Open the middle drawer."

Shin's mouth watered in anticipation. She rarely ate beef or pork, but right now she craved it, especially cold ribs. Joining everyone else, she took the containers and a fork and napkin into the great room and joined her father on the plank floor, but she sat on an oversized, hand-made fringed deerskin pillow. Normally, she wouldn't sit on someone else's pillow without asking, but she and her mother had made it for Laura as a birthday gift. Shin loved this view point because from here she could see the wide-open space and tall roof lines of the entry hall creating the feeling of free flowing *chi* energy. The entrance hall displayed a portion of Laura's collection of English riding paintings by Booth Malone and Andre Pater and even an original by Sir Alfred Munnings.

Grayson caught a glimpse of the natural slate clock on the fireplace mantle. "It's after one in the morning. What are we going to do about the sweat lodge?"

The plan had been to fast for the night and then ride to another part of the farm for a sweat lodge, where five of Grayson's viators would meet them. The three terminally ill men and two women were doing a modified fast at a local hotel, drinking only water and juice, and eating only fresh fruit and crackers to help their stomachs tolerate their pain medicine and any other medication. Grayson's farm manager would drive them to the sweat lodge, arriving mid-afternoon, so the horseback riding clan had time to relax before the work began.

Thundering Cloud swallowed a slice of salami and spread Brie on a cracker. "We can do two sweat lodge ceremonies. One, for the viators as planned, and then we can do our own the following day. I can still perform the ritual for your viators."

"Great idea," Tate said.

Grayson dripped mustard down his shirt. He dabbed it with a napkin, spreading the thick substance.

Cia laughed. "Money doesn't buy class, does it?"

For a split second everyone was shocked at her crassness, but before there was a chance to react Grayson showed his friends he wasn't insulted. "No. Money doesn't buy class."

Everyone roared in hysterics again.

"I'm filthy," Grayson said, now standing. "Let's go for a swim."

Moments later, fully dressed, he swiftly went through the swinging double doors and jumped into the deep end of the tepid indoor pool.

"I'm game," Shin called out, playfully following.

Thundering Cloud looked at his son and stood. "It's not skinny dipping in the lake, but I bet it'll feel good after all we've been through."

After stripping down to their boxers, father and son did cannon balls into the pool splashing water over the sides. By now, Cia was floating on her back, relaxing her muscles, oblivious to everyone. Shin sat on the lower step in the pool and wrung out her hair. Grayson slowly swam a lap just to stretch out. Exhausted,

Wisdom of the Horse

he hadn't considered how difficult it would be to swim in jeans, a belt, and a flannel shirt.

Shin climbed out of the pool, wrapped an oversized Egyptian cotton towel around herself, and managed to remove her clothes without anyone seeing any parts they had no business seeing. She spotted a large empty tray on the table by the hot tub and grabbed it. A few minutes later she returned from the great room with their food and drinks. The others were out of the pool - clean, refreshed, and ready to polish off what they had started eating before the hilarious uproar.

"Got any smoke?" Thundering Cloud asked Grayson.

Cia was startled. It sounded like college again, but these were grown, respected, spiritual, wise men.

"Always," Grayson answered casually. "Want some?"

Tate answered for his father. "Sounds good."

"Bring enough for all of us," Shin added.

"Not for me. I don't like pot," Cia said. "I'll just get another beer. Anyone else want one?"

"It's not pot. It's Vision Blend. You drank it as tea out at the campfire. We smoke it too," Grayson explained.

"Seriously?" Cia asked.

"It's perfectly legal and there's no marijuana in it. It's a blend of herbs that give you a slight buzz and blissful lightness," Shin explained.

"Vision Blend?" Cia questioned. "That's why I felt so relaxed?"

"Probably," Tate answered.

Cia grinned. "I thought it was just getting away into the wilderness and being with all of you – and the horses."

"That was probably most of it," Shin said, "but the Vision Blend enhanced the feelings you already had. That's what's great about it – it's subtle, but definitely good."

"It's a pain reliever too," Grayson said. He turned a lot of his viators on to it – the ones who didn't want to smoke pot or didn't want to spend that much money on pot.

"I'm not really a smoker. Can you make me another tea of

it?" Cia asked.

"No one waits on anyone here," Grayson said. "You know where the kitchen is. Mugs are to the left of the sink and there's an Insta-Hot in the center island. You'll see the tea strainer next to the mugs – bring it and we'll fill it out here."

Cia liked how Grayson was just a down-to-earth everyday person. Every once in a while it hit her that he was 'rich as shit', but it didn't make him act superior.

Grayson went to his bedroom to discard his wet clothes and slip on a pair of frayed, gray sweat pants and a tee shirt that said, *"Cowboys are bad lovers because they think 8 seconds is a great ride."* By the time he returned, everyone had discarded their clothes and wrapped themselves in plush, oversized Egyptian cotton towels. They were sitting around the table by the hot tub. Thundering Cloud rolled five cigarettes made from the Vision Blend and passed them around. Everyone lit up and relaxed as Cia quietly sipped her tea, eager to feel so relaxed again.

A half-hour later, Shin excused herself to one of the guest suites upstairs. Her eyes grew wide when she walked in and found two queen-size beds constructed of lodge poles and a sitting room with two moss green, overstuffed suede chairs and matching ottomans facing a river rock fireplace. The bathroom had a rustic décor with a sunken tub and a steam shower constructed of copper-colored slate.

Tate, exhausted, wasn't about to go to bed before Grayson or Cia left first – and separately.

Thundering Cloud sprawled out on a padded lounge chair, his hands behind his head, feeling grateful for his own world of modest means and spiritual wealth. He wondered what it was like to be Grayson – a wealthy white man who desperately wanted to be an Indian and says he'd love to have lived in the early 1800's in a tribe with many wives.

Grayson rolled one more Vision Blend cigarette, lit it, took a big hit, and then passed it around

Thundering Cloud chuckled. "*Wasichu's* give ridiculous names to horses and pets."

Wisdom of the Horse

Grayson rolled his eyes. "Any horse will be renamed once Tate spends any time with it. He's renamed at least a half-dozen of ours," he told Cia.

Tate grinned and suggested they go to sleep. His father and Grayson agreed.

"Do you mind if I soak in the hot tub for a while?" Cia asked.

"Go ahead. We won't look. Your bedroom is upstairs at the end of the hall. Everything you need should be there," Grayson said.

Two hours later, Grayson woke, hungry and thirsty. On his way to the kitchen he spotted Cia sprawled out on the wide leather sofa in front of the massive stone fireplace in the great room. She was reading *Spirit Healing*, a book she found on the sculptured elk antler end table.

"Can't sleep?"

"Don't want to,"

"Why?"

"I'm pretending I live here."

"Pardon?"

She pulled a soft, woolen Navajo blanket over her chest and hugged herself. "I'm pretending I live here – in this dream house on this dream farm with all of these Native American and natural artifacts. And being close friends with the Crows. I'm pretending I'm living your wife's life."

Grayson lowered himself into the buckskin chair and looked into her bloodshot eyes. "Envy is your enemy."

"I can't help it," she admitted as she placed the open book face down on the coffee table. "It's easy to say you shouldn't envy anyone when you're the one who has everything you want in the world."

"Material possessions are superficial and don't bring contentment. What I value about my life is my peace of mind and my relationships with people and animals, and my connection with nature and the spiritual world."

"I value those things too, but I have to worry about money

every month." Tears glazed her eyes as she struggled to hold back a real gusher.

Grayson tented his fingers and contemplated his words. Finally, he said in almost a whisper, "Tell Shin these kinds of issues. She'll direct you on how to reach a path to ask the spirit guides for their help."

His message echoed in her mind and soul. She nodded. An instant later she closed her eyes and drifted into a deep sleep.

Chapter 26

Laura woke up in the hotel room in Louisville feeling uneasy. The digital alarm clock read 5:18 A.M. She debated between going back to sleep or calling room service for coffee and French toast. Tossing the blanket aside she realized she had fallen asleep reading the novel that lay open on the fitted sheet. Where had she left off? What was going on in the story? Ah, now she remembered. It was because of the story she closed her eyes to visualize herself in the situation of the character in the book. Laura wanted to see if she could imagine herself killing a man in defense of her daughter. In the book, the mother had intended to incapacitate the rapist who was attacking her daughter, but she wasn't successful and the rapist slashed the mother's arm and torso with the knife he had been holding to the daughter's neck while raping her.

Laura read the pages and thought the woman was crazy to take the chance of incapacitating the man. She closed her eyes and pictured herself in the situation with Heather and saw herself killing the rapist. Apparently she fell asleep before she found out if the mother survived and if the rapist continued with the daughter. She shuddered at the thought. Part of her wanted to throw the novel away, another part wanted to know what happened. Laura had no idea there was a rape in the book. It wasn't the kind of story she would choose to read.

Cali Canberra

Sitting up in bed, she wished she could reach Grayson and ask him to convince Brett to persevere throughout the remainder of the show. Talking man to man, Grayson would encourage Brett to do anything in his power, so long as it was ethical, to achieve his longtime goal of winning a National Championship, the High-Point Horse Achievement Award, and the Amateur Achievement Award. She reminisced about how Grayson had once been such a competitive person in the show ring.

That was before he met Tate and subsequently his father, Thundering Cloud. She thought back to when Grayson met Tate at an equine clinic on relationship training - her husband attended the clinic because his favorite horse, Rambo, (who had always been easy-going) suddenly wouldn't let Grayson catch him in the pasture. After years of riding Rambo, he had to patiently lure the horse with treats or corner him in the pasture and ease up to him with the halter. Then Rambo started turning his hind end to him when he went to the stall to get him out.

Grayson heard about Tate and his Native American horsemanship methods and decided it couldn't hurt to go to a clinic. During the clinic, Grayson bought Tate's book and asked some questions while he was getting it autographed. It was then that he learned Tate's parents lived close to their Oklahoma ranch and Tate visited his parents often. Grayson persuaded Tate to work with him one on one. Tate asked if he could bring his father who was also a skilled horseman, as were many of his elders. Grayson agreed, and that's how he met Thundering Cloud. They've been close friends ever since. Grayson's life changed in ways Laura could never have imagined.

The memory Laura recalled in the hotel room made her heart thud in her chest. She ran her fingers through her hair, thinking about the time Grayson asked her to go on a trail ride because he needed to talk about something. The first two hours of the ride were unusually quiet and uneventful. When they reached the lakeside, Laura spread out a blanket and unpacked the food and wine. After a glass of Merlot, Grayson took her in his arms and began to weep.

Wisdom of the Horse

"What's wrong?" she whispered in his ear.

He lay down on the blanket and took her hand in his. "I got a phone call yesterday from a woman I used to live with. She broke it off with me because she said I was a workaholic and she couldn't take it anymore. Anyway, she never told me she was pregnant with my child – we didn't speak after I moved out. We weren't angry with each other. It's just that I thought she wanted to meet someone who would give her what she needed and there was no point in me staying a part of her life under those circumstances. We went our separate ways and I dove into my work even more until you and I met."

He paused, nervous to see his wife's reaction. She had none - yet.

Grayson continued, studying Laura's face. "Susan, the woman I lived with, called yesterday and informed me I had given her a daughter."

Laura nodded her head calmly, believing he really had been blindsided by Susan. Besides, money wasn't an issue – Grayson should support his daughter.

"As it turns out, my daughter has leukemia. Fortunately, she's been in remission for quite some time." Waiting a moment to let it sink in, his heart fluttered. "The problem now is that her bone marrow is destroyed. Her cells are dying and no new red or white blood cells can be produced. She'll develop anemia, making her more vulnerable to infection which can be fatal. Susan called me because my daughter needs a bone marrow transplant. They can't find a suitably matched donor and she had no alternative but to call me. I'm the most likely to be a correct match, having a tissue type called 'HLA' - Susan isn't a match," he said through tears that made it almost impossible to talk.

Laura held him tight, powerless to stop crying with him. They rocked back-and-forth in each other's arms. There was nothing to consider. "Of course, you'll get tested. You'll help her."

"I have to."

"I know. You have to."

Devastated, Grayson felt like a spear had seared his heart. He didn't even know his daughter – didn't even know she existed until the day before. "Shit," he said, dropping his chin to his chest.

"What?"

"I didn't even ask her name." He collapsed back on to the blanket. "I can't believe I didn't even ask what my own daughter's name is. What kind of a person am I?"

Laura intertwined her fingers through his then leaned back down to hold him. "You're a wonderful person, Grayson. You were shocked at the news of having a teenage daughter and that she's dying."

The word just about killed him. He hadn't digested the word 'dying', although he knew it was the case – unless his bone marrow matched.

"This is the most grueling thing I've ever faced in my life. Worse than any business problems, being sued, losing my parents…worse than anything. She's my flesh and blood," he cried out with anguish.

"I understand."

He held her tight. "I would feel the same way if it was Heather or Brett. I love them. They're like my own – you know that, don't you?"

"I know. And they know. They think of you as their father."

"Why won't they call me Dad, then? Why do they keep calling me Grayson?"

Laura frowned. "I suspect Drew asked them not to. I never felt I should request they call you anything in particular. But I'm certain they love you like a father."

The horses were tied on a picket line and Laura's horse began to paw the ground. Laura reluctantly left Grayson's side and moved her horse to a place with more grass to eat. As she did so, Grayson asked her if she would go with him to the hospital to get tested and to meet his daughter, whatever her name was. Of course, she didn't hesitate to agree.

To everyone's relief, Grayson's bone marrow was a match. He visited his daughter, Lana, daily during her two months of recovery in the hospital. They got to know each other and eventually he was able to get her to talk about what it was like living with leukemia. Once she was released from the hospital, he and Lana saw each other frequently and talked on the phone almost daily. He loved being her father. Laura could see a light in his eyes she had never seen before. The only thing she regretted was that he was away from her and her children so much due to his new relationship.

In May of that year, Grayson bought Lana a brand new, fully loaded, cherry-red Mustang GT for her high school graduation present. A week later, he and Lana went to a Jimmy Buffet concert together. She drove them in her new car. At almost midnight Laura received a frenzied telephone call from Susan. Grayson and Lana were hit head-on by a drunk driver and both were in critical condition. Laura, Heather, and Brett rushed to the emergency room of the hospital. On top of having a head injury and massive contusions, Grayson's heart failed from the stress and panic of pulling his daughter out of the car just before it burst into flames.

Laura would never forget his recounting of what had happened. At first there was pain and suffering, but then he instinctively fought to survive. He felt his body go limp and no more air flowed through him. His heart stopped. At that moment, the moment of death, there was no more pain. He heard himself pronounced dead, then heard a ringing noise and saw a long dark tunnel. He saw his own body and watched the medical team work on him. He met other beings of light and saw his life review that would ultimately help him evaluate his life. During all of this, there was only calmness and peacefulness. He knew that he was dead yet he knew that he still existed. He remembered thinking that it was infinitely more natural not to breathe than to breathe. He became enlightened by the awareness that you are not your body - it's just something you wear while living on the earth. In his moments of death he felt relieved to no longer be encased by the trappings of the earth or be subject to its rules. Yet, he wanted to have another chance to be back with everyone he loved – a chance to live a life of meaning. At some point he reached a barrier to final death and knew he had to go back – to be there for Lana and everyone he loved. In his temporary death he felt joy and peace, but he wanted to return to life as we know it. He was slammed back into his body again, aware of the agony. They called it a medical miracle.

Lana had severe internal injuries including a collapsed lung. After lingering on and suffering for ten days on life-support in intensive care, Lana died with both of her parents at her bedside.

Devastated, Grayson quit his job as director of sales at an advertising agency. A few weeks after losing Lana, he began seeing a grief counselor and realized it was time to reevaluate his life. He needed to decide what kind of survivor he would be. The counselor pointed out how suppressed grief torments you in ways you can't control. Grayson knew himself – he needed to be with people he could express his grief with so that it could be released. He joined a support group in order to learn how to make the process of mourning a healing journey by moving through grief thoughtfully. During his mourning period he discovered that this devastating loss was his challenge to grow. It would require painful change, but his whole life had changed since the moment he found out about Lana's existence. When the death of anyone close to you comes to your door, nothing is ever the same again. There is an emotional wound that needs to be healed through a healthy and positive process.

Eventually, knowing there was no way Grayson would move to Florida, Laura suggested they move to the Oklahoma farm full-time, at least until he knew what he wanted to do with his future. Laura's father had given her the secluded 4,000 acre property her grandfather had homesteaded because she was the only family member who loved the rugged lifestyle, nature, and horses.

Over the years, when Grayson, Laura, Heather, and Brett flew to the Oklahoma farm on weekends, holidays and for the summers, Grayson's horses always let him approach them in the pasture and the stalls. After Lana died and they moved to the farm full-time, the trouble with the horses began. A couple of months

Wisdom of the Horse

later, Grayson met Tate and then Thundering Cloud. Over time, he grew into a kinder, gentler, more compassionate and spiritual being – all because of his friendship with Thundering Cloud and the world he opened up to him.

A year or so after Lana's death, Grayson began talking about how he didn't miss working in the advertising field, but he really missed his former co-worker and best friend, Doug, who had always played hysterical practical jokes. He and Doug were traditionally the life of the party. As bonded as they were when it came to having a good time, Doug wasn't the kind of guy to be there when times were tough. They drifted apart. From time to time, he thought about contacting Doug, but he hadn't taken the initiative.

Eventually, Grayson had the opportunity to sell viatical investments – a business he was drawn to because he could help the terminally ill and their families and make a substantial profit doing so. When he heard about the profitable opportunity, his instinct was to call his old friend and see if he wanted to sell viaticals with him. Laura quickly reminded him that Doug was too much of a happy-go-lucky kind of a guy to sell something so serious. Knowing Doug, he'd find a way to make a joke out of investors profiting from death. Grayson realized immediately that Laura was right. He began selling the investment anyway because he would be able to be at the farm more than he would have with most other business opportunities.

He wasn't a workaholic in the sense of time spent with the actual business. He spent a lot of his time with the terminally ill trying to help them spiritually and giving them an opportunity to enjoy the pleasures of being with the horses and out in nature. He shared lessons with his clients he had learned from the Dalai Lama about how in the moment of death, if we make a special effort to generate a virtuous state of mind, we may strengthen and activate a virtuous karma and so bring about a happy rebirth. As a gift, he gave each of his clients a framed quote from the Dalai Lama saying: "If we wish to die well, we must learn to live well. Hoping for a peaceful death, we must cultivate peace in our mind, and in our way of life."

As Laura sat in bed alone in the Kentucky hotel room, she reminisced about Grayson. She yearned to talk to him. Wide awake, she decided to call room service. Dialing the hotel phone and waiting for them to pick up, she powered on her cell phone even though she wouldn't need it for hours. When the phone powered on it beeped, indicating she had voice mail. Anxious to find out who called, she hung up the hotel phone and pressed the numeral one on her cell phone to connect her to voice mail. The message was from Grayson – he was back home and safe. Laura felt like a twenty-year-old in love for the first time when she heard her husband's voice. It was gentle yet masculine, just as he was as a man, as a husband. She wished Lana hadn't died, but she loved his transformation after losing her. Of course, she loved Grayson when she married him, but there were so many things she had hoped to change about him. Like most wives, she couldn't change him. Life's circumstances changed him to be the best person she could ever imagine. If only his gift of spreading laughter would return.

In Kentucky, it was 5:30 A.M., an hour later than Oklahoma. She debated whether or not to wait for a more reasonable time to call her husband now that she knew she could reach him. He was often awake early, eager to watch the sunrise from the screened porch overlooking the pasture with a large pond. When weather permitted, he'd turn out Chief (formerly Rambo, until Tate renamed him) in the pasture with a couple of geldings so he could admire them as he woke up to freshly brewed coffee and read the news on his laptop. After a few moments' consideration, she decided he wouldn't mind waking an hour or so earlier than usual. He could go back to sleep after they talked if he was still tired. Laura dialed.

"Hello."

Laura hung up, feeling bad about dialing the wrong number at such an ungodly hour. This was another reason why she needed to learn how to enter phone numbers into speed dial on her cell phone. She carefully redialed and confirmed the number on the cell phone screen before she pressed 'send.'

"Hello," the same woman answered on the first ring.

Laura's heart dropped out. Who was this woman answering their phone? She never considered Grayson having an affair, let alone in their house.

"Hello?" Cia repeated.

Laura cleared her throat. "Who is this?" she demanded.

"Cia. Who is this?"

"Let me speak to my husband," she said assertively, hoping it would take several minutes for him to get to the phone.

Cia shook Grayson awake. Groggy, he mumbled something she didn't understand.

She pressed the cordless phone into his hand. "The phone's for you."

"Yeah," Grayson mumbled.

"Who was that?"

"Laura. I'm so glad to hear your voice."

"I asked who answered the phone," she said coldly.

"Oh," he said, suddenly wide awake. "That's a friend of mine."

"That's all you have to say? A friend of yours? You're sleeping with a friend?"

Grayson smiled, not realizing how hurt and angry Laura felt in that moment. "I'm not sleeping with her. We're in the great room. She was sleeping on the sofa and I must have fallen asleep in my chair. You know I always fall asleep here."

Laura hoped his innocence was true. "No sex?"

"Of course not!"

"Not anything intimate?"

"No. Nothing. I swear," he said, feeling bad he made her question him, while flattered that she would think another woman would find him desirable.

Laura took a breath so deep he could hear it over the phone. As she exhaled loudly, she decided to believe him. "I suppose you'll tell me how this happened? Your camping trip cut short and you ending up sleeping," she said drawing out the word, "in the same room as another woman."

"If it makes you feel any better, she's not my type," he said aloud without considering Cia's feelings.

Cia stuck her tongue out at him and then showed him a broad toothy smile to let him know she wasn't mad. She grabbed the phone. "Laura – hi – it's Cia. Your husband didn't come on to me. I didn't come on to him. I seriously doubt he has any interest in me. Plus, I'm happily married anyway."

Before Laura had a chance to respond to the rambling stranger Cia handed the phone back to Grayson and went to the bathroom.

"It's me again," Grayson said.

"She sounds like a lunatic."

"I was thinking the same thing, but as it turns out, she just says what's on her mind. It's kind of charming in its own way."

"Charming?" she said, kidding as if she were jealous.

"Don't worry. If I'm ever going to screw around, it won't be with her."

Laura believed him. "Good to know. Who should I be worried about?"

"No one. I don't want anyone but you."

"Music to my ears." Laura hoped he was being honest.

They spent over an hour on the phone catching up about what had happened the previous day and evening, including that she had given Brett permission, and the funding, to go into a partnership with Greg Bordeaux.

Chapter 27

Thundering Cloud took a shower while Shin and Tate went to the pasture with the horses. Grayson grabbed a two pound bag of carrots, slipped on an old pair of shoes, and joined them.

Considering the horse's workouts over the previous twenty-four hours, and the one coming up to ride to the sweat lodge, Grayson suggested they give all of the horses Bounce Back with their morning grain.

"What's that?" Cia asked.

"It helps horses recover from hard work and from injury," Shin explained. Her parents fed the supplement to rehab horses.

"We use it all the time," Grayson said. "Laura started using it and it worked wonders. Now all the horses get it when they're in rigorous training or competition. I've never heard of anyone not happy with the results."

"Is it like Conquer?" Tate asked. He had been giving Canku Conquer ever since it came on the market.

"No," Grayson said. "I use Conquer on two of my retired broodmares, though. Conquer is a hyaluronic acid, whereas Bounce Back is an herbal supplement for joint support. It's great for convalescing animals. It's designed to make them more comfortable."

Grayson returned to the house, took a long, hot shower, shaved, and dressed. While the others showered and dressed, he made a second pot of coffee and called Brett in Kentucky. Grayson convinced him to ride in the classes he had entered, especially after what had happened to Accomplice, his reining horse. Grayson said that if he wanted to stop showing after the Nationals that was understandable, but he should at least go out with a bang, if possible. He reminded Brett that reaching that level of achievement was something he had worked toward for years and it would be ridiculous not to compete when he and Campala were there - ready, willing, and able.

Brett didn't say so, but part of him hoped that they did poorly because it would be easier to walk away from the show world. The other part of him wanted to do well; to at least win one championship or reserve championship. If that happened, he could say he stopped because he wanted to - not because he and his horse didn't make the grade.

Brett told Grayson how excited he was to become involved with Greg. As a silent partner, he would have very little work to do. Greg preferred to continue operating the business alone. He simply needed capital. Brett wanted to start earning a living, and Greg agreed to pay him a percentage of the after-tax profits for ten years. Brett thought the arrangement was ideal because it would allow him plenty of time to train and condition Accomplice and Casino for competitive trail riding and he could help with the rescue horses.

Grayson would love to have Brett work with him in operating the hospice and equine rescue program, but he had to talk to Laura about it. He didn't suggest the idea to Brett, wanting to discuss the pros and cons with Laura first. They were already concerned that it seemed he had little interest in being out in the real world, so to speak. Working full-time at the new enterprise would isolate him in a way he'd never experienced before.

Grayson wished Brett luck at the show and said win or lose, he was proud of him, and he should enjoy himself.

Chapter 28

Cia was deciding which horse to ride. She couldn't ride Maya today – the mare wasn't in condition to ride again for at least a week after the adventure of the previous day and night. Temptation, the most affectionate horse toward Cia, would have to be ridden in a cut-back English saddle because of his high-set withers and long back, but Cia was afraid to be without a horn on a horse she had never ridden. The next easiest horse could be ridden English or Western, but that horse made her feel uncomfortable with his indifference toward her. She was afraid he wouldn't behave if he didn't even like her when she was on the ground.

Thundering Cloud suggested Cia ride Temptation, the Quarter Horse gelding, since she felt a connection.

"I agree with Dad," Shin said. "Anyway, you learned to ride bareback and you did great. You've got good balance."

Finally, Cia chose Temptation. The horses were already immaculate and their feet had been cleaned. Bruce, the farm manager, tacked up the gelding and then gave Cia a leg up and adjusted the stirrup leathers for her. Cia cued Temptation as she did Maya and Cabaret. Temptation responded equally well. Her apprehension vanished and the pleasure showed on her face.

Shin and Cia rode together behind the men so they could talk alone.

"You look deep in thought," Shin said.

"Yeah," Cia replied. "I've got a big decision to make."

"About?"

"Jeffrey has a business opportunity that he doesn't want to pass up and it would require us to relocate."

"Isn't that good news? I thought you didn't like living here."

"I don't like living here. Or, I should say, I didn't. But now that I'm in therapy with you and taking care of Ambra and horseback riding, I'm starting to like it. In fact, I love it. Except the town. I'm getting so much out of our relationship and the experiences with the horses, and I don't want to lose all that. But, then again, I can't stand this town and Jeffrey not being able to earn a good living and all the limitations revolved around not having enough money."

"It must feel good to finally know you at least have an option. Until now, you felt stuck, as if your life could never be different."

"Now I see my life can be different. In fact, it is different from when I first came to you. But in one way, I still feel stuck in this town," she said. She wished she could explain herself, but she couldn't tell Shin that she was afraid of taking the chance of moving and being discovered.

"Where would you move?"

"Somewhere out west."

"That sounds great. I'd come visit you if it was somewhere pretty."

"Do you think the Martins would sell Ambra to me if I have the money?"

"No way. Jane told her parents, her doctors, and everyone else that Ambra and the foal she's carrying are the only reason she's able to push herself so hard to heal and move on with her life. The whole family is hoping Ambra has a stud colt to replace their stallion that perished."

Wisdom of the Horse

"I didn't think about Jane. I feel so insensitive. Anyway, I'm going to hate to give Ambra up. Elizabeth and I are so attached already. And it would be so cool to be there when she has her baby and to raise a foal."

"I understand. Maybe you'll get the opportunity with another broodmare though. By the way, now that Ambra's walking sound again, I would think you could ride her as long as you take it easy," Shin said, referring to the mild case of founder.

"Really? We would love that! Your mom's Chinese herbs really did work on her. It's amazing. To be honest, I didn't put much faith in the idea of herbal remedies for something so serious."

Shin shooed a fly off of Cabaret's neck. "It's obvious that your own change in diet and the herbs are working. You must be out of most of your pain also."

"I don't have any physical pain," Cia said, never expecting to say the words. "Your mom knows what she's doing with all that Chinese medicine and energy balancing. Meditating has helped release my pain and relieves a lot of stress."

"Good. Anyway, in regards to you possibly moving, I'm sure you could find another therapist you're comfortable with."

"What if I don't? And what if I can't buy a horse? What if I can't find a place like your parents' and I can't be around horses anymore? There's so much to worry about if we move."

"Are those the things you're worried about?"

"Yes," Cia said, unable to tell the whole truth.

"It's a big decision. You have to choose between the known and the unknown. With the unknown, you'll at least have money, therefore more opportunity to make things happen."

"I know."

The horses began trotting without being prompted. Cia lost her balance and got a little scared.

"You need to learn better balance both in life and on horseback," Shin said.

Cia furrowed her brows as she regained her composure on Temptation. "You said I had good balance."

"For a beginner, you do. But you've got more to learn and you need practice. It's critical for your physical and emotional health. For harmony in life and on horseback, you must be balanced."

"I thought I was balanced on horseback," Cia said insecurely.

"For walking and cantering when a horse isn't acting up, you're fine. It's much more difficult to be balanced when trotting because of the difference in how the horse moves. The lengthening and shortening of the body is different, and how the horse's feet land is different. Besides, I meant that for a beginner your balance is good, but you really need to perfect it."

"Why? I'm not going to compete. If trotting is harder, I just won't trot."

Shin laughed. "It's not always your choice if the horse is going to trot. It may only be a few strides until you bring the horse back to a walk or push it back to a canter, but horses trot on their own all the time."

"Oh."

"You need better balance for safety. Look at it this way: if you were walking on a wide bridge you wouldn't need that much balance. But if you were on a narrow bridge with no railings you would need more balance. The narrower the bridge, the greater the balance you would need because the exposure to danger is more severe. The greater the exposure, the greater the potential for loss – and for gain."

"For gain? How would there be a potential for gain when you're risking safety?"

"The gain is in the confidence and the adrenaline rush derived from the achievement. If you had been on the narrow cliff with my brother and dad, you probably wouldn't have survived because your balance is not perfected like theirs is. Your lack of balance would throw your horse out of balance and in a situation like they were in, it could have been fatal. Right now, for instance, if Temptation startled or did a crow hop or a fast 180 degree turn and took off running, your balance would probably not be sufficient to keep you from falling off. You never know

Wisdom of the Horse

what will happen where you'll need a perfected sense of harmony and balance. Or, how would you like to be responsible for a horse to be sore and possibly develop an injury because you ride with too much weight onto one side? It would be like you carrying a fifty pound purse on your right shoulder for hours on end and never getting relief. What do you think that would do to your body?"

"I'd have to compensate to balance the purse. But I'm human. A horse is huge. I don't think it would matter that much if I lean a certain direction."

"That's where you're wrong. Very wrong. Anyway, let's work on learning how to trot."

Cia thought Shin was exaggerating, but she didn't voice her opinion. "You make it look so easy."

"Let me show you how to sit a trot," Shin told Cia and then explained what she was doing.

Cia tried, but found herself sliding in the saddle and coming down too hard on Temptation's back, just as Shin had expected she would.

"Actually, it's easier to post at a trot because the horse's back will push you out of the saddle and you'll feel the diagonal much easier. I'll teach you how to post."

Cia held Temptation back as Shin trotted off. "No. I'm not ready," she yelled out.

Shin circled around at a trot and then brought Cabaret back to a walk. "You cantered yesterday."

"I know, but that was easy – you just sit your ass down and move with the horse," Cia said. "Posting is too hard. Don't push me."

"Are you afraid of falling?"

"Yes. Of course. And of looking stupid."

"Don't worry about how you look. You won't be a real horseperson until you take your first fall. Everyone knows that," Shin said lightly.

"I'm not taking a chance of ruining the rest of this trip by getting hurt. Let me do what I'm comfortable with," Cia pleaded.

Cali Canberra

They walked at a brisker pace, Cia developing more confidence and gaining a better seat the longer she rode English. She didn't comment once about not having a horn. They talked more about Ambra's emotional and physical progress. The mare was now eating enough to gain weight, but she still wouldn't tolerate anyone except Elizabeth to walk directly up to her and pet her. Everyone else still had to slowly ease their way closer to her with their hands out in a non-threatening manner. If, and only if, Ambra extended her neck toward them and sniffed at their hands, could they continue slowly proceeding toward her and pet her. The transformation from leeriness to acceptance was undisputed when Ambra lowered her head and licked her lips. Cia was certain she and her daughter also experienced a positive transformation since Ambra and Heyoka were under their care.

Cia told Shin about Elizabeth playing fetch with Heyoka in the paddock and Ambra watching the ball so closely, the brilliance returning to her eyes. She said Ambra didn't even mind it when Heyoka kept running under her belly to retrieve the ball, so finally, Elizabeth crawled under her several times, and Ambra was aware but not phased.

Shin continued to wonder why Cia's daughter never came outside when she visited. On two occasions she had brought gifts for the girl - first an age-appropriate book about horses, and then homemade chocolate-covered strawberries. She couldn't imagine Cia not bringing Elizabeth outside to receive the gifts or at least have her come out to thank her. The child didn't even come outside for the paddock cleansing ceremony. Most children would have had a natural curiosity and want to join in the dancing, drumming, and burning of herbs. Shin assumed the reason Cia never invited her into the house was because she was embarrassed about the meager furnishings. It certainly wasn't a lack of hospitality. Cia always served cold beverages and healthy snacks and they'd relax on lawn chairs in Ambra's paddock, talking for as long as she would stay.

Finally, Shin asked the question she had been wondering about for quite some time. "Why don't you ever talk about

Wisdom of the Horse

Elizabeth unless it has to do with Ambra or Heyoka?"

"I don't want to," she responded mechanically.

"That's probably because it's one of the most important things you need to address. Do you have a bad relationship?"

Cia didn't answer.

"Cia, I need to know so that I can help you."

She tensed up and offered no reply.

"Have you taken your depression out on your daughter? If you've abused her, I promise – I won't report you. I'll help you deal with the frustrations that led to the abuse so it can stop. I promise – I just want to help."

Cia's eyes widened. She finally responded. "I've never harmed Elizabeth! I've never even thought about it. I love that child."

"What is it, then?" Shin asked gently.

"I don't want to talk about it."

Shin stopped her horse. It was time for tough love. "If you don't tell me the truth right now, I'm going to canter off as fast as Cabaret will go, meet up with the men, and we'll all ditch you. You'll be on your own out in the wilderness," Shin said unethically, but not meaning it.

"You would do that to me?"

"Test me. I'm counting to five and then taking off if you don't spill your guts about whatever it is with you and your daughter. One – two – three…"

"Fine! My daughter is deathly afraid to leave our house. She had anxiety attacks when we tried to push her, so we stopped and she got worse. Until Ambra and Heyoka came, she wouldn't even take one step outside. It's been a huge accomplishment for her to just go to the paddock - and as you saw, she won't come outside if anyone else is there. She's petrified of strangers."

Shin rode up close and hugged Cia the best she could from horseback. "I'm sorry to hear it, but it's not that horrible. You'll do things to get her over her fears and then everyone will live a normal life."

"She'll never get over her fear. We've tried everything we've read about in books and on the internet. Don't get me wrong - I love her with all my heart, but I thought I'd raise a child, do all the things moms and their daughters do, then she'd go off and live her own life as an adult and hopefully give me grandkids. I won't have any of that."

Shin became suspicious. The story was certainly sad and frustrating, but she suspected there was more to it. "Why haven't you talked about this before?"

"I just didn't want to."

"Why not? Elizabeth is an incredible part of your life. We need to talk about your feelings. Like you said, you thought you'd do all the things mothers and daughters do. I don't suppose you've been able to do much of anything most mothers and daughters do."

"I'm missing out on so much. And so is my husband."

"I'm confident we can get your daughter over her fear. It may take some time, but we'll get there. You just need professional help. We'll talk about it in our sessions."

Cia cried so hard she bounced in the saddle. Each time she landed on his back, Temptation flicked his ears in agitation and threw his head in the air.

"Let's get off for a while. I need to stretch," Shin said diplomatically.

Cia was glad to straighten her sore legs. She continued sobbing and when her nose started running she had nothing to wipe it with. Shin suggested that she use her horse's tail. Cia laughed at the idea, almost forgetting she was so upset. Not wanting to use her clothes, she used Temptation's tail to wipe her nose. It smelled surprisingly good.

They hand walked their horses for a while, stretching their legs and talking. Eventually, Cia confided that she felt guilty about putting Jeffery in a life to support an unhappy wife and child.

"You're not as unhappy as before you started seeing me, are you?"

"No. Actually, not nearly. At least I'm not thinking I want to be dead anymore. But still…"

Wisdom of the Horse

"Sometimes your thoughts are your own worst enemy. You shouldn't feel guilty. Having a child with an emotional problem or phobia is not your fault any more than it's your husband's fault," Shin said, her arm now wrapped around Cia.

Cia stopped walking and turned away. "It is my fault."

Shin stopped beside her. "It's not. Stop blaming yourself."

"You don't understand."

"Try to make me understand."

Cia tossed her reins to Shin, sat down on the ground, and covered her face with her shaking hands as she once again cried uncontrollably. Shin gave her a few minutes to purge the repressed tears from her system. She found two trees nearby to tie the horses. Temptation was outfitted with a halter under her bridle for such an event, and Cabaret wore a bitless bridle. Shin took two extra long lead ropes out of her saddle pack and tied the horses with quick-release knots. This far away from Grayson's, if they got loose the worst thing they would do was run at full speed to the men and their horses, which were still within sight, albeit far in the distance.

Back at Cia's side, she sat down and put her arm around her. "Tell me everything. You're still holding something in," she said, studying her face.

"I can't tell you."

"Yes, you can. Whatever you're keeping buried has gotten to where it consumes you. It's both pain and an excuse to not live your life. It's pain in that you hate whatever happened that you feel like you have to hide, but it's also become a handy excuse for not reaching the challenge of being productive and progressing through life in a normal and happy way."

"You'll call the police."

"I won't. I promise."

"No matter what?"

"I told you. If you've abused your daughter I won't call the police. I'll help you stop."

"I didn't abuse her. Neither did Jeffery."

"Then what?"

There was silence for quite a while as Cia's face was lost in thought. The secret she tried to bury churned inside again. Blood drained from her face as she whispered, "I kidnapped Elizabeth when she was a toddler."

Chapter 29

"We've always been so worried her biological parents would recognize her that we kept her in hiding until we moved to Oklahoma. By then she was afraid of being around other people and of going outside because she was afraid a stranger might come. We didn't mean to make her afraid."

Astonished, adrenaline raced through Shin's veins. She swallowed hard, unsure of how to respond. Finally, all she could say was, "Seriously?"

"Yes. That's why this is all so messed up. I love Elizabeth, but now Jeffrey and I are going to live our entire lives in hiding and raising this emotionally disturbed child that's not even ours."

Still in shock and with a million questions reeling through her mind, the first thing Shin asked was how and why they kidnapped a child. Cia told her story.

When living in Santa Fe, New Mexico, she and Jeffrey had tried to have a baby for two years. Eventually, they went to a fertility specialist who discovered severe endometriosis that affected both the fertilization of the egg and implantation of the embryo in her uterus. Spending more than she earned in a year, they went through invitro fertilization three times with no success. Heartbroken, they still yearned to have children and knew the adoption process for infants was incredibly difficult and could

Cali Canberra

take years.

On a summer day when they were heading back home to Santa Fe from a week long beachside vacation in Corpus Christie, Texas, they stopped at a convenience store on the outskirts of San Antonio to use the restroom and buy sodas. While there, they saw a toddler in the rear seat of an unlocked car, unattended. They looked around for what felt like quite some time, waiting for the parents to return to the car, which they didn't.

In one spontaneous moment when the child started crying, Cia reached into the car's open window, unhooked the seatbelt, and rescued the child. Initially, her instinct was to simply calm the child until the parents returned – and she wanted to chew them out for leaving the child alone. Before Jeffrey knew it, Cia was in their car cradling this sweet smelling child in her arms. The child stopped crying immediately. Without another word, Jeffrey jumped in the car and turned on the ignition. He looked to his wife in shock. One word turned their lives upside down. "Drive!" she demanded.

Jeffrey drove away inconspicuously as Cia held the child in her arms, feeling the little heart beat, seeing the trusting eyes staring up at her as if she were the most important person in the world.

Shin held Cia's trembling hand. "No one followed you?"

"Jeffrey kept looking in the rear view mirror and nothing happened."

"I can't believe the parents didn't call the police and have a search party out or something." A level of discomfort she had never experienced crawled on her skin.

Cia looked her in the eye for the first time since they had brought up anything about her daughter. "We never even heard anything on the news or read anything in the newspapers about a kidnapping. We felt so lucky. You wouldn't believe how scared we were. But still, we were worried someone would recognize Elizabeth. We basically avoided letting her be seen by anyone. It was so difficult to live that way. After a few years we moved here because it's so small and isolated, but we're still scared someone will recognize her if she looks anything like her biological mother or father."

Shin still had a million questions. "What did you tell everyone you knew about where this baby came from out of the blue?"

"We said we had an opportunity to adopt her. No one questioned it since they knew about my inability to get pregnant."

Shin shook her head. "Your parents even believed you?"

"My parents don't speak to me because I married Jeffrey. So, they don't know about Elizabeth. Jeffrey's parents died when he was very young. His legal guardian used their life insurance to keep him in boarding schools most of his life."

"Didn't friends ask how you got a baby so quickly?"

Cia shook her head in reply. "No one asked. They were just happy for us."

Shin's thoughts spun a million miles a minute. There was a long silence she didn't know how to break. She didn't know what to do from this point forward. Eventually she spoke. "We need to get back riding to catch up with everybody else."

They mounted the horses.

A storm raged in Cia's mind. She still didn't feel a weight lifted off her shoulders because Shin didn't know the whole truth about her and Jeffrey being in hiding. They were already in hiding and on the run when she kidnapped Elizabeth. But that was because of Jeffrey. Until he was caught, Cia thought her husband earned his living by custom developing and manufacturing electronics devices and computer programs. It wasn't far from the truth, but she had no idea how he had used his degree and knowledge from MIT.

And she had no idea he was putting hundreds of thousands of dollars into a foreign bank account. She thought he earned $200,000 a year and was perfectly content to live with their combined income.

After Jeffrey's arrest she found out he and a few MIT associates actually made a living by traveling around the country and electronically tripping slot machines to make them pay off. When she bailed him out of jail he promised her he'd never break the law again. With the help of a top-notch lawyer, he plea bargained with the authorities. He surrendered all of their assets and cash and he testified against his accomplices. Ever since, they've been in the witness protection program, but they worried there could be payoffs and leaks – his associates lost too much not to hold a grudge. He feared his associates (who each pulled down over a million dollars a year, tax free) would retaliate if they knew where he was.

While Cia thought she was happily married to a successful entrepreneur, she had been a talented artist with a gift for painting murals and unique high-end faux finishing. It had taken over two years for her to get fairly steady work through interior designers and referrals and she had just begun building a nice portfolio when Jeffrey was arrested. Now she couldn't pursue her career because she could no longer be bonded and insured with her fake identity and they would need to live in, or near, a large and affluent population which they could not afford financially or for the risk of being found.

Jeffrey encouraged Cia to at least paint on canvas for personal pleasure, but she didn't want to work on such a limited and small scale. Her heart wasn't even into trying. At this point, all she really wanted out of life was to go back to being Jordan and Sarah Mathews, living where they wanted to, with legitimate careers, a nice house, health insurance, credit cards, friends, and their daughter. If only Elizabeth were their real daughter.

Until meeting Shin, feeling imprisoned by their limited and suffocating world, life had become a nightmare. Sometimes she felt that living a lie and knowing they would be living a lie for the rest of their lives was far greater punishment than being childless and Jeffrey going to prison.

Chapter 30

"You're going to turn us in, aren't you?" Cia asked, referring only to the kidnapping.

As she spoke, reality struck her down as powerfully as a tornado - she and Jeffrey didn't have much of an exit plan. In the event they needed to pick up and leave in an emergency, they hid a thousand dollars in a five pound coffee can, but they hadn't discussed where they would go or how they would get there, assuming they couldn't drive their own vehicles. Now Cia had caused the likely emergency and there was no way to warn Jeffrey about what she had done. When he suggested she try therapy, he trusted her to not to put their secret lives in jeopardy.

Her heart raced. Her hands began to tingle. What had she done? Had she blown the Jeffrey's opportunity to start a new life for their family? Where would they go if they had the chance to get away?

Shin didn't answer and Cia didn't have the guts to ask again.

The women returned to the trail. In the distance, they saw the men heading back toward them.

"Keep walking. I'm going to tell them we're okay. I'll be back," Shin said. Shook up from her patient's confession, she wasn't thinking clearly. She assumed Temptation wouldn't follow when she asked Cabaret to sprint into a gallop.

Cali Canberra

Temptation took off following Cabaret. Cia stayed on by grabbing hold of his mane and relaxing her body as Shin had ingrained in her. "Relax your body and then relax the horse," Shin had said over and over. It worked. Cia moved in rhythm with the stride and didn't pull back on the reins. Shin heard pounding hoof beats behind her and continued to gallop as she turned around to make sure Cia was okay. Out of Cia's control, Temptation closed the gap between himself and Cabaret. Cia smiled from ear to ear in spite of what was just discussed. Within moments the horses galloped at a nice smooth pace next to each other, and for several moments Cia couldn't think about anything else except for how free she felt riding like the wind.

~ ~ ~ ~ ~

Now that Shin knew why Cia was an emotional wreck, there was so much to consider. She had promised Cia that no matter what her secret was, she wouldn't tell. She was a therapist and there were confidentiality issues. This was not a plan for a future crime to be committed. When she pressured Cia to confess her secret she couldn't have known it would be that someone's child had been stolen. Another family was suffering and wondering if their child was dead or alive, safe or abused, happy or sad. She couldn't decide whether or not she should tell her father and get his advice. What if he turned Cia in? She had no idea how he would feel about an issue like this. If anything, perhaps she would wait and talk to her mother about it.

Chapter 31

Laura and Heather nibbled on lunch in the sky box as they thumbed through the show program looking for the two-page color advertisement picturing Brett showing Campala at the Regional Championships – he had won Reserve Champion and they were advertising for the public to look for the team at the U.S. Arabian Nationals. Before they found the ad, Laura got a call from Grayson's office on her cell phone.

Misty, Grayson's secretary, was frantic. Tim Tortola, Grayson's business partner, was in his office with an FBI agent.

"I can't reach Grayson. I don't know what to do," Misty added hysterically.

Laura gasped. She swallowed, but her mouth was dry. "The FBI?"

"Yes."

"Why is the FBI questioning Tim?"

"I don't know. The agent was looking for Grayson but since he's not here –"

Laura cut her off. "Looking specifically for Grayson?"

"Yes," Misty answered. "The agent asked if Grayson was here. I said I didn't expect him back until late next week and then he said he has your address in Oklahoma."

"He'll never find him – he's camping with some friends and

some viators. I better call the farm manager and tell him not to let them know where they are."

"Isn't that obstructing justice? I think they can arrest you for that."

Laura hesitated. "I'm not obstructing anything."

By now, Heather had caught the gist of the phone call. Her stepfather was the most honest person she knew and he couldn't hurt a fly. Whatever this was about was all a mix up. She was absolutely certain – as certain as her mother must be.

"Are you sure that's what you want to do?" Misty asked in a disapproving voice.

Laura looked to the ceiling. She took a deep breath and long exhale as she gathered her thoughts. "I don't want to ruin their trip – not just my husband's, but everyone's."

Misty didn't know Laura well enough to give her personal opinion. "It's your husband."

"Please tell Tim to call me on my cell as soon as he can," Laura said, then abruptly disconnected the call. Her thoughts wandered a dozen directions as dead silence hung in the air.

Heather racked her brain trying to think of whether or not she had ever heard anyone in the family talk about knowing a criminal attorney. Nothing rung a bell. They weren't that kind of family. They certainly used lawyers enough for business matters, but never criminal that she knew of. She didn't recall Grayson or her mother mentioning a friend or distant family member being a criminal lawyer either. Whom should they call? Regardless of knowing that Grayson couldn't have done anything wrong, she knocked over her can of soda from the coffee table as she jolted out of the chair and began to pace.

A few minutes later Laura tried to call Bruce, the farm manager. There was no answer and the answering machine didn't pick up. He had probably left the cordless phone off the hook and run the battery dead. It was a bad habit he had, making it frustrating when they needed to reach him by phone because he rarely turned on his cell phone, not wanting to be interrupted while riding or from whatever he was working on.

Wisdom of the Horse

Laura finally told Heather everything Misty had said. They agreed that they needed to get their pilot to fly them back to the farm as quickly as possible. Laura and Heather knew where the group would be. They'd ride out, find Grayson, and tell him what was happening.

"What about Brett?" Heather asked as an afterthought.

They opened the sliding door of the sky box as the announcer called in a Western Pleasure class. Heather looked in the show program and realized they had missed Brett's class. All the work he had done and the stress he had gone through, and now they missed seeing him compete. The women haphazardly gathered their personal belongings from the sky box. They wouldn't be returning. With bags full of merchandise and brochures in tow, they headed for the barn to find Brett. Huffing and puffing from the brisk pace and carrying so much, they discussed whether or not they should tell Brett the truth and take him back with them or if they should concoct another story, leaving him undistracted to compete in the class that evening and the class the following morning. Almost completely out of breath, they agreed to be honest with Brett and let him make the decision on his own to compete or return home.

Brett stood beaming outside the stall as he hung the Championship ribbon and the garland of flowers he and Campala had won. Laura approached him with tears streaming down her face, partly in pride seeing he had won, partly regretful that she hadn't seen it even though she was less than a hundred feet away. She hated to ruin his 'moment' when she told him she and Heather were leaving and why. He'd need to make a decision about what he wanted to do.

Chapter 32

Early that morning, Joel, one of Grayson's farm hands, drove out to the camp in a loaded down 4WD Suburban to set up. First, he began burning wood and heating rocks for the sweat lodge. After stoking the fire, he set up the tents and put sleeping bags and pillows inside. After eating lunch, he arranged folding canvas chairs around the fire pit. His last morning chores were to sweep the debris off the picnic tables and set the coolers of food and drinks out, along with the paper goods.

Later in the afternoon, Grayson, Shin, Tate, Thundering Cloud, and Cia arrived invigorated in spite of having had very little sleep, a busy morning, and a long ride. Grayson thanked Joel for the work he had done and told him to relax until they needed him for the sweat lodge ceremony. Joel asked if he could ride Chief for a while. Grayson agreed so long as he restricted the ride to a walk and stayed away from the rocky areas once he crossed the bridge over the nearby river.

Now that they were at camp, it dawned on Cia that she needed to decide between staying close to Shin to make sure she wasn't telling anyone else about her crime, or taking time alone to assess her options.

Wisdom of the Horse

~ ~ ~ ~ ~

"You know how everything your clients tell us is intended to be in confidence?" Thundering Cloud asked Grayson.

"Yeah."

"Is there any reason we couldn't broach a confidential subject with a client?"

Grayson frowned. "What do you mean?"

Shin didn't seem to have any more of a clue than Grayson did as to what her father was trying to say. This wasn't like him.

"This reminds me of high school," Thundering Cloud said. "but this is important," he said to Grayson.

"What? Spit it out!"

"Cia told Shin something that very well might have a critical connection with something Cynthia told us."

Shin was really confused now. "Cynthia? What's she got to do with this?"

"We're all trustworthy. We need to forget any confidences. What exactly are you getting at?" Grayson asked his friend.

"This is for the greater good if my instincts are correct," Thundering Cloud said as he rubbed the stubble on his chin. "Do you remember what Cynthia used to do for a living?"

"How could I forget?"

"Do you remember the story about the time when her car broke down? The reason she was fired from her job?"

"How could I forget?" he said once again.

Shin was still in the dark.

"Cia kidnapped a kid seven years ago," Thundering Cloud said as if it weren't any big deal. "The kid that was stolen from Cynthia just very well might be the kid Cia and her husband kidnapped. Cynthia said it happened in San Antonio, didn't she?"

San Antonio was not what Grayson thought about. "Cia kidnapped her daughter?"

"Yes," Shin said. "Cia's daughter is almost nine years old. When she was kidnapped no one seemed to be looking for her – at least it wasn't on the news or in the newspaper. Can you two please tell me what on earth you're talking about?"

Once Grayson considered the correlation, he told Shin the story. Cynthia was a registered pediatric nurse. After she worked in a hospital for a couple of years, and then for a pediatrician, she was approached by a man who claimed she could make over a hundred thousand dollars a year using her skills but not working very many hours. Skeptical, she heard the man out. He was a lawyer who specialized in private adoptions. She took the job, part of which was to get unwed pregnant women to give up their babies for adoption. The firm paid all of the pregnant women's living expenses, doctor's bills, and hospital bills. After the birth and turning over the baby, the biological mother received $10,000 to start a fresh life.

Cynthia made most of the arrangements. She also took possession of the babies and took them to the lawyer's office if it was a local adoption, or if it was an adoption out-of-state, she took the baby to the adoptive parents. The lawyer handled all of the legal documents and financial issues. Cynthia was paid $10,000 for each successful placement. The adoptive parents paid a minimum of $50,000 in legal fees for the adoption – and some up to $100,000.

Once, the lawyer assigned her an unusual case - the placement of an eighteen-month old girl. Cynthia spent time with the unwed mother and then made all of the arrangements. A few days later, she picked up the little girl in her own car, as she always had - and then her car broke down on the interstate. There was no cell phone signal and she didn't want to wait for police. She wasn't too far from an exit, so Cynthia carried the little girl and the car seat and walked to a convenience store. She used the pay phone to call the lawyer so that he could make arrangements to pick them up. No one answered the office line or the lawyer's cell phone.

It occurred to Cynthia to call the adoptive parents, but then she remembered she had left their phone number in her briefcase in her car. She pleaded with the only employee in the store to let her borrow her car just long enough for her to retrieve the phone

Wisdom of the Horse

number. The woman was hesitant, and before she made a decision, Cynthia realized she must have locked her keys in her car—resulting in the impossibility of getting the phone number. She called information, but the telephone operator said it was an unlisted number. She kept trying to call her office, but still there was no answer. They must have been out to lunch or in a meeting.

By then, the child squirmed uncontrollably in her arms and she wouldn't stay in the car seat Cynthia put on the floor. She couldn't let the toddler walk around or she'd pull everything off the shelves. There was no alternative except to ask the employee if she could put the child in her car, strapped in the car seat with the windows down, while she kept trying to call her boss. The employee handed over the car key; Cynthia strapped the little girl in and gave her a small cuddly stuffed bear she had thought to carry in her purse. She went back-and-forth between the car and the pay phone. Still, she couldn't reach anyone. She assumed the little girl was hungry and thirsty so she searched the store for something relatively healthy to eat and drink. Cynthia wasn't worried about the child's safety because the majority of the time she had a view of the car from most places in the store - and in all that time only a few customers came inside the convenience store. While Cynthia was inside, she noticed a married couple for a few moments, but they came and went quickly.

Before returning to the car with the food and drink, Cynthia attempted to reach the lawyer one more time. This time, the receptionist answered but put her on hold before Cynthia had a chance to say anything. Finally, the lawyer took her call. Cynthia told him everything. He was glad she didn't call the police for assistance with her car and insisted he'd be there as quickly as he could. It would be about an hour from his office in San Marcos, which was midway between San Antonio and Austin. She didn't know how long she was on the phone, but it didn't seem long. When she stepped outside and approached the car she saw the child was gone. She almost collapsed. How could she have done this? She rushed back inside and asked the employee if she saw anything; she hadn't, she was stocking shelves. The employee said they should call the police. Cynthia had a feeling that the lawyer would want to know first. She said she'd call the police from the payphone, but she called the lawyer first and explained what had happened. He insisted she not call the police no matter what the store employee said and assured her he'd get there as quickly as humanly possible.

In less than forty minutes the lawyer arrived and swept her away without a word to the convenience store employee. He told her they couldn't call the police – there was a chance that if his practices were investigated, although it was unfair, it could be construed that the way he handled the adoptions was not legal because of the amount of money his firm made from the transactions. The lawyer convinced her to take $100,000 severance pay and to keep her mouth shut. Cynthia was very worried about the child's safety, but the lawyer convinced her that if someone stole the child it was because they wanted to raise her – to take good care of her and give her a good home. Not totally convinced, and not at all comfortable, she took the check and never contacted the lawyer again. She assumed he called the adoptive parents and told them the mother had changed her mind. If Cia's daughter was the same child - and it sounded like she must be - that was the explanation as to why no child had been reported missing or kidnapped.

Shin, Thundering Cloud, and Grayson agreed that Cynthia needed to tell her story to Cia. If this was in fact the same little girl, Cynthia would at least die with the peace of mind knowing the child had a safe and loving home. She had always thought her illness was a result of karmic forces and that she was being punished for losing the little girl in her custody. Cia and Jeffrey could live without guilt and without the fear of being caught. There would be no need to remain in hiding in the small, remote town with little opportunity.

~ ~ ~ ~ ~

Cia's arm tired from grooming the horses. She returned to

Wisdom of the Horse

the campfire and happened to be near Grayson when he retrieved his cell phone from his saddle pack. Without pause, chills ran down her arms, bile rose in her throat, and fear consumed her. She had assumed there was no means of communication since there hadn't been the previous day. She and Shin hadn't spoken again about her crime and now she wondered if Shin had used Grayson's cell phone to notify the police. She thought she'd have two days before she were in real jeopardy if Shin felt an obligation to turn her in.

Grayson called Bruce to give him the go-ahead to bring the viators. After he hung up the phone he looked at Cia appraisingly. He bit his lip as if he were considering something important. Finally, he asked, "Do you believe things happen for a reason?"

Convinced he must know of her crime, her face flushed, "Most of the time. Why?" She waited for him to tell her he knew what she had done.

Grayson did his best to sound casual. "Shin said you hate the house you're renting and that it's a little dilapidated."

"That's an understatement." Thoughts floated in her mind about how she may have blown their option to move out west.

"Well, the property I bought for the hospice and equine rescue program has an old house on it. It needs a good amount of work, but you and your family are welcome to move in and really make it your home. Fix it up the way you'd want. Under the carpeting there are old, plank hard wood floors. If you want the carpet removed, and want to do the work to fix up the planks, it would look a lot better. I'll put in new bathrooms and a new kitchen in whatever style suits your taste. You can do whatever you want as far as the rest of the house goes."

Cia was flabbergasted. Relief flooded every cell in her body. "Seriously?"

"Sure."

"How much would the rent be?"

"Nothing. Not money at least. Perhaps either you or your husband could handle the administrative end of the property. Are you or he any good with computers?"

"Both of us are. In fact, Jeffrey even knows how to do programming," she said. It took all of her willpower not to boast that he went to MIT and could do far more than programming.

Grayson smiled. "I'd love to talk to him. Hopefully, there are ways I could use his computer skills for our horse operations and for my viatical business. Our computer systems aren't state-of-the-art anymore. Hopefully he could help us out with getting what we need. Of course, I'd pay him for his services."

Cia beamed for a moment and then remembered the jeopardy they might be in if Shin went to the authorities. "That sounds wonderful," she said, faking her enthusiasm.

"The place definitely needs to be painted, but don't worry about doing the work. I'll hire a painting crew."

Her first instinct was to tell him that she had once been a successful muralist and faux painter, but she restrained herself. If he knew, he would likely inquire about her background and how she ended up in southeast Oklahoma. "I'd appreciate it if I can pick the colors. Would you mind if I kind of play around with doing some faux techniques? I've always admired it and would love the chance to try it," she said, torn between excitement and frustration.

"Do whatever you want. Treat the house as if you own it. If you turn out to have a knack for the faux work, I'll pay you to do the offices and the recreation room. That way you can make some extra money and get more hands-on experience."

He sensed her lack of genuine enthusiasm, certain it weighed on her mind that she had told Shin about the kidnapping. He assumed she regretted the disclosure. Surely she was terrified of the consequences. Who wouldn't be?

He sat on a folding canvas camp chair and rubbed his hands together quickly. "I know this is none of my business," he said, then paused for what seemed like minutes to Cia. "but you don't seem to be using your potential. I can see you have compassion, but you're struggling with something deep inside yourself."

She simply nodded, acknowledging his observations. There was no point in making friends with this generous man. No point in giving a meaningful response.

Grayson sat, letting her think about his comment.

"Life as we know it can change in an instant," she snapped suddenly, surprising even herself. She'd probably be disappearing into yet another new life as soon as she could get back to Jeffrey. That is, if they weren't arrested first.

He nodded in agreement. "I can assure you, I'm aware of that – and the viators can tell you the same thing. Each of them were handed a death sentence by their physicians."

"I'm not feeling sorry for myself, if that's what you're thinking."

He furrowed his brows, acting baffled by her comment. "Why would it cross your mind I would think that?"

Although no one else was near, she lowered her voice as if she didn't want anyone else to hear her. "I don't know why I said it. I guess I was thinking that if I were terminally ill I'd be feeling sorry for myself. I don't know."

He thought for a minute. "When I get to know my clients, my viators, if they want to die in peace, I teach them lessons about life, which are also lessons about death. We discuss what they can do to help cleanse their soul. For example, I encourage them to confess things they've done wrong in their life and then make right whatever they can."

She bit her fingernails, nervously listening.

When no response came forth, he continued. "Leaving the world with a clear conscience helps people die without as many regrets. But as you probably have already experienced, living with a clear conscience allows more opportunity for inner peace. Personal integrity allows you to be guilt free, which in turn leaves you open to being a better person with more to offer the world. These things alone will bring personal happiness."

"Why are you telling me this?"

"I didn't plan to. Trust me. Our conversation took its own path. It had its own destiny. Like everything in life, one thing leads to another and the next thing you know you might surprise yourself. Sometimes the surprise is a good thing. Sometimes not."

Cali Canberra

She nodded in agreement. "I can be impulsive," she stated and then went back to chewing her fingernails.

He thought he knew what she was referring to, but couldn't let on. "Being impulsive can be freeing and liberating. You should be glad you have the ability. Too many people can't go with the flow of things. They're so uptight they have to plan everything in their day and their life."

"I could never be like that. I need an unstructured life."

"Same here. That's why I didn't have a set time for the viators to arrive. By the way, I want you to meet Cynthia. I think the two of you should get to know each other."

"Why?"

"Cynthia's very open and honest about life. It's refreshing. Of course, she jokes about it and says she wasn't that way until she knew she was dying!"

Cia almost smiled. "I guess it would be easier to be honest if you know there are no consequences – at least not long-term consequences since you wouldn't be alive long-term."

"Anyway, you should get to know her today." He stood, wordlessly ending the conversation. Perhaps another time he would explain to her that he believed the things you do in life have resulting consequences in death and the after-life.

Cia was glad to have a few minutes alone to consider asking Grayson if she could use his cell phone. If she did, she'd call Jeffrey and alert him about what she had done and tell him to figure out an escape plan – maybe even come pick her up if she could find a way to get directions. She didn't know exactly where she was in regard to driving since they had started out at the far end of the National Forest, then rode the horses through the forest to Grayson's house, then rode horses out to the camping area on his property. She knew there was a way to drive in to where they were because there was already a Suburban and the viators would arrive by car. Her thoughts swarmed around like bees outside a broken hive. It took a level of self-control she didn't realize she possessed not to ask Grayson if Shin had used his cell phone and not to ask if anyone else there had a phone with them. The

Wisdom of the Horse

suspense of not knowing if Shin had called the police drove her mad. If she simply came out and asked Shin directly, how could she be sure of an honest answer? Perhaps there was an excuse she could fabricate to leave camp with the driver who was bringing the viators. There was so much to consider.

Chapter 33

The $60,000 yellow Hummer H2's tires kicked up clumps of mud as Bruce, Grayson's barn manager, arrived at the sweat lodge and camping area with five people tightly squeezed into the rugged SUV powerhouse. Bruce turned off the Bose stereo and the DVD navigation system that entertained his passengers. He removed his ash-colored Stetson and carefully placed it on the front seat while he unloaded their belongings. Cynthia, Alison, Les, Randy, and Dat introduced themselves to everyone. Thundering Cloud greeted them as old friends, except for Alison whom he hadn't met. He made a special point of making her feel comfortable - she was putting her future in his hands. Whether she believed it or not, the purifying ceremony in the sweat lodge would help her.

Cia's possible option of leaving the group seemed quelled. Bruce, now tending to the horses, was obviously staying. At a moment when she didn't think anyone was paying attention, she approached him and asked to borrow his cell phone. Wordlessly, he handed the phone over. She wandered a reasonable distance away - not so far as to look secretive, but far enough that he wouldn't be able to hear. Her hands trembled as she dialed her home number. Four times in a row, each time she anxiously

Wisdom of the Horse

dialed, before she finished she realized she had pressed a wrong button on the keypad and needed to start over. Still trembling, she slowed her movements to get the number right. Just as the phone began to ring Shin silently approached her from behind and put a hand on her shoulder. Cia jumped, startled and frightened. The phone fell to the damp maple leaf covered ground.

"You shouldn't do that," Shin said, squatting down to pick up it up.

Cia couldn't tell if Shin's words were intended to be threatening. She stood speechless.

"One of the points of this trip is to have no access to the outside world," Shin said as she looked at the screen and read the number Cia had dialed.

Cia blinked nervously. Her voice rose. "Have you had access?"

"Since you told me your secret?"

"Of course that's what I'm referring to."

"No. I haven't."

Cia gave her a speculative look. "What are you going to do about what you know?"

"Just don't make any phone calls."

Without giving Cia a chance to respond, Shin walked away with the cell phone. She returned it to Bruce and instructed him not to allow Cia to use it again.

~ ~ ~ ~ ~

Two years earlier, to construct the *Inipi*, the Lakota sweat lodge, Thundering Cloud, Tate, and Grayson cut red willow branches and then fastened them together using only the willow bark. Using a stake and a rope to position them, they placed eight lodge poles equidistant from the center into holes chipped by a pickax. They then tamped dirt around the poles with an ax. Over the frame they placed heavy waterproof and flame resistant canvas. Inside, old blankets filled in any gaps of light because the *Inipi* must be completely dark during the ceremony.

Cali Canberra

In the center of the lodge they dug a shallow pit to serve as a round fireplace which represents the center of the universe, where *Wakan Tanka* holds His power which is the fire. For the heated rocks they built a platform out of firewood and placed it the center of the fireplace, located 15 feet west of the *Inipi's* door which faced east, for it is the direction that the light of wisdom comes from. Outside, about ten paces east of the lodge door, they constructed a sacred path leading to a sacred fireplace for the 'eternal fire' where the rocks for the lodge are heated. They made an offering of tobacco in the earth altar, and then invited the spirits. After the lodge was built, Roy Stone, a Lakota medicine man from Rosebud, South Dakota, blessed it.

One of the Seven Sacred Rites of the Lakota is the sweat lodge ceremony. The construction techniques and the ceremony have changed very little in the course of thousands of years. Various American Indian tribes perform their sweat lodges a little differently from each other. The Cherokee's form of Lodge, known as *Asi*, is used strictly to facilitate Healing and for no other purpose. Thundering Cloud's ceremony combined Lakota and Cherokee ways. When he performed ceremonies for non-Indians he did not reveal all of the Native American rituals and prayers – only enough of them to offer spiritual healing and purification. There is much disagreement among the Lakota community and other tribes about allowing access to Native American religious activities such as the sweat lodge but Thundering Cloud saw it as bringing greater awareness and understanding of American Indian beliefs.

~ ~ ~ ~ ~

Sunset faded as twilight took over. When the full moon and bright stars lit the sky, Grayson asked the viators to change into their shorts and tank tops and to bring the towels from their tents.

Thundering Cloud sat with his *Chunupa Wakan*, his Sacred Pipe, in the *Inipi*. Next to him was a tall stoneware bowl of water. Cynthia, Alison, Les, Randy, and Dat entered clockwise and sat

Wisdom of the Horse

on their towels in a circle around the *Pita Hochokan*, the fire pit. A large stone sat just inside the door. Joel pulled the heated rocks from the outdoor fire pit using a rake and passed them inside with a pitchfork. Thundering Cloud maneuvered the first four rocks around the pit using a deer antler until each rock was positioned at the four compass points – North, South, East, and West. Joel piled the rest of the hot rocks on top. With each rock, the heat climbed. Calling in the spirits, Thundering Cloud tossed dry sage onto the rocks. They ignited and filled the *Inipi* with a pungent aroma. The lodge door was closed when all of the glowing red rocks were inside.

Thundering Cloud chanted ancient prayer songs that had been passed from one generation to another. When it became unbearably hot, the door to the *Inipi* was opened to let some steam escape. The viators gave personal prayers when the door was open. After some time they passed around the Sacred Pipe.

"The struggle of being in the hot *Inipi* is like the struggle of the Native American way of life," Thundering Cloud said. "Native Americans have been able to face adversity with grace and dignity just as you will face ending your Earth Walk with grace and dignity."

He prayed for all of Creation and then told a story. "It has been said that there was once a man who prayed for a million dollars when he was in the *Inipi*. His medicine man wondered how a million dollars could come to the man. Perhaps through an inheritance? Or through gambling? The medicine man did not think the prayer was a good one. Later, he found out that the man's prayer was granted. He was in a car accident in which his whole family died and he survived. His insurance company paid him a million dollars."

After the story, the viators sipped hot sage tea to flush the impurities from their bodies. One by one, they exited the *Inipi* feeling simultaneously drained and uplifted. Once they cooled down, they feasted on food and drink. Grayson, Tate, Shin, Cia, and Thundering Cloud refrained from eating in order to prepare for their own sweat lodge ceremony.

Chapter 34

The following morning, Grayson approached Cynthia. "How are you feeling?"

"Worse than ever before. I don't know how much more I can take." Her eyes watered around the edges. The daily malaise had become unbearable. "I'm ready for the butterfly."

His throat constricted. "You're sure you want the butterfly?"

"Yes. I've thought about it a lot. I'm ready. That's one of the reasons why I came here – to tell you I'm ready."

His solar-plexus burned. He wanted to tell her he didn't think she should give up on life so soon, but it wasn't his place to influence her decision. Conflicting images filled his mind as he thought of his ability to change the lives and deaths of others. "There's a butterfly in the Suburban," he said. Without knowing its purpose, Joel had brought the butterfly in the jar with holes in the top.

"I didn't know you'd have one with you. I'm not doing it here," she said.

"You know me. I'm always prepared. The butterfly will survive about a week in the jar."

Wisdom of the Horse

Cynthia nodded. She had expected a protest and now didn't know if she was glad there wasn't one, or if she wished he had tried to convince her to wait. She looked toward the corral filled with the five horses eating flakes of hay. No words came to mind, so she didn't speak.

"Do you still want to ride a horse?" Grayson asked. "Often, experiencing the connection can help heal the nonphysical aspects of your life."

Feeling an emotional quagmire, on the one hand she wanted to do all the things she had never had a chance to do while she was physically fit. On the other hand, she was ready to leave the earth and move on to a place free from pain and suffering. The inevitability of her death, combined with feeling insignificant to the world because her body was deteriorating, made lingering on feel pointless. "Actually, yes. I would like to try riding."

They walked to the corral, Grayson carrying a camp chair. He suggested Cynthia sit and calm her mind, gaze at the horses, and focus on whatever feelings came to her. In his experience, horses transmitted energy to everyone, but most especially to those who suffered physically or emotionally. Some horses remain aloof to what they sense about humans, but others are highly sensitive. As a result, highly sensitive horses are fearful, or aggressive, or they gravitate to people and intuitively nurture the person's spirit.

Cynthia took in the beauty of all the horses. She was instantly drawn to the large, soulful eyes of one horse in particular. She felt an internal transformation when they made eye contact. She stood up, drawn to his presence. Grayson observed how both of their postures shifted. Cynthia went from looking exhausted, beaten by the world and hopeless - to that of peace and serenity. The horse went from being on guard for predators, protecting the small herd, to looking docile. He responded to Cynthia authentically, giving her his undivided attention, waiting for her signal to approach.

"What's that horse's name?" Cynthia asked as she pointed to the dark bay gelding.

"Cabaret."

Cali Canberra

The moment Cabaret heard his name, his head elevated a few inches and his ears pointed toward them. His stance became proud and elegant.

"He's the only one I feel drawn to," Cynthia said, feeling fully engaged in the moment. "There's something about him in particular. I can't explain it."

Cabaret kept his eye on them as Chief took over the position of being on watch for predators.

"Take the time to find the words, even if you don't verbalize your thoughts. It will help you get in touch with your deepest feelings," Grayson said.

Cabaret tentatively walked toward them, sensing Cynthia wanted to be near him, but also sensing some fear. Cynthia leaned across the fence and with her thin and delicate fingertips she reached toward his forehead. Energetically sensing her hand, Cabaret turned his head before she touched his face, his blind spot. He stepped forward, positioning himself where she could reach him. She slid her hands down the long, strong muscles of his neck and shoulders. Cabaret arched his neck slightly and communicated that this was the place to keep contact. Cynthia stood on her toes attempting to reach over the fence to hug him.

Grayson offered to bring Cabaret out of the corral. Cynthia, anxious and excited, worried that he would easily hurt her frail body but part of her sensed he would be gentle. She didn't know if it was possible for horses to have feelings like humans, but it seemed to her that this horse was conveying compassion. She thought he was telling her that if she would allow it, he could make her let go of the sadness simmering beneath her surface.

Cabaret nuzzled her neck and back as she sat in the chair. An insight crossed her mind. The connection she felt was more than physical. Eventually, she told Grayson she'd like to try to ride if he thought it would be safe. Almost instantaneously, he effortlessly picked her up from the chair if she were no more than a feather and placed her on Cabaret's back.

The horse relaxed into the sensation of her energy, immediately causing her to mirror his actions. The two melded

Wisdom of the Horse

as one. Grayson led Cabaret down a wide trail that ended with the view of a small clearing lit up by the vibrant colors of the fall foliage. Cynthia rode in a slightly hypnotic state, the freedom and energy of movement bringing back memories of when she was strong and healthy and active. Horseback riding diffused the inward rage she felt about her debilitating health. She hadn't realized it until that moment, but inactivity due to her weakness was the very thing that made her want to die sooner, rather than at the last possible moment. Before she was given her death sentence, she loved to hike, mountain bike, explore caves, snorkel, and do aerobics. The rawness of the realization felt as devastating as a recently broken heart. Somehow, riding felt effortless while simultaneously triggering the sensation of all of her muscles and joints moving. This triggered her self-awareness and it occurred to her that ever since her health problems had become significant, her self-image had shattered. Tears poured down her face like opening floodgates. Grayson lifted her from Cabaret and motioned for her to sit on a boulder.

"It's fine to cry," he said, stroking her hair.

Cabaret stood next to her, his head hanging near hers, his soft breath upon her face.

"I thought I was cried out. Where do all the tears come from?" she wondered out loud.

Grayson smiled tenderly but did not speak. Sometimes silence was a gift.

Eventually Cynthia stood again and hugged Cabaret. "He doesn't care about how sick and weak I look, does he?" She thought of how her husband rarely touched her anymore, fearful it would hurt her. She craved the physical contact but didn't know how to tell him without sounding as if she was soliciting sympathy. She could tell that Cabaret sensed her needs and she thought he had the level of wisdom most humans strive for.

Grayson placed Cynthia back on Cabaret and began leading them to the campsite. "I want you to tell Cia your San Antonio story."

Her face twitched. "Why?"

Cali Canberra

"If you tell her your San Antonio story you should ask her about her San Antonio story. She'll probably tell you. If she does, you'll both be better off."

Cynthia chewed the inside of her lip as the possibilities formed in her mind. Her San Antonio story was like living with a stone in her shoe for the rest of her life. It didn't matter that she wouldn't be arrested and it didn't matter that she was paid $100,000, enabling her to travel the world. While she was on an African safari, she began feeling sick. When she returned home, she was diagnosed with lymphoma. Convinced it was karma, she thereafter lived a life of various degrees of suffering.

Tired of the pain, exhaustion, and weakness, she wanted the butterfly – a beautiful symbol of the metamorphosis of life, death, and rebirth. She desperately wanted the butterfly. Not a drug overdose. Not a plastic bag over her head. Not carbon monoxide poisoning. The only way she could imagine dying was by being closed in her master bathroom sprawled out on her airbed and releasing out of a jar the beautiful and rare *Lachrymosa codriceptes* – 'winged death' – a unique and intensely poisonous butterfly of the Yucatan.

Grayson could get the special butterflies with a twenty-four hour notice. He promised to help her die when she was ready and still of sound mind to make the decision as to the right time.

Chapter 35

Joel kept the rocks hot by fueling the fire throughout the night. He and Thundering Cloud went through the same ritual as the previous day, arranging the hot rocks inside the *Inipi* for the ceremony.

Grayson sat to Thundering Cloud's left side, Tate to his right. Shin and Cia sat across from them, forming a circle.

"I understand the sweat lodge is for healing, but why are we doing it?" Cia asked Thundering Cloud.

By the light of the hot rocks, he looked into her eyes which seemed almost empty. It was a look he hadn't seen before. "Being in the sweat lodge is going back into the womb, into Mother Earth. You come out born again."

"That's what I need. To be born again. Can I get a different name and everything?" she said, half kidding, half serious.

"Maybe we'll give you an Indian name."

"Do we talk while we're in here?"

"Sure," he said, hoping she would consider opening up about how she got her daughter. "Tradition dictates that nothing said inside an *Inipi* can be repeated outside the lodge. There is total anonymity so that participants can speak with absolute honesty. Talking is part of the ceremony. In fact, everything involved with the Lodge is part of the ceremony, including helping to gather the wood for the fire."

While everyone else was in the sweat lodge, the viators relaxed, grateful for another glorious day on Earth. Cynthia stared into the distance thinking about how most things were meaningless in the face of death. Alison wrote in her journal about her sense of feeling connected to nature and the other viators. Les, Randy, and Dat played cards.

When Cia had had enough of the heat and steam, she backed out of the *Inipi*, appreciative of the invigorating fresh air. Not long after, Shin found her sitting on the broad flat rock at the river. Filtered sunlight broke through the brightly-colored, huge oak, maple, and elm trees. They wordlessly nodded to each other and then Shin opened a small notebook and began reading.

"What are you reading?"

Shin set the notebook down behind her and splashed river water on herself to cool down her body. "Some notes I took about the things I want to think about during this trip." She had done the same thing many times – brought notes from books jotted on index cards with her on a trail ride. She sat and read and pondered the ideas while she let the horse graze and rest.

"Would you consider sharing?"

It was a reasonable request. Shin read the quote she wrote from Jamie Sams book, *Dancing the Dream*. "It is important to remember that every time we think we have no more to learn in any given area it is our weaknesses, not our strengths that will be tested. Often we are tricked into learning something new when our own behavior creates the need. In the Native American tradition, we call this trickery Coyote Medicine."

Reminiscing, Shin thought back to a bitter cold November day, the first day at an Equine Affaire in Massachusetts when she visited with her brother while he set up his trade show booth. Tate patiently listened to her describe what she had been doing. He reached under his covered table and presented her with a gift - a wooden carving of a coyote. He told her she needed Coyote Medicine. She smiled at him, knowing he was right.

Cynthia, looking increasingly frail and weak, wandered over to the women. A brilliant shaft of light illuminated her. "Do you mind if I talk with Cia alone?" she asked Shin.

The tips of the trees swayed from the light morning breeze. In slow motion, vibrant colored leaves drifted through the air and landed on the ground. The contrast was chilling after having been

Wisdom of the Horse

in the *Inipi*. "No problem," Shin answered. "I need to change clothes anyway."

Cynthia sat on a dry boulder across from Cia. "Grayson asked me to talk to you."

Cia gave her a long inscrutable look. "He wanted me to talk to you, too."

Cynthia told Cia her abbreviated San Antonio story. Her own words sounded strange and apart from her, completely opposite of the person she had been before the incident, and even more so afterwards.

At first, Cia couldn't assimilate her thoughts. Was she dreaming? No. This was why Grayson said she should talk to Cynthia. This was real. "It was me and my husband in the store. We took the child," she said at last. "I thought there was a neglectful mother and that I was rescuing her."

"You kept her?"

"Yes, of course. We love her. We named her Elizabeth." Cia went on and told Cynthia her San Antonio story without telling her anything that happened after they drove off.

Cynthia wailed, releasing the festering grief and guilt stored in her heart, soul, and body for all these years. The child she was entrusted with had always been safe and loved. Cia's admission and sincerity in her love for the little girl was an enormous gift.

Sharing their stories changed their lives at the drop of a coin. Cia could be certain no one was looking for Elizabeth. Now they could be more aggressive with her to be around people, to overcome her phobia. Their lives had to change. Normalcy was suddenly a possibility.

"You met Elizabeth's biological mother. Do you know anything about her background?"

"I do. There's no family history of health problems. That should be a comfort," Cynthia said, remembering the story in detail because while she was in college she had gone on a Taglit-birthrite Israel Hillel trip. Her mother was half-Jewish, but she never learned about Judaism, let alone observed the religion. Cynthia had been curious and took advantage of the free trip offered to any young Jewish adult in the 18-26 age range who has never before visited Israel on a peer-group program.

She went on to tell Cia all she knew. "Your daughter is Jewish. Her biological mother, Rebecca, was a foreign exchange student in Israel at the Hebrew University of Jerusalem, in the Religious Studies graduate program. She fell in love with a handsome young Orthodox Jew from the beautiful ancient city of Tzfat. They dated for over a year, and in respect for Jewish tradition kept *shomer negiah*. Do you know what that is?"

Cia nodded. As an only daughter of Orthodox Jews, she knew all about *shomer negiah*, one facet of someone's level of observance of their Jewish religion. The Torah restricts absolutely all physical contact between men and women as a safeguard against the development of improper relationships and premarital intimacy.

Cynthia continued. "When Rebecca graduated, she was heartbroken about leaving Israel and returning to the United States. The young man was very close to his family and could not imagine living in any other culture, so as much as he loved her, they would probably never see each other again. On her last night in Israel, they could not resist the pleasures of the flesh. They made love, each for the first time in their lives. Six weeks later Rebecca discovered she was pregnant. She didn't believe in abortion and could not imagine giving the baby up for adoption.

Her parents were very disappointed in her, but accepted her decision to keep the child. Although her parents allowed her to live in their home and gave her money for living expenses, they had no intention of parenting the baby. They owned a diamond import business which required buying the diamonds overseas and traveling throughout the United States selling to jewelers.

Rebecca's pregnancy was easy and there were no complications in giving birth. The first couple of weeks of motherhood were life altering. She didn't know what she would have done if her mother hadn't stayed home with her and taught her what she needed to know. But then, her mother went about her own life, tending to their business enterprise. The baby refused to breastfeed

Wisdom of the Horse

and tended to be colicky. Without a husband at Rebecca's side, loneliness overwhelmed her. She was home alone, a single mother getting no sleep and not seeing an end to the crying and diapers. She began suffering from what her physician told her was post-partum depression. After over a year had passed, even with the financial and emotional support of her parents, she couldn't imagine getting anywhere in life on her own. Worse, she could no longer envision the future she had dreamed of and worked toward. Her plan had been to teach Religious Studies. How could she pursue such a career when she was an unwed mother? Emotionally, she was hanging by a thread. That's when Cynthia and she met.

Cia was enthralled by the story and then chuckled. When Cynthia asked what she found humorous Cia told the story of her parents disowning her because she married outside of their faith, and by doing so she wouldn't have Jewish children. The women laughed together, far longer and far harder than the circumstances warranted. Perhaps they both needed the release. The women stood and hugged, weeping about the gift they had given each other, thanks to Grayson.

Cia's indescribable burden was lifted. The authorities had never looked for them and never would. Grayson was willing to hire her and Jeffrey, providing them a much nicer place to live - a place to really call home, a place with horses. Now they had another option to moving away from Shin and the horses so that they could make a better life for themselves.

A moment later, reality hit her like a jolt of caffeine. She and Jeffrey would still have to be in hiding. The whole problem with their life wasn't just Elizabeth. There was still the lingering fear of Jeffrey's former business partners finding them. Her temporary elation and relief quickly dissipated. She had to think things through.

Cia backed away from Cynthia and looked at her appraisingly. "Why does Grayson know what you told me?"

"I told him and Thundering Cloud. They said I should clear my conscience and make things right – it would help my soul, in life and in death."

"Does anyone else know?"

"I haven't told anyone except my husband. I trust they haven't, either."

The women parted. Cynthia returned to her tent to be alone, to absorb the import of what she now knew for certain. For the first time in years, she felt free.

Cia remained at the misting river, deep in thought. Shin must have told her father or Grayson. Otherwise, why would Grayson know to talk to Cynthia or her about it? She wasn't completely surprised Shin had gone to someone she trusted and respected for advice, but still, there was a sting of betrayal. She supposed it didn't matter at this point. But then again, just because Shin told Grayson the secret, it didn't mean Shin knew Cynthia's secret. If Shin didn't know Cynthia's secret, there was a chance she called the police. The uncertainty was grueling. If Shin called the police and she was arrested, stealing the child was still probably a crime. When all was said and done, from a legal point of view, would it even matter that no one was looking for Elizabeth and that she and Jeffrey gave her a loving home?

Chapter 36

Shin and Cia checked on the horses. When they returned, Thundering Cloud and Tate were out of the *Inipi*. Father and son didn't bother making plates – they ravenously ate directly from the platters with their fingers. Once their appetites were satisfied, they joined the group around the campfire.

"I hope everyone is comfortable," Grayson said.

"I am," Les said. "By the way, have you heard about the man in the park dying of cancer?" he asked, his voice intoning the beginning of a joke.

"No," Randy replied.

"Well," Les continued. "This man was sitting on a park bench and he sees a frog near his foot. He picks up the frog and places it next to him, and to his surprise, the frog starts talking. The frog says, 'You don't look happy. If you kiss me, I promise I'll turn into a beautiful woman and I'll satisfy your every need. I'll make passionate love to you whenever you want, as often as you want.' The man didn't kiss the frog or respond. The frog repeated himself and then said, 'Can you hear me? Am I speaking loud enough?' The man replied, 'In my condition, with cancer and all, I think I'd be better off with a talking frog to entertain me than to have a woman to make love to.'"

Everyone laughed, the women louder than the men.

Randy spoke up. "I've got a good one. When Beethoven died he was buried in a churchyard. A few weeks later the gravedigger heard sounds coming from the area of his grave. He brought the priest over to listen. The priest sat next to the grave and listened. 'That's Beethoven's Ninth Symphony, being played backwards,' he finally told the gravedigger. They continued listening. Then the priest said, 'That's the Eighth Symphony, and it's backwards, too.' A few minutes later, he said, 'There's the Seventh... the Sixth...the Fifth... the Fourth...' Suddenly, the realization hit him. 'There's nothing to worry about. It's just Beethoven decomposing.'"

Everyone laughed hysterically.

"I've got another one," Les said. "A lawyer named Strange died, and his friend asked the tombstone maker to inscribe on his tombstone, 'Here lies Strange, an honest man, and a lawyer.' The inscriber insisted the inscription would be confusing - people would think that three men were buried under the stone. He suggested an alternative – 'Here lies a man who was both honest and a lawyer.' That way, whenever anyone walked by the tombstone and read it, they would say, 'That's Strange!'"

Again, everyone laughed until Grayson used a serious tone when he thanked everyone for joining him for the weekend.

Cynthia tried for a smile but it was so faint no one could tell. "I wanted to give my husband a break. He feels he shouldn't enjoy the things he wants so that he can keep me company as I'm just wilting away waiting to die. I feel so guilty. What else can I do but to give him space? Anyway, Grayson said he'd let me ride if I came. He got me up on Cabaret. I've never ridden before and I actually loved it. I've always wanted to ride but was too afraid of getting hurt. Now, I'm so far gone I guess it doesn't matter! Anyway, if I didn't do it on this trip, I'd never do it. That's one of the things you think about when you know your days are numbered." She began crying and wordlessly got up and wandered to the corral.

Thundering Cloud was glad she was drawn to the horses - and Cabaret in particular. Horses could help heal her soul and bring light to her spirit. No one could help the condition of her body, but it was where she would journey next that needed direction.

Cia tried to conceal her glistening tears. Now that was a woman with real problems, she thought, feeling guilty that she

Wisdom of the Horse

had felt sorry for herself.

Alison said, "Grayson thought it would be a good idea for me to get to know him better so that he might be able to serve me better, as he put it. His company bought my life insurance policy last year, and other than accepting the money, I kept my distance from him – or at least tried to. He kept sending me inspirational e-mail messages, and flowers, and invited me to other events. I just shut him out. I'm single – my husband left me when he couldn't cope with my cancer. I don't have kids. Anyway, a few weeks ago, Grayson asked if I was shutting the whole world out just because I'm dying. When I admitted I was, he and Thundering Cloud came knocking on my door in Tulsa and practically begged me to come this weekend. I couldn't say no, and to be honest, I'm grateful they pushed me so hard. Just talking with the others who are in the same miserable predicament has helped so much. And being able to pet the horses and watch them interact has been a wonderful distraction. Thank you, Grayson."

Randy eagerly took his turn. "I'm here because I'm helping Grayson get the hospice and horse rescue operation going. Until three years ago I was in the horse business. My ALS progressed to the point I couldn't work. I used to train and show stadium jumpers. Unfortunately, I never had much of a relationship with the horses – I just used them to get the job done, win a ribbon or trophy, and have a more valuable product to sell. I regret it now, but you can't go back. Seeing Grayson using horses as companions to feed the spirit, I grew envious. Anyway, I'm glad I'm here and hope to get to know all of you better."

"My name is Dat," said the Vietnamese man. "I'm here because my wife said she would kill me herself if I didn't come." His fist covered his mouth as he coughed, his lung cancer announcing itself. "Grayson told her about the trip so she would convince me to come. I've been to discussion groups with Grayson and Thundering Cloud, but I've never taken Grayson up on his numerous invitations to visit his farm. Of course, now I'm very happy to be here. I had no idea what this would be like. I've only lived in the city," he said with his heavy accent. "I brought something to read to everyone that I found in this Jamie Sams book, *Dancing the Dream* that Thundering Cloud sent me. I read English, so do not worry," he added.

Dat looked down toward the book and laughed until he doubled over.

"Go on, Dat," Randy urged.

Everyone wondered what could be so funny.

Finally, Dat pulled himself together enough to start reading, "My Cherokee grandpa took me to a fishing hole," he said and then broke out laughing again.

Everyone joined in, becoming giddy. Grayson laughed so hard he nearly choked on the tea he had just sipped. It felt so good, as if other than the previous night, he had held back genuine laughter for years.

Shin laughed hysterically. She leaned over and whispered to Cia, "I peed in my pants, I'm laughing so hard."

"Again?" Cia asked loudly, then about fell out of her own chair laughing.

Tate looked at his sister and loudly asked, "Did you pee yourself again?"

Shin blushed.

Thundering Cloud said, "You've done it all your life. You need to do Kegle exercises like your mother told you."

When everyone finally calmed down Dat started over and read, "My Cherokee grandpa took me to a fishing hole and asked me to throw a rock into the pond. He asked me what I saw, and I replied that I saw a splash. He asked me what else I saw, and I said a circle of water and another circle and another circle. He then told me that every person was responsible for the kind of splash they made in the world and that the splash would touch many other circles, creating a ripple effect. I sat and watched the water until he asked me to notice the muddy bank where we were sitting. He pointed out that one of the circular waves made by my rock was lapping at my feet, having found its way back to me. Then he told me that we all need to be careful of the kinds of splashes we make in the world, because the waves we create will

Wisdom of the Horse

always come back to us. If those splashes were hurtful, we will not welcome them back, but if the splash and the waves were made from goodness, we will be happy to see them come home."

Chapter 37

Just after Laura, Heather, and Brett boarded their plane, Tim called Laura. He sounded calm, but Laura knew he had nerves of steel and the ability to discard his emotions. Being disconnected, Tim kept everything about their business on a purely professional and economic level. So, when Tim told Laura that Misty shouldn't have called and that there was nothing to be concerned about, she didn't believe him, even for an instant.

Once back at the Oklahoma farm, the Suburban and the Hummer were the only vehicles that would make it out to the sweat lodge and campsite after such hard rains. Both were gone, presumably already at camp. By early afternoon, Laura and her kids tacked up their horses and rode the longer trail because they knew Slim Shady, Heather's Thoroughbred (a gift for her 21st birthday), wouldn't cross the creek water if he couldn't see the bottom. A competitive horse, Slim had loved water - until he got the scare of his life when Heather rode him on a cross-country course and jumped him over a wide water jump where he didn't make his mark. He slid out from under himself in the mud, landing on Heather, knocking her unconscious and breaking her leg. Slim panicked when his back leg cast itself under the jump rail and when mud got in his eyes and inside his ears. Ever since, Slim Shady refused to ride through water if he couldn't see the bottom. Today, no other horse was in condition enough to ride out to the campsite and back – she had to take Slim Shady even if it meant a longer journey.

Shin was spreading out flakes of hay for the horses when Laura, Heather, and Brett unexpectedly appeared.

Wisdom of the Horse

"Where's my husband?" Laura asked before Shin had a chance to greet them.

"I'm not sure. He and Dad were fishing the last time I saw him, but that was at least an hour ago. Is everything okay?"

Heather slid off Slim Shady and patted his sweaty neck. Brett did the same, then loosened Casino's girth and removed his tack. Laura remained astride Touché, anxious to find her husband.

"Where can we put them?" Heather asked Shin, referring to the horses.

"Will they go on a picket line?" Shin asked, thinking it unlikely.

"Casino will," Brett said. Arabians were quick to learn so it didn't take much work for Brett to show Casino how to stand tied to the line.

"I've never put Slim on one. Maybe you can just hold him," Heather told Shin as if it were an order rather than a suggestion.

Shin raised her brows and kept her thoughts to herself. "You'll have to try him on the line and stay with him to see if he'll be calm and safe."

"I can't. I've got to see Grayson," Heather said.

"I'm not standing around holding your horse," Shin told her and went about her work. Aside from the idea of not wanting to hold the horse, she didn't like the tall lanky Thoroughbred. He had a mean look in his eye.

"Brett – will you hold him while I go with Mom?"

Brett looked at her like she was out of her mind. "I missed showing in the rest of my classes at the Nationals to be here. I came to see Grayson – not to hold your horse. Why don't you do the ground work with him that the rest of us have done? You're so irresponsible sometimes."

"Don't do this right now," Heather said, exasperated. "I'll just put him in the corral with the other horses – one more horse won't matter."

Shin aggressively stepped in front of Heather and put her hand out to block her movement. "You can't. There's not enough room, and your horse is enormous. He could seriously hurt one of them if he wanted to be Alpha."

"Take out your horse so I can put Slim in. This is important," Heather demanded as her mother strode off on Touché.

"What's wrong?" Shin asked suspiciously.

Brett decided he may as well be honest. People would find out sooner or later. "We need to warn him that an FBI agent is trying to find him."

Shin almost laughed. She couldn't imagine that Brett wasn't teasing. Grayson was the most honest and generous man she had ever heard of.

"He's serious," Heather said, reading Shin's expression.

"Fine. But I'm not just standing around holding your horse. I'll work with him on the picket line. Somebody has to teach this horse the whole world's not about a fancy show barn, show ring, and perfectly groomed cross-country jump course," she said, more snippety than she intended.

Heather handed Slim Shady's reins over. She briskly walked off with Brett without saying another word. They found their mom at the river's edge talking to Thundering Cloud. They overheard him telling her that Grayson was in a tent talking with Cynthia.

"Why?" Laura asked.

"She feels lousy. He took her a Kava Kava and ginseng blend tea to uplift her," Thundering Cloud replied.

"Is it some Indian or Chinese concoction?" Heather interjected.

Thundering Cloud chuckled at her immaturity, not even considering being insulted. "He bought the tea at a health food store in Dallas. Who am I to judge?"

"Which tent?" Laura asked.

"I'll show you," Thundering Cloud said as he threw the last pebble from his weathered hand into the rushing water.

Laura swiftly dismounted Touché, ran his stirrups up, pulled the reins over his head to lead him, and walked alongside him with her children. Thundering Cloud pointed to the darkest green tent. As they approached, Laura instructed Brett to hold her horse. She wanted to bring him out alone. She'd be right back.

Wisdom of the Horse

Cynthia's tent door was zipped closed, but the window flaps were open for air circulation. Sunlight flooded through the windows. Just as Laura was about to call out Grayson's name, she glanced into the tent window. Her eyes grew wide. As she watched Grayson and Cynthia in what seemed to be slow motion, she unconsciously shifted her weight from one foot to the other. Blood drained from her face making her look like a kabuki doll – a white face with too much contrasting makeup. Her heart raced and her hands trembled. She couldn't bear to watch. She abruptly turned away, as if not witnessing what Grayson was doing would nullify his actions. All she could do was replay his words in her mind. He had always said that he didn't want the viators to be alone when confronting their death. Often, in one powerfully moving moment, he tested their limits and his own. He said when death was near, there was an incredible sense of connectedness. She could never truly understand because, unlike Grayson, she hadn't had a brush with death.

Quietly, Laura walked away from Cynthia's tent without disruption. She struggled to try to make sense out of what Grayson thought was the right thing to do. When she approached her children, all words eluded her. Brett and Heather's eyes danced inquisitively as they repeatedly asked what was wrong. She offered no direct reply.

Chapter 38

Shin removed the manure piles from the corral as she kept a watchful eye on Slim Shady who stood calmly on the picket line. Tate came to check on Canku. Shin told him that Laura, Heather, and Brett had come claiming that the FBI was looking for Grayson. Tate grunted, assuming it was a bad joke. Shin invited Tate to go for a ride. He thought riding sounded like a good idea. His idea of communing with nature didn't include being with terminally ill people.

Temptation was acting restless and had begun picking on the other horses. Shin always enjoyed riding a horse she hadn't been on before and after Cynthia spent time with Cabaret and rode him, he seemed relaxed for a change. There was no sense in getting his adrenaline pumped up again. Slim didn't seem as if he would have a problem being left alone in the company of the other horses. Brother and sister headed through the woods to the clearing to find their father. They wanted to let him know where they were riding.

While still in the thick of the woods, Shin and Tate spotted their father with a hand on Laura Solvan's shoulder. Laura looked to the ground, sobbing, her arms wrapped around herself. Shin and Tate scanned the area. Tate contemplated interrupting his father, but he and Shin decided against it. They'd wait to see how long the encounter appeared emotional.

Scanning the area, they spotted Heather and Brett on the far side of the clearing walking toward their mother. Laura saw them and yelled out that she needed time to talk with Thundering Cloud alone. Heather and Brett retreated and sat on a fallen tree. Touché patiently followed.

Wisdom of the Horse

Laura was compelled to tell Thundering Cloud what she saw in Cynthia's tent and how difficult it was for her, even though she knew what Grayson was doing. Thundering Cloud and Laura were the only people Grayson confided in. She also had to tell him that an FBI agent was looking for her husband. She didn't want anyone else to know. Grayson couldn't risk losing credibility and respect if anyone saw him being arrested, if that's what the FBI was going to do.

Shin and Tate decided to remain hidden in the woods. They watched their father cup his hand over his mouth in deep contemplation and tap the toe of his boot on the dirt – a clear sign that this must be serious. The discussion between their father and Laura was very quiet, their body language intense. Becoming increasingly curious, Tate eased up closer, hoping to hear something. He could not.

Thundering Cloud advised Laura to return home with Heather and Brett. He'd find Grayson and alert him about the FBI agent. If Grayson wanted to leave, he could always take a vehicle and leave Oklahoma quickly, if that's what he wanted to do. Laura gathered herself and did as he suggested.

Shin and Tate strode out of the woods and called their father's name.

If a red man could ever turn white, Thundering Cloud did. He wondered if his children had seen or heard anything he and Laura had said.

Instinctively, Shin and Tate chose to act as if they didn't know anything was going on. "What's Grayson's family doing here?" Tate asked, nonchalantly.

Thundering Cloud couldn't tell the complete truth. Looking to the sky as if he were evaluating the type of cloud cover, he said, "Laura needed to get a message to Grayson and she didn't know he brought his cell phone with him since he usually doesn't." He cleared his throat. "It's a beautiful day to ride," he added, as if the observation made everything sound logical.

"I thought Brett was showing at the Nationals," Tate commented.

"Something came up."

"Want to go for a ride with us?" Tate asked, forgetting he and Shin had planned to ride alone.

"After I tell Grayson something, I'll go."

"Can we grab some food before we head out? I'm already hungry," Tate said as an afterthought.

"Good idea," Thundering Cloud said. "I could use a sandwich."

Thundering Cloud went to Cynthia's tent and found Grayson had left. Cynthia didn't know where he had gone. He asked the others and no one knew exactly where he went – they just saw him walk off down toward the clearing a minute ago. Thundering Cloud jogged toward the clearing and called out his friend's name. There was no reply. He called out louder. Still, there was no reply. He'd ride with his family and then he'd tell Grayson Laura's news when they returned. It wouldn't be all that long.

The Crows prepared and then ate thick, stacked, rare roast beef sandwiches with provolone, sliced avocados, and sweet onions on 9-Grain bread. For desert, they splurged on thin slices of dark chocolate and raspberry swirl New York style cheesecake.

Brett and Heather pleaded with their mother to tell them what was wrong.

Laura refused to tell them anything. She couldn't put them in the middle of this mess. "We're going back home. Give me a leg up, Brett."

It was better that they didn't know anything – at least for now. How could she tell her children that Grayson had just given Cynthia a jar with a butterfly? Sure, Cynthia asked for his assistance in her suicide, but still, he was effectively killing her. Within a couple of hours of the butterfly landing on her she would be dead from anaphylactic shock. The butterfly toxin would cause a fatal systemic reaction. Cynthia's throat would swell closed. She wouldn't be able to breathe, and she'd experience a sudden decline in blood pressure. Without medical assistance, she would die. It would be a quick and relatively painless death - and one she had surely even pleaded for.

Chapter 39

Cia roamed in an isolated area with boulders set high on a ridge overlooking a valley that generations ago was dotted with grazing buffalo. Shin had taken her there earlier and suggested she spend time alone to reflect upon the admission of her secret and where they might take their therapy sessions from this point forward. Shin didn't tell her that she knew Cynthia's San Antonio story. Cia was petrified of Shin being out of her sight for so long, especially knowing there were at least two cell phones Shin could use to call the police – but there was no way Cia could refuse the suggestion of taking time to think things through about her therapy.

The Crows rode their horses to the ridge in order to let Cia know they were going riding.

"Where's Grayson?" Cia asked, not letting on that she was worried about the honesty of their story. "I guess I ought to know since all of you are leaving."

"I don't know. But if you see him, please tell him we went riding and that we won't be gone long," Thundering Cloud said. "Cabaret seems perfectly content alone in the corral."

Bruce was still out riding Chief, so finding the Crows horses gone, Grayson took Cabaret out of the corral, tied him to a tree, brushed him down, and cleaned out his feet. A few minutes later, Cabaret was tacked up and ready to ride. Grayson grabbed a bottle of spring water for his saddle pack, mounted the eager horse, and rode off into the woods heading the opposite direction of where he anticipated anyone rode.

It never got easier helping someone die, especially when his personal opinion was that they could endure more time on earth. He needed time alone to commune with nature and pray that Cynthia wouldn't suffer in her last hours. At the first opportunity to take off cantering, Grayson signaled Cabaret, which didn't take much leg. The wind blowing on Grayson's skin and the exhilaration of feeling as if he were almost flying through the air helped him cope with life – and death.

The only people back at camp were the viators and Joel. Bruce had at least an hour before he planned to start packing up and then drive the viators back to town where they'd stay in the motel overnight before leaving for their own homes the following day.

A black Suburban unexpectedly appeared, a blue light flashing on the roof, but no siren. The sight was startling. No one had a clue what was going on.

As an imposing, tall man dressed in a suit exited the vehicle with the blue light still flashing, Cia was just about to come out of the woods and into the clearing of the camp area. She spotted the vehicle and the man. Her body fought the instinct to collapse. Scared and angry, she turned around and darted into the shadows, trying to flee the area as quietly as possible. Shin had called the police. Damn. She needed to disappear in the woods even though she didn't have a clue where to go. Her instinct was to avoid the trail system for a least a little while. As quietly as possible, she navigated through sparse vegetation.

The instant she was far enough away from the campsite for anyone to hear her footsteps, she ran down the first riding trail she came upon. When her chest began burning and heaving and she could run no further, she stopped to catch her breath – seething about Shin's betrayal. No wonder Shin and her family took off on horseback – they turned her in but didn't have the guts to see her arrested and taken away. Fury buried itself deep inside her, provoking an adrenaline rush. She'd be damned if she didn't try to escape and get to Jeffrey. She ran as if her life depended on it – in a way, it did. Eventually she ran so hard her lungs didn't want to work. She collapsed onto the damp ground, her breath coming in short gasps, and the pulse points in her temples and neck throbbed. She didn't have a clue where she was or what direction she was heading.

Back at the campsite, the tall, imposing man in his suit flashed a shiny badge in a leather holder as he said, "FBI."

Joel looked around to see if they were surrounded. They weren't. Maybe there was a way out of this mess. He wished he hadn't brought his flask of cheap whiskey and wished even more that he hadn't finished half of it off in the last hour. When he had started drinking there was no reason not to. He planned to sleep it off in his tent, so why not dull the ache he felt being around all these terminally ill people? In hindsight, he should have stayed clear-headed and kept the bottle back at his double-wide.

Reacting to the FBI badge, Joel clumsily reached down to the sheath on the outside of his left boot, pulled out a long, wide knife and grabbed hold of Dat, the nearest person to him.

Joel tried to look crazed. "Stop right now or I'll kill him."

Joel would never really hurt anyone, even if they were dying, but he needed to bluff. He was on parole. If he was arrested, he'd definitely end up in 'McAlister', the Oklahoma State Penitentiary. The maximum security prison sentence was mandatory for a third felony offense. The last thing he wanted was to be in Warden Mike Mullin's prison. It was a well known fact that he ran the place with an iron fist.

No one could believe what had just happened. Dat had fought in the Gulf War but nothing there scared him like this. In the Gulf, he expected the enemy. In the Gulf, he was armed and prepared to defend himself. Here, he trembled, fighting the reflex to collapse.

The man raised his hands as blood drained from his face. "Wait a minute –"

Joel cut him off and an exaggerated, mean expression took

Wisdom of the Horse

over his normally placid face. "Get down on the ground face first and keep your arms above your head." He couldn't believe what he was doing and saying. It was like he was outside of himself watching this happen. Why, he wondered, didn't he just do right by Grayson? Grayson was the first person who really believed in him, giving him a second chance at a straight-laced life.

Cynthia, Alison, and Les were scared for Dat, worried about how the scene might escalate. Randy remained calm. Almost entertained. Accepting of the fact that he was going to die soon anyway, he found himself wishing Joel had grabbed him instead of Dat, who looked petrified.

The man sprawled out face down on the damp earth in his $1,500 Giorgio Armani suit. A mixture of dirt, mud, and twigs imbedded into the watchband of his Rolex. His soft leather Salvatore Ferragamo shoes became caked with debris.

"Everyone just stay where you are while I think," Joel demanded. He gently pushed Dat up against a nearby tree, planting himself a foot away, his knife pointing near Dat's abdomen.

The man slowly raised his head. "It's not what you think –"

Joel kicked muck and leaves in his face. "Shut the hell up!" he screamed.

Dat couldn't help himself. "Joel, what are you doing?"

Joel ignored him.

The man didn't think there was any alternative. "The badge and the blue light are a joke – I swear, they're just a joke," he got out before Joel could stop him.

Joel didn't know what to do.

Still calm, Randy called out to Joel. "What if he's telling the truth? What if it was really a joke?"

The stranger spoke loudly, this time in a pleading voice. "I swear to you, I'm a friend of Grayson's. This was just supposed to be a prank!"

Joel shook his head and lowered the knife. He didn't know what to think. He began pacing like a trapped tiger. An uncomfortable silence blanketed the air. It seemed as though even the birds and the crickets fell silent. Dat dropped to the ground and slouched with his back against the tree, his arms hugging his knees.

Out of the blue, Bruce rode up on Chief and surveyed the scene. It didn't take more than a moment for him to see the desperation and panic-stricken look on everyone's faces, including Joel's. Bruce walked Chief directly to Joel, and in one swift movement he dismounted only inches from his bewildered co-worker and friend. Without resistance and before a word was uttered, Bruce took the knife from Joel with one hand as he held Chief's reins with the other. He took Joel by the forearm and led him a few yards away. With an upward nod of his head and his body language, Bruce signaled Dat to join his friends.

Dat was safe, although no matter what was happening Bruce knew Joel's nature enough to be certain that everyone had always been safe. Joel might not have a lick of sense, but he'd never hurt anyone.

The man in the suit slowly regained his stance but held his arms away from his body. He shook in his shoes, unsure what to expect next.

Bruce took in a deep breath, not unlike an older brother patiently waiting to have his questions answered. "What's going on?" he quietly asked Joel, without anger in his tone.

"The guy's FBI. I'm going to the Pen now. I can't believe I screwed up again," he said as if his actions were beyond his own control.

"What did you do this time?" Bruce asked.

"You know all that cash Grayson gave me to buy used tack for the rescue horses?"

Bruce bit his lip. He knew what was coming. He told Grayson not to trust Joel. He said that trusting Joel with a substantial amount of cash was like giving an alcoholic an open bottle of his favorite liquor and telling him not to drink it. But Grayson insisted that for Joel to continue gaining self-esteem he needed someone to demonstrate that they believed he could be trustworthy. After all, Grayson said, Joel's not wanting for a roof over his head, for food or for a vehicle to drive, or the gas to operate it, and he gets a good salary - there's no reason for him to steal anymore.

Wisdom of the Horse

"You stole all that tack you came back from the horse shows with, didn't you?" Bruce said accusingly.

"Yeah. The locks them people use ain't worth shit. They were practically askin' for it." He spit on the ground trying to sound tough.

"That's bullshit. You know better. If it isn't yours, you don't take it no matter what. Besides what you did to those people, look at what you're doing to yourself for no damn reason. You had it made working for Grayson. Sometimes you're such an idiot."

"You gotta help me. I can't go to the Pen. Help me out of this," Joel pleaded.

Bruce felt an obligation to follow Grayson's example, helping to redeem the misguided young man. He pondered the predicament.

Seeing that Bruce had Joel under control, Randy told the filthy stranger to speak up.

The man in the suit called out loudly, "I swear. I'm not FBI. It really was a joke. Let me prove it to you."

Joel didn't believe him and told Bruce so. Neither of them responded to the stranger. Joel pleaded with Bruce to let him take Chief and ride away before anything happened. He begged for just one more chance. If Bruce would let him escape, he'd leave Oklahoma and start fresh somewhere else. He promised he'd safely ride Chief to the barn and put him up in his stall before he took off. All he needed was some time to get away.

Against his better judgment, Bruce agreed. He gave Joel, still tipsy from the whiskey, a leg up. When Joel settled in the saddle and had the reins arranged between his fingers, he quickly apologized to the viators for putting them through everything and then galloped away on Chief.

Once again, the stranger told Bruce that everything had been a joke and offered to prove it.

Bruce's instinct was to believe the man since he hadn't pulled out a weapon and Joel obviously hadn't taken a weapon from him. "How can you prove it?" he asked more out of curiosity than disbelief.

"Check my wallet and the phony badge. The names don't match. Look at the light on the Suburban – it's a cheap piece of crap."

Bruce considered this, too. It sounded believable. He calmly walked to the Suburban and in the rear seat he saw two Gibson acoustic guitar cases, a pair of folded jeans, and a long-sleeved Hilfilger shirt. On the floor was a new pair of Timberland boots with the price tag attached and new socks sat on top of a case of beer. A black straw Resistol cowboy hat sat on the front passenger seat. Sure enough, the blue light was made of cheap plastic and charged by batteries. He didn't bother to check the stranger's identification.

It was obvious to everyone that the suit wasn't an FBI agent and that his story must be real – it was a joke.

Bruce chuckled, glad Joel had the shit scared out of him. He'd wait until he thought Joel was back at the barn and would phone to tell him that he'd try to give him one last chance. He wouldn't tell Grayson what happened. He'd try to convince the rest of the group to keep it to themselves so his job would be protected, as would his relationship with Grayson. He felt pretty confident that he could appeal to everyone's sense of reason when they heard about Joel's upbringing – his mother was a prostitute and his father was a drunk that beat the hell out of him if he didn't steal food and clothing for the family. He grew up without morals and proper guidance. He'd urge them to give the kid another chance.

"So, who are you?" Bruce finally asked the stranger.

"Doug. Doug Niller. Grayson and I go back to his days at the ad agency. We always were the jokers around there. We lost touch after his daughter died and I thought it was about time I made the effort for us to get together again."

Bruce grinned. "He told me about you. Said you were a hell of a funny guy. The life of the party. He's brought up getting in touch with you, too."

Doug nodded. "He ever get a new guitar?"

Bruce shrugged but didn't reply.

Wisdom of the Horse

"He can play an acoustical guitar better than any non-pro I've ever met. He can sing pretty well, too."

"Never heard him play or sing," Bruce said.

"I don't doubt it. I play also. The last time we saw each other he was clearing out his office and he gave me his guitar to remember him by. He said music had left his life when Lana died. Of course, I kept it, knowing he'd be ready for it someday. That's why I'm here. I brought it for us to play together. His business partner, Tim, told me where he was and what he was doing here. It stood to reason that this would be a good time and place for him to start strummin' and singin' again. Music heals the soul."

By then, the viators had gathered around and overheard their conversation. Randy took the liberty to bring the guitar cases from the back of Doug's vehicle. He wasn't the greatest, but he could play a little and carry a tune.

"You may as well get comfortable," Bruce said. "I see you've got a change of clothes in the car."

Randy spoke up. "Mind if I reacquaint myself with a Gibson?" he asked Doug.

"Not at all. Mine's in the black case. Help yourself," he replied, then went to the far side of the Suburban to change out of the filthy suit and shoes.

Randy unpacked the case, found a pick, settled himself on a dry bale of straw and tapped a foot as he settled the instrument against his body. His eyes sparkled for the first time in months. It occurred to him what a mistake it had been to quit playing just because he was dying. It felt natural to strum out the chords.

Doug returned dressed in his comfortable clothes and with a big cooler. "Are you guys allowed to have beer?"

"It's not gonna kill us," Les said jovially as he held out his hand for the first cold one. He popped the lid and took a nice long gulp as everyone else took a can.

To everyone's surprise, Dat asked Randy, "Do you know the Gordon Lightfoot song *Heaven Don't Deserve Me*? My wife and I listen to it all the time. We're kind of morbid I guess, but somehow that song seems to make us feel better."

Cali Canberra

By now, Doug had his own Gibson out. In response to Dat's request, he and Randy began picking D – G – A – D.

In unison, everyone sang:

> I'm not afraid that when I'm dying
> There'll be no one to hold my hand
> If there's a God up there he loves me
> As much as my old woman can
> I don't intend to be a martyr
> I don't give a damn what people say
> And if I never get to heaven
> Heaven don't deserve me any way
>
> I've tasted life both good and evil
> At times I was cruel and did not pay
> And if I never get to heaven
> Heaven don't deserve me any way
>
> I don't know what it was I came for
> But I've enjoyed it up 'til now
> If there's a friend who ever needs me
> I'll do my best to help somehow
> I don't intend to keep no secret
> I don't give a damn what people say
> And if I never get to heaven
> Heaven don't deserve me anyway

Randy was in his element. All physical pain was forgotten for the time being. The moment brought to mind an e-mail from Grayson about living every remaining day doing joyful things and being of service to others.

The Crows came upon Cia in the forest, collapsed from exhaustion.

Cia looked up from the damp ground. Her expression showed a mixture of fear and anger. "You promised," she yelled at Shin.

Shin furrowed her brows wondering what Cia was referring to. Her father dismounted his horse and helped Cia stand up. At first, she tried to pull away from him, and then quickly realized there was no point.

"It looks like you could use a ride," Thundering Cloud said, ignoring the tension in the air.

Before Cia had a chance to refuse, Thundering Cloud eased her close to Temptation and gave her a leg up to ride double with Shin. Cia supposed there was nothing she could do at this point – she was caught. They were taking her back to the FBI agent.

"You promised you wouldn't turn me in," she said resignedly into Shin's ear as she held her thumbs in Shin's belt loops.

Surprised, Shin replied, "I didn't."

"Bullshit."

"Dad – you or Grayson didn't call the police, did you?"

"Of course not."

Cia didn't respond. She didn't believe them, but they didn't seem like they were lying.

Fifteen minutes later they rode up to the campsite and found everyone singing and drinking beer. It was obvious to Cia that she was so paranoid that she somehow imagined the scenario she had run from. They put the horses in the corral and joined the others.

Doug introduced himself as a friend of Grayson's. "He wasn't riding with you guys?"

"No. I guess he went off somewhere on Cabaret," Thundering Cloud said.

Moments later everyone was drinking beer and singing along with Randy. In between songs, just as Bruce commented on what a great day it was, the sound of whinnying and galloping hoof beats approached.

It was Grayson on Cabaret. Three miles out, to Grayson's

Cali Canberra

astonishment, Cabaret had done a 180 degree turn and uncontrollably galloped back to the campsite. There was nothing Grayson could do to stop him.

Cabaret did a slide stop into the clearing in front of the startled group. The rambunctious gelding swung his head up and down as if feeling gleeful.

Grayson's eyes sparkled at the scene in front of him. "What are you doing here?" he asked Doug with a huge grin spread across his face. This was just the kind of surprise he needed. There was nothing like the idea of rekindling a friendship.

Grayson dismounted as Doug broke into the James Taylor song, *You've Got A Friend.*

Everyone rocked their bodies and sang along.

Sitting in the round, descended through space and time, everyone's spirits vibrated to the communal energy. Grayson was anchored by his friend's presence.

Cabaret wandered behind Cynthia and rested his chin on her shoulder, giving her the strength and courage to tell Grayson she'd wait for the butterfly. She moved her line in the sand. This day of being out in nature with new friends, horseback riding, and singing, brought new hope.

Now Grayson knew why Cabaret bolted, disobeying his every command. *Suktanka Woksapa* – Wisdom of the Horse.

Thanks to my sponsors whose products I personally use & endorse- Cali

TUCKER TRAIL SADDLES

EQUILITE — Natures Best Botanical Blends

TURTLENECK BY PAINT ROCK DESIGNS

HEALING TREE®
Wound & Skin Care Treatments for Horses & Pets

KINETIC TECHNOLOGIES

boink
Equestrian designed and tested riding apparel

Vet-A-Mix
Equine Products

ZAREBA®
SMART SYSTEMS FOR ANIMAL CONTROL

Tucker Saddlery 800-882-5375 tuckersaddles.com

Tucker Saddlery, maker of trail saddles with the patented Gel-Cush™ Shock Absorbing Seat for Ultimate Trail Comfort, is the leading manufacturer and designer of trail saddles and equipment. For 30 years Tucker trail saddles have set the standard in quality craftsmanship and innovative design. Tucker trail saddles are made in the USA. Contact Tucker for a free color catalog.

Equilite, Inc. 800-942-5483 equilite.com

Equilite Inc. - *Nature's Best Botanical Blends*™   Creators of the world famous Sore No More™, the all-natural arnica based liniment line, as well as a complete line of high quality herbal supplements, including Bounce Back™ - and the Botanical Animal line of Flower Essences for all animals - *Behavior Modification in a Bottle*™. Only the best for your animals!

Healing Tree Products 800-421-6223 healing-tree.com

Healing Tree Products are the first to perfect the 'science' of combining proven naturopathic ingredients and remedies with powerful pharmaceutical agents. Healing Tree products are specifically designed to work together, enhancing each others curative qualities and healing properties.

Paint Rock Designs 888-371-1519 paintrockdesigns.com

Horse blankets, sheets, custom show bags, trail riding accessories, home accessories, halters, and leg care. Unique turnout rugs designed for extreme weather conditions. Guaranteed to keep horses dry. Flexible elastic necklines snug up comfortably to prevent wind, rain, sleet, and snow from blowing in around the neck. Detachable elastic belly and leg straps, anti-bacteria lining, stainless steel hardware, and easy-on 1 ½" front buckles. The 1680d ballistic nylon shell has a two year guarantee and the company offers an unlimited customer satisfaction guarantee.

Boink 800-471-4659 boinkcatalog.com

Designed by a rider, Boink's apparel is comfortable, functional, and appropriate for schooling or recreational riding. Winter, summer and all-season pull-on breeches are complemented by coordinating tops, and are made of high quality performance fabrics. Not just for riding, many of the jackets and tops cross over into regular sportswear.

Kinetic Technologies 877-786-9882

Kinetic Technologies, manufacturer of *Conquer*, produces a full line of medically researched and clinically proven neutraceutical supplements for the veterinary, animal health, human health, and wound/skin care industries.

Vet-A-Mix 800-831-0004 lloydinc.com

Vet-A-Mix, manufacturer of *Thyro-L*, produces products that are used to aid in the treatment of diseases and nutritional deficiencies.

Zareba Systems 507-684-3712 zarebasystems.com

Zareba Systems - Experts in Animal Control. Helping to keep animals safely contained in electric fencing. Zareba has everything needed to design and build a quality fence that keeps animals in (or keep predators out), installs easily, requires little maintenance, and is affordable. The EZEE Corral encloses 900-square feet and uses all white components for greater visability.

A special thanks to authors Bill Paul & Cindy Paul who gave me permission to use part of the story from their historic novel, *Shadow of an Indian Star*.

The wilderness horseback riding scene in *Wisdom of the Horse* where Thundering Cloud tells the story to his daughter about Smith Paul's discovery of the horrific scene of dead horses in the valley came directly from *Shadow of an Indian Star*. I love their novel, and highly recommend it.

www.shadowofanindianstar.com

Shadow of an Indian Star
is an epic novel which chronicals three generations of a brawling pioneer family, their friends and enemies, and the women who helped battle tragedy, corruption and their own inner demons to save themslves and the Chickasaw Nation from annihilation.

Cali Canberra's emotionally charged tale is a crime story that revolves around the moral and ethical issues of selling high-end horses for record prices.

Rene Killian, a female bloodstock agent, plays by her own set of rules in her continuous pursuit of the almighty dollar. Trying to claw her way to the top, she's caught in the political crossfire between some of the horse industry's most influential breeding farms and her own investors. Jared, one of her biggest spending clients, has threatened to destroy her. Now, she'll go to extreme measures, including blackmail and extortion, to get Jared out of her life. In the midst of her problems, she has an affair with a respected equine attorney who discloses confidential information about his own family and wealthy clients, in order to win her affection.

Criminal behavior, greed, jealousy, betrayal, seduction, friendship, and even romance inhabit the pages of this critically acclaimed, unpredictable no-holds-barred reality-based story.

Trading Paper
A MYSTERY NOVEL ABOUT THE HORSE BUSINESS

Cali Canberra
Author of Never Enough!

The best selling novel that took the horse world by storm..

Trading Paper offers an unparalleled insight into the lives of some of the top players in the horse business. Find out what made this unique industry tick.

Cali Canberra takes us on a wild ride of intrigue, murder, manipulation, corruption and suspense with an insider's eye toward the inner workings of an industry previously reserved for the rich and famous.

Fast paced excitement awaits the reader with every twist and turn of this intricate story, told from the perspective of numerous characters whose varied lives and professions are intertwined with at least one visible common element - their love of horses. The legal entanglements catapult into motion a chain of events that effect the entire Arabian horse industry in a way in which it will never recover.

At the peak of the Arabian horse industry in the 1980's, St. Louis businessman Johan Murphy takes time out of his stressful life to meet with his unscruplulous new lawyer. Caught between a rock and a hard place, Murphy's finances prohibit him from making the upcoming installment payment on his champion mare, *Love Letter*, an Arabian he recently acquired at a prestigious Scottsdale auction... setting the stage for the demise of an entire industry.

Vivid characters such as: the owners of Scottsdale's Vintage Arabians, Greg and Marcie Bordeaux, who with intuition, ingenuity, and chutzpay, turned their hobby and passion into a fullblown industry, with them at the helm; Brian and Dean Pondergrass, the most prolific horse trainers and showmen, celebrities themselves within the industry; Johan Murphy, a rough and tumble produce industry mogul, wants desperately to be accepted; Shawna Sanders, an award winning investigative television news journalist and her flamboyant Broadway director/movie producer husband, Ryan Sanders.

Excerpt from *Trading Paper* by Cali Canberra

"I understand. Let's talk about how the prices got so high," she said diplomatically.

Greg knew better, but he hoped that Jessica wouldn't bring up the escalating prices again. He drank down the last of his bottled water as he composed his thoughts. Honesty and truth are two different things, he thought to himself.

"There were several other farms in Scottsdale at the time. All of us owned a lot of land because it was so undervalued when we bought it. From time to time, we'd end up talking at a show or some function, and it would get around to how expensive it was to add fencing and more barns to accommodate more horses, whether they were our own or our client's. None of us could even come close to breaking even financially... especially with the labor and feed costs to take good care of the animals," Greg said.

"Go ahead," Jessica said, trying to keep an open mind.

"So, one night, a group of us went out to dinner together after a local show and got talking about forming a consortium. The purpose was to turn this expensive hobby into something we could all turn a profit from. We discussed having about six or seven farm owners in the group. By the end of our long dinner and drinks, a couple of them didn't want anything to do with our plan, but five of us survived and formed the consortium," Greg said, intentionally omitting the details of the plans they schemed.

"What did the five of you do?" Jessica asked.

"A week later, we had a twelve hour long closed door meeting. No interruptions. We ordered in food and beverages and we stuck to business. We decided that it would be easy to take a leadership role and turn Polish Arabian horses into an actual industry. We just needed to devise a plan and follow it. We agreed to be friendly competitors, but we also all needed to work together to grow an industry from what was, at that time, a casual hobby. The horses were a hobby that we couldn't make a profit at.

"I still don't understand how you got people to pay such high prices for the horses," Dolan interjected, getting impatient. He could see that Greg was skirting around the details.

Greg took a deep breath before he continued. He needed to set the scene, or they would never understand how and why things happened as they did.

"I'll get to that in a second. First, we decided that it was fine to have just the everyday kind of person buying and showing the horses, but we needed to get more wealthy people involved...like the Thoroughbred business. We talked about how wealthy people wanted everything to be first class... their country clubs, cars, houses, boats, clothes, jewelry... everything. So it was obvious that they would want the farms they did business with to be first class also."

"Makes sense," Jessica admitted. Now that she had money, she didn't want to have her horse at a run of the mill looking barn.

"So, we needed to build fancy facilities and have fancy marketing materials. We would have to wine and dine our clients. That would cost us a lot of money," Greg reasoned.

"So, it was a catch 22?" Dolan asked.

"Not really. The other three gentlemen in the group were quite well off on their own. They just didn't want to pour even more money into their farms than they already were, if it wasn't going to make a profit,"

"I can see that," Jessica said, nodding in agreement while she sat back in her chair. There was nothing to really take notes on in this point of his explanation.

"So, anyway, we all agreed to build our farms as spectacular and prestigious as we could imagine and afford... and to have professional people do our marketing materials in a first class style and quality."

Jessica shot straight from the hip. "What about you? How did you and Marcie come up with the money?"

"A couple of ways. After I explained my business plan and our goals to Marcie's parents, they wanted to help us expand the business. When I told them that we needed to upgrade and add on to the farm to accommodate all of the potential business that was out there, they could see that it was necessary also. To help us out, they gave us a gift of $250,000 and three Pure Polish mares that were in foal.

"We spent some of the $250,000 on working with architects drawing up plans... and they made us a detailed model to display in my barn office. While the architects were working on our project, we bought and imported Lancelot, a Swedish National Champion Stallion. We paid an equine attorney to take care of the legal end of a stallion syndication... we offered the very first stallion syndication in the Arabian breed. We also spent, what at the time, was a lot of money, on marketing materials to market the stallion syndication."

For a change, Greg was just describing the facts without a hint of arrogance, Jessica thought. Maybe she jumped to an unwarranted conclusion earlier. She would reserve her judgment for later when she got to know him better.

Marcie's eyes showed that she shared her husband's pride of accomplishment as she listened to him continue. Jessica was surprised that she seemed to be listening to him as if Marcie were hearing the story for the first time herself. Was there a chance that she didn't know very much about how her own husband had built up their business? Jessica couldn't imagine herself being that uninvolved in the details of her and Turner's life. They shared almost everything.

Greg kept talking. "Each of the other people in the consortium bought one or two shares of the Lancelot syndication to help me get it rolling. Then, just by my reputation and Lancelot's show record and pedigree, along with people seeing my plans for the farm development, they were impressed with the syndication. All of the shares sold out within about six months. I guaranteed to buy any shares back at a ten percent discount if they later wanted out of the syndication and there wasn't an actual resale market developed yet," Greg boasted as he sat up tall and puffed his chest out just enough to display his self-confidence.

Here comes that arrogance again, Jessica thought.

"Sounds like good business," Dolan said, knowing that Jessica thought the same as he did about their client's attitude.

"How much money did you bring in from the syndication?" Jessica asked. She was taking notes once again. The details might be important later. There was no way to be certain at this point in the game.

"There were 75 shares at $75,000 each…" Greg started to explain as if he were totally numb to the incredible dollar amounts.

Jessica interrupted him. "I thought a syndication was when someone buys lifetime breeding rights to a stallion… when they get one breeding a year until the horse dies or becomes sterile."

"That is how it works," Greg said, confused by her statement.

"Why would people pay that much money?" Dolan asked.

"Because we did projections showing that each breeding would sell for $10,000 the first year, $20,000, the second, $30,000 the third. The projections didn't show any further appreciation past the third year."

"So what you're saying is, that according to your projections, in the first five years people would make back $120,000?" Jessica asked, adding the figures to her notes and double-checking that she wrote them correctly.

"Even better than that… we let people buy the shares on five year terms. That way, *every dollar* they invested was fully depreciated on their taxes for that year… including their mortality insurance and their pro-rata share of expenses, *and* even trips to Hawaii for syndicate share holder meetings," Greg said with a huge grin on his face. Somehow, he forgot about the circumstances that led him to his explanation.

Jessica wrote furiously. Dolan asked the next logical question. "So, did your projections pan out?"

Marcie had to chime in and answer. "Yes! In fact, in the fourth year, the breedings were selling for $35,000 each, *if* someone could even buy one. Lancelot was such an outstanding sire that most people used the breedings on their own mares. I think there were only about 20 breedings for sale the fourth year." Her eyes were sparkling now, with no trace of the tears that consumed her earlier, other than the fact that her make-up had disappeared.

Copyright © 2001, 2006 by Cali Canberra

Buying Time
THE SEQUEL TO TRADING PAPER
A novel about the horse business

Cali Canberra
Author of *Trading Paper, Never Enough!* & *Wisdom of the Horse*

The fact-based fast moving story, *Buying Time*, is full of morally challenged characters who resolve their problems in unforgettable and unconventional ways.

Canberra unveils how industry insiders prolonged the demise of the lucrative horse industry and what triggered its collapse.

Cali Canberra sets a fast pace of excitement in the high-stakes world of the decadent 1980's. Using Trading Paper as the backdrop, Canberra has cleverly created a stand-alone story utilizing several key characters from her first book. She has molded some wildly colorful individuals that help to unfold this topsy-turvy tale of murder, manipulation, suspense and big business.

The story, which sweeps from the Arizona desert of Scottsdale to mountainous Santa Ynez, California, from the bluegrass horse farms of Kentucky to Florida's horse capital in Ocala - will keep you captivated. By spattering the novel with references to real-life businesses and individuals, Canberra has intentionally blurred the line between reality and fiction. This gripping story exposes the darker side of the horse world while entertaining and educating the reader.

Self-appointed industry kingpin, Greg Bordeaux, weaves his way from riches to ruin in his quest to create, develop and sustain a market for the horses he loves. Bordeaux is faced with the undaunting task of overcoming insurmountable obstacles from an unscrupulous attorney to an unsolved murder in which he is a key suspect. In the middle of his living nightmare, he is bombarded with family in-fighting, the era's biggest stock market crash and a major overhaul to the federal tax code, eliminating the incentive for buyers to pay outlandish prices for horses.

Excerpt from *Buying Time* by Cali Canberra

A few moments passed when the pallor hung in the air again. Greg shouldn't have stopped talking.

Once again, Nick's face turned solemn as he boiled under the surface about the newspaper article and the problems with the Murphys, Vintage clients being deposed, and everything else that had transpired without his knowledge.

"I don't know how we got off track," Nick said. "I need to weigh my options."

The color drained from Greg's face.

"Options?" He was well aware that his fate hung in the balance of what Nick would tolerate.

Nick, sitting behind the massive desk, pursed his lips - his index finger tapped a crystal paperweight with a horse embedded in the design. He wondered how Greg had kept the problems with Johan a secret from Ron.

"If it weren't for me bailing you out, you'd be bankrupt and probably in jail. Did you think I was going to hand over that kind of money without expecting to be kept informed?" He raised his bushy eyebrows to emphasize the question.

Greg swallowed hard before answering. "I had no alternative but to take your money. I know that. I've thanked you. And I said I'm sorry for not keeping you informed."

Striking a deal with Nick improved his odds for the business to grow exponentially. Two years ago, there had been a remote possibility that Greg and his sales team could have sold enough horses to pay the enormous past due tax bill, but he wasn't confident it could be accomplished before his father and the public discovered their financial predicament.

Greg lacked sophistication, but he didn't lack ambition. He had spent all the Vintage Inc. cash reserves on buying two thousand acres of undeveloped woodlands and pasturelands in LaGrange, Kentucky. Until he invested in land, what had felt like an endless stream of money from the Scottsdale and California operations began flowing into the simple basics of land development in Kentucky. The stream went dry. In less than two years, Greg borrowed from one bank to payback another.

Eventually, he was strapped for cash to the point he was unable to pay the taxes. By the time everything on the farm was leveraged and payments were late, he finally went to Ron and confided to him that he was a drowning man. Ron arranged restructured payment plans with the banks and approached Nick, a client of theirs.

Nick, a land developer and racehorse breeder by profession, arrived in the nick of time. Thanks to Ron, Nick bought a financial interest in Vintage Incorporated, which included the Scottsdale real estate and all business assets and inventory of Vintage Arabians and the sales company. In addition to the credit line and cash Nick infused, he contributed his farm and horses in Ocala. Once business arrangements were worked out, the undaunted team, led by Greg, remained the major force in the industry without anyone knowing any of their dirty laundry.

Nick stood. "When you approached me with your proposition, you swore you didn't care about making money. You said you just wanted to stay in the horse business."

Greg's face flushed. "But you - "

Nick spun on his heels and faced him. "Don't you interrupt me, Bordeaux."

"But - "

Nick glared at him. "If you interrupt me again, I'm out of here. So is my funding and my credit. And you can be sure that I won't bail you out of L'Equest."

"Screw you. I have every right to defend myself."

"Screw me? Every right? No - you don't have any rights with me unless I tell you that you do," Nick said as his lips pursed and his thick chest puffed out.

Greg nodded and kept his trap shut.

"The problem is Bordeaux, you got greedy. Remodeling that house in Equestrian Manor - it's still not finished. Then you buy a $500,000 motor coach without asking me and you start wearing fur coats. You look like a fag – I don't know if you think you're impressing people - "

This time Greg had to speak his mind. "You're the one who insisted I should create an image of success – of having money to flaunt. Marcie picked out that coat for me. People know I'm not a fag."

"When I told you people are attracted to people of wealth, I assumed that you would consult with me on what you had in mind. Only a handful of people will know about the motor coach or the Equestrian Manor property – it's in a gate-guarded community for god's sake. You need to have things that everyone can see."

"I can't have something just for me? Me and Marcie? You can't tell me where to live."

"I can and I will," Nick said. "Sell that place. Consult with me from now on. You're not going to burn through money unless it's for things I approve of."

"You're a silent partner," Greg said defensively.

"The day we met you didn't have two nickels to rub together. All you had was a herd of horses and not enough buyers for the prices you were establishing. Now banks are loaning money, buying notes from you, and the client base is growing – you know it's because of me and only me."

"I recognize that. But you agreed to be a silent partner," Greg said.

Greg certainly wasn't going to remind Nick that it was really himself, his father, Thomas, Ron, and his sales staff - Larry Brown and Mike Wolf - that were